The Sweet Smell of Magnolias and Memories

Center Point
Large Print

Also by Celeste Fletcher McHale and available from Center Point Large Print:

The Secret to Hummingbird Cake

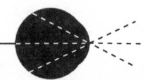

This Large Print Book carries the Seal of Approval of N.A.V.H.

The Sweet Smell of Magnolias and Memories

Celeste Fletcher McHale

CENTER POINT LARGE PRINT
THORNDIKE, MAINE

This Center Point Large Print edition
is published in the year 2017 by arrangement with
Thomas Nelson.

The text of this Large Print edition is unabridged.
In other aspects, this book may vary
from the original edition.
Printed in the United States of America
on permanent paper.
Set in 16-point Times New Roman type.

ISBN: 978-1-68324-441-7

Library of Congress Cataloging-in-Publication Data

Names: McHale, Celeste Fletcher, 1961– author.
Title: The sweet smell of magnolias and memories / Celeste Fletcher
McHale.
Description: Center Point Large Print edition. | Thorndike, Maine :
    Center Point Large Print, 2017.
Identifiers: LCCN 2017013446 | ISBN 9781683244417
    (hardcover : alk. paper)
Subjects: LCSH: Large type books. | GSAFD: Christian fiction. | Love
stories.
Classification: LCC PS3613.C4998 S94 2017b | DDC 813/.6—dc23
LC record available at https://lccn.loc.gov/2017013446

For my precious Aunt Betty who believed in me even when I didn't believe in myself.

And for Candy Sue. I know you are still in there somewhere. We miss you.

Prologue

He kissed her again.

"Don't lose that number, Jacey," he said, the rain beating down on both of them, stinging and biting their bodies. He quickly shoved the card into her pocket.

"Wait, let me write down mine too," Jacey said, frantically grabbing the pen, then dropping it into the water. "Oh no."

"There's no time," Colin said. "You have to go. Get in the boat. Find me. Call me."

"I will. I promise," she said. "Be careful, Colin. Please be careful."

"I will," he said. "Now, go. Hurry!"

She climbed into the boat, soaking wet, shivering, and as hungry as she'd ever been in her life. She ached all over. There were scrapes and cuts and bruises all over her body, and mud caked her hair. But all of those things seemed minor compared to the pain she felt leaving him behind. Tears filled her eyes as they sped away, and she watched Colin standing on the rooftop until he disappeared from her sight. Then she finally allowed herself to cry. She held the young boy in her arms and felt every ounce of fear she'd carefully hidden for the past seventy-two-hours stream down her face. She'd wanted to sob a dozen times before now, but crying would have been an indulgence. Floods were no time for indulgences.

She watched the tops of trees as they flew by— the only scenery in this watery world, save for a stray rooftop that appeared from the shadows every now and then. She still had no idea where she was or where she'd been, surely having drifted miles away from her original destination. Three days before, she'd been chasing a story she was writing for a regional Southern magazine. A story about rural life in a modern world . . . which seemed like a whole different existence now. She knew she had been forever changed by this experience and was anxious to be home—to open her laptop one day soon and transfer the feelings from her mind to written words while her heart was still raw.

Surely they would find civilization soon. They could have been anywhere on the map, floating on top of a city or a valley or a school. She wondered how long it would take before she could lie down at night without hearing the rolling and almost constant threatening thunder that made her want to scream and cover her ears. She took a deep breath. It was nearly over. Couldn't she relax now? She felt a cautious relief begin to seep in. Soon, they would be back on solid earth, and she would very well kiss the ground when they got there. They were going to be all right. She looked down at the boy in the boat, and he grinned broadly at her, his dimples cutting into his cheeks. She kissed his forehead and hugged him close against her. Then she smiled at Lillian and her other three boys. They were going to make it.

Just as that thought entered her mind, she heard screams and a deafening boom. She felt a quick and hard jolt, then a flying sensation. The last thing she remembered was being submerged in water. Again.

Chapter One

"I thought this day would never come," Willow Washington said as she swirled around in front of the full-length mirror and admired her reflection in the yards and yards of silk and lace and pearls. "I can't believe I'm getting married today."

"I can't believe you made us wear these dresses." Jacey Lang frowned and smoothed the taffeta on her skirt. "I can't decide if I look like an overgrown sweet potato or the Great Pumpkin. How many yards of material gave their lives for these puffy sleeves? What were you thinking?"

"She was thinking she wanted all eyes on her," Georgia Bankston said, smoothing down her twin pumpkin dress.

"That's *exactly* what I was thinking, smarty-pants," Willow said, never taking her eyes off the mirror. "And this is exactly how I always dreamed of looking like as a bride."

"You do look beautiful," Jacey said. "I just don't think it was necessary to make us look quite so . . . bad." She tugged underneath her skirt.

"Haven't you heard?" Willow mused. "Orange is the new black."

"Well, tonfetti ain't the new cotton," Jacey said. Willow and Georgia laughed. "It's *taffeta*,"

Georgia said. "And it really isn't that bad. I mean, we make the dresses look good, huh? Or I would, minus the extra twenty pounds I'm dragging around."

Jacey pulled at the material. "It's Velcro," she said. "And you aren't fat. Everybody gains a little weight now and then." Jacey adjusted the baby's breath entwined in her chocolate brown hair and tried to appreciate the dress. Didn't work. It was, indeed, awful.

"Everybody except you," Georgia said.

"I gain a little sometimes," Jacey protested.

"Do not," Georgia said.

"Do too," Jacey answered.

"Stop!" Willow said. "The color of your dresses is gorgeous, and so are both of you. Do you realize how pretty the pictures will be?"

Jacey raised her brow. "Whatever," she said, pushing the dress down against her legs again. Of course it popped right back into place. "It's your day, Willow. I guess I can take it. For a little while."

Willow smiled at the mirror again and Jacey chuckled. Willow was on cloud nine and paying little attention to Jacey's whining.

"You really do look incredible," Georgia said. "Does a wedding gown just automatically make a woman gorgeous?"

"I'm gonna say an emphatic *no*," Jacey said. "Remember Tara Davis's wedding?"

"Ohhhhh . . . ," Willow and Georgia said in unison. Then all three observed a moment of silence.

"A psychedelic chicken comes to mind," Jacey said. "Or maybe an ostrich. And big dresses. Big hair. Giant hair, actually."

"I understand trying to be unique," Willow said, "but the colors."

"And the boas . . . ," Georgia added.

"And the live swans dyed magenta," Jacey said. "That has to be against some sort of animal cruelty code."

"Didn't seem to bother the swans while they were bobbing for bugs in the champagne fountain," Georgia said.

"Tara should've worn white," Willow said. "Brides should always wear white. Even if they aren't as pure as the driven snow."

"Like Tara," Georgia said.

They laughed.

Jacey looked at her friends and felt a little twinge of sadness. She'd met them both on their very first day of college at LSU. They were scared freshmen trying desperately to act like they knew what was going on, but all three of them were lost looking for orientation. They struck up a conversation in the quad and realized they all lived in the same dorm. By the end of freshman year, they'd become fast and loyal friends. The summer before their sophomore year, they moved into a condo off campus. Three years after graduating, they still lived together. At least, Jacey and Georgia would. Willow would be moving out when she returned from her Jamaican honeymoon, which was the sad part. Still, Jacey was happy for her friend and knew Colby would be a great husband. Willow would make him happy too. Assuming he liked ramen noodles.

Jacey loved these women. They had been there for each other through some of the worst parts of their lives. Willow had lost two of her grandparents in the last two years. Jacey and Georgie had spent many hours consoling her, letting her talk, holding her while she cried. Georgie had gone through a breakup that had changed her entire life. She'd been with the same boy since she was fourteen years old. He was the only love she'd ever known—and to find out he had cheated on her not once, not twice, but many, many times had nearly killed her. And what Georgia and Willow had done for Jacey after the flood . . . Jacey squeezed her brown eyes shut. She didn't want to think about that today. Or about Colin.

"Okay, ladies, it's time." The wedding planner appeared at the door and announced the occasion in her game-show-host voice. That ultra-excited tone made Jacey and Georgia want to crack up, but Willow loved the girl and her enthusiasm. Even if it did make them feel like they'd just won a new car. Jacey and Georgia smiled at each other.

"Wait," Jacey said, tugging at the front of her dress. "Let me fix my cleavage."

"You wish there was some cleavage to fix," Georgia said.

"I don't want the good Reverend Willis to faint when he sees all this," Jacey said.

"You're right," Georgia said. "I bet those double-As will change his life."

"Girls!" Willow said. "Stop fussing. It's *time*. Besides, Reverend Willis is sick. He sent another guy."

"Maybe he's old and blind," Georgia said.

"Like Reverend Willis," Willow and Jacey said in unison.

"Okay, enough," Willow said. "Let's get this party started."

Months ago Jacey and Georgia had both been given the title of maid of honor. Willow had said there was no way to choose one maid of honor, so both her best friends accepted the prize. Jacey and Georgia walked down the aisle together, smiling and nodding acknowledgments to the packed church. When they reached the altar, they stood facing the crowd and waited for Willow, who walked down the aisle on her father's arm.

Willow didn't disappoint. She was absolutely glowing—as perfect as any bride ever. Jacey snuck a look at Colby, who looked like he was about to burst into tears at the very sight of her. Jacey weighed that a moment, trying to decide if it was cheesy or really, really sweet. Sweet won in the end, and she gently nudged Georgia to look.

"Who gives this woman in marriage?" the minister asked.

Jacey shivered all of a sudden. Déjà vu. The words had nearly made her hyperventilate, although she didn't know why that question would've made her think she'd been in this same spot before. She couldn't recall anyone inquiring *her* father about marriage.

"Her mother and I," said Ben Washington, Willow's dad. He kissed Willow and placed her hand in Colby's.

The congregation sat down and Jacey, Georgia, and the groomsmen turned to face the minister.

"Friends, family," the minister began, "we are gathered today to join Willow Mist Washington and Colby James Frost."

Jacey felt strange all of a sudden, like she was in a vacuum. She was never nervous in front of a crowd. What was wrong with her? She picked at her bouquet and moved her shoulders around. The post-trauma anxiety that had plagued her for months was threatening to rear its ugly head in the form of another not-so-pretty panic attack. *Not today, please, not today,* she thought.

15

"Stop fidgeting," Georgia whispered.

"I can't help it," Jacey whispered back. "Something's freaking me out."

Jacey decided it was best to concentrate on the minister's words and stop feeding her fear. After all, if she didn't give it any energy, the anxiety couldn't . . . Wait . . . wait . . . *what?*

She jerked her head up and stared at the minister. "Colin?" she whispered, much, much louder than she'd intended.

The minister stopped and looked at her, his face registering an equal amount of shock. "Jacey?" he whispered back.

But Jacey had gone deaf. At least temporarily . . . the roar in her ears a buffer for the sound of her own voice. "Are you a . . . *preacher?*" Oh my, had she thought that out loud?

Colin stared back at her like a deer caught in headlights. Finally, composure took over and he said, "Yes, yes, I am. Uh, sorry about that interruption, folks . . . Let's get started again, shall we?"

Jacey grabbed Georgia's hand and squeezed it so hard Georgia whispered, "Ouch!" a little too loud.

Willow stared at them and whispered through gritted teeth, "Georgie!"

"Sorry," Georgia said, and not so softly. "Go ahead, uh, Reverend."

Jacey stared at Colin the rest of the ceremony.

She couldn't decide if she wanted to throw her arms around him, punch him in the face, or take off running. One thing was for sure: This reception was going to be interesting.

Chapter Two

Colin stood at the altar posing for pictures with the bride and groom. How long was this going to take? This was the first wedding he'd ever officiated. Was taking pictures with the minister normal? Why did they need a picture of him? For proof? They already had a license. What he wanted to do was run into the reception hall and find Jacey. He was just as stunned as she had been when she said his name in the middle of the ceremony. What was she doing here? Where had she been? And why hadn't she contacted him after the flood?

He knew it sounded crazy—so crazy he'd never said it out loud—but he wondered if he had fallen in love with Jacey during those three days on a roof. At least, in deep like or maybe infatuation. Whatever it was, he'd wanted to explore it, and he thought she might have felt the same way. He knew what happened to them wasn't ordinary, and maybe even quite extraordinary. He hadn't talked about it with anyone because he didn't want to defend it or debate it. He just accepted it.

Before they were separated, he'd made sure she had every contact number he had. When the men who rescued Jacey and the others got to them, the first thing Colin did was ask for the ink pen in the man's pocket. Just holding the cheap ballpoint pen had made Colin feel like he'd won the lottery. Finally, a way to be sure she could find him again when the disaster was over. He wrote down his numbers and stuffed the paper into her pocket. So why hadn't she ever called him? Not even once to see if he'd survived. He knew what had happened between them on the roof was . . . special. He'd been around the block enough times to recognize the look on her face and the promise in her eyes.

"Okay, Reverend, I think we have all we need. Thank you so much." As soon as the photographer freed him, Colin bolted for the door in search of the fellowship hall where the reception was in full swing. He almost made it.

"Oh, Reverend," Mrs. Perkins, the church pianist, called to him. "I need to send a book to Brother Wilson. I just hate that he is sick, and I'm hoping this book will make him feel better. It's about orchids. He grows orchids. Did you know that?"

Colin shook his head. "No, ma'am, I didn't," he said. "I'll be happy to take it to him for you."

"Just follow me to my car, if you will," she said.

Colin followed her toward the parking lot, matching her snail's pace step for step.

"Folks say I'm crazy to park my car clear across the parking lot, but I think it's good for my

19

arthritis," Mrs. Perkins said as she crept across the asphalt. "Don't you think so?"

"Yes, ma'am," Colin said. "I'm sure it's good for you." He wanted to snatch her up in his arms and run to her car, grab the orchid book, tuck her safely into her seat belt, and sprint to the reception before Jacey disappeared again. But he just kept moving . . . and envisioned turtles lapping him and Mrs. Perkins as she talked about her new-and-improved titanium hip.

He thought he was home free by the time he got back to the side entrance of the fellowship hall when he was stopped by a teenage boy with pimply cheeks and a frightened look on his face.

"Um," the boy said. "Do you have time to talk to me for a minute?"

"Of course," Colin said. The deck was stacking against him yet again. "How can I help you?"

"I can't talk to Reverend Willis," the boy said as tears filled his eyes. "I'm afraid he'll tell my parents."

Colin studied the boy for a moment. Whatever this boy's problem was, it was real trouble. At least, in the boy's mind it was. "Let's go inside," Colin said. "I'm sure we can find an empty room to talk in."

The grateful and relieved teenager followed him back into the church. Colin glanced over his shoulder at the doors of the fellowship hall. Jacey would have to wait. At least he hoped she would.

• • •

Jacey sank down in her chair and was swallowed by the huge orange dress. She scanned the crowd. Where was he?

"Wow," Georgia said. "Just wow . . . I can't believe Lover Boy is a preacher."

"Keep your voice down," Jacey said.

"He's a *preacher,*" she said again. "Yikes . . . that's gotta sting."

"It's not like I knew that," Jacey said. "He wasn't wearing a name tag that said 'Brother Colin.' He was wearing jeans . . . and flip-flops! Is that the regular reverend uniform?"

Georgia took a sip of her wedding punch. "You're going to hell."

Jacey slapped at her arm. "Georgie!"

"Well, let's recap, shall we? You spent three nights on the roof. Two of those were wrapped up with a man you'd known for exactly that long—and he's a *preacher.* Somehow you went all gaga over him, then never saw or heard from him until a year later, when he shows up to conduct the marriage ceremony for your best friend." Georgia paused and took a deep breath. "In the meantime, you spent the last eight months or so going out with anybody that has a pulse in some sort of misguided effort to forget this man whom you've decided isn't worthy of your affection because he's a man of God. Is that about right?"

"Do you know how messed up that sounds?" Jacey asked.

"I know exactly how messed up that sounds," Georgia said. "That's why I said you were going to hell."

"I don't care if he's a . . . ," Jacey began. "What I mean is, it isn't that . . . I was on a roof. In a storm and a flood. There was no feather bed, wine, or roses. It wasn't a seduction. I didn't do anything wrong."

"Still . . . there was some kissy-kissy smooch-smooch, and you came back in *L-O-V-E*. You've been ruined ever since. And now . . . you find out he's a preacher and you're hiding from him." She looked squarely at Jacey. "You couldn't hide from Helen Keller in that dress, by the way."

Jacey cringed.

Georgia scanned the crowd. "If he's a preacher, where are his big-haired wife and eight tiny children?"

Jacey winced. Oh no. What if he had a wife? And a kid?

"Of course, that would be fast work, but still," Georgia said. "It's possible. The man apparently moves fast."

"You're so funny," Jacey said.

"Oh, I know, right?" Georgia shrugged. "But we aren't talking about me. So, what's your deal? You've been pining away for him all this time. Why are you hiding? Why?"

Jacey didn't answer right away and finally shrugged. "I don't know."

"Is he not the way you remember him?" she asked.

Jacey shook her head. "No, he's *exactly* the way I remember him."

"I was wondering, because he is delicious!" she said. "All that dark hair and those velvety brown eyes . . . Delicious!"

"Stop," Jacey said. "Isn't that like . . . sacrilegious? Can you say that about a preacher?"

"I can," Georgia said. "I'm not the one who sucked face with him."

"Ugh," Jacey said. "I'm mortified."

"Because he's a minister?" Georgia asked.

"No, of course not," Jacey said. "That would make me an awful, horrible person, wouldn't it? But . . . okay, yes. It's exactly why. I can't hook up with a preacher."

"He's still a guy," Georgia said. "He's just a guy who prays."

"I pray too, Georgie," Jacey said. "But I'm no preacher."

"You certainly aren't," Georgia agreed.

"What is that supposed to mean?"

"You're a serial dater," Georgia said and laughed.

"A what?" Jacey asked.

"Don't get all bent out of shape at me," Georgia said. "Willow's the one who came up with that."

"A serial dater? Explain that, please," Jacey said. "What does that even mean? Is that a thing? That's not a thing."

"Well," Georgia began, "you go out with a guy once or twice. Then you never see him again. Especially this past year. It's almost pathological. After you got well, you turned into a man-eater. You were never like that before."

"I acknowledge I have been on several dates this year. But I was just—"

"Several dates?" Georgia interrupted. "You went out with three different guys *last week*."

Jacey snapped her mouth shut. Georgia was right. She realized that. She'd dated a lot this year, but she was just trying to shake the memory of Colin. She thought if she dated enough men, surely one of them would make her forget those velvety brown eyes and strong arms. Not that it had worked, but she had given herself an A for effort. She'd managed to make a couple of new friends in the process, so it wasn't a total wash . . . but there certainly hadn't been any sparks flying around. Besides, it wasn't just her dating habits that had changed. It was everything. There was Jacey Before the Flood and Jacey After the Flood—the version who didn't want to continue watching life from the sidelines, who didn't want to be afraid to try new things, new food, new places. New Jacey took risks she'd never taken in the past and didn't want to waste a single day of her life. Jacey Squared, as Georgia called her.

"Look," Georgia said. "You've just been different this year. That's all. That's not a bad thing. You've done a ton of things that were *very* atypical for you. Zip-lining, that whole Mardi Gras spectacle, riding on the back of a Harley with that guy . . . Python or Cobra or Garter Snake, whatever his name was. I get it. You almost died. It was a wake-up call. You've been through a lot and you want to embrace life. There's nothing wrong with that."

"Thank you for approving," Jacey said, chuckling.

"That's precisely why you need to give this guy a look. And you really are a serial dater. Willow banged that nail on the head." Georgia stood up and gave Jacey her cup of punch. "Here," she said. "Hold this. And writhe in your man-eating shame. I'm off to make someone dance with me in the Baptist church. So, will they send the dance police or just deacons with pitchforks or something? How does that work?"

Jacey watched her walk away in a puff of orange and laughed in spite of her torment. She had no doubt Georgia would find somebody who would be happy to oblige.

Jacey didn't know if she qualified as a serial dater, but Georgia was right about one thing: She really was a different person after the flood. But it wasn't just because of Colin. She was running from something and she knew it. Somewhere in the mysterious shadows of her brain, where memories hovered just out of reach, there was something she didn't *want* to recall. When a sight or sound or smell threatened to retrieve one of those memories, she ran. But she always remembered Colin, quite vividly and frequently. He was the first thing she thought of in the morning and the last thing she thought of at night.

When she was still in the hospital after the flood, she tried to find Colin, but to no avail. She asked nurses and doctors and janitors to find the shorts she was wearing on that roof, the same ones she'd worn during the accident. Each of them said they'd been cut from her when she came in and certainly were thrown away. In those first days, the answer always made her cry. She could remember him shoving the wet, soggy scrap of paper into the pocket of those shorts, and she remembered him telling her not to lose it. She had wanted to tear the paper in half and write down her own number, but the pen had fallen from her shaky hands into the water. After that . . . nothing. It was as if someone had reached inside her head and physically removed the memories. Her next recollection was of waking up in a hospital bed surrounded by tubes and monitors and hushed tones.

Willow and Georgia couldn't believe Jacey

had no more information about Colin than she did. But while you're sitting on top of a house in a storm of epic proportion, you don't chat about jobs and favorite restaurants and movies. It wasn't exactly a typical first date. They had been in survival mode. They talked about repairing a boat, about the lightning that popped around them. They soothed a near hysterical mother and her horrified children. Yes, there were sweet moments, stolen kisses shared and promises made, but very little background information exchanged.

She knew he liked The Eagles because she'd heard him humming "Hotel California" one night as they tried to sleep, during one of those hallowed moments when the rain had let up and the panic had dissipated. She began to sing softly while he hummed the notes. Then he began to sing with her. Even Lillie had joined in. It was a sweet little memory she clung to. A minute and a half or so of happiness, brought to them courtesy of Glenn Frey and his tribe. She thought of that moment often after the flood, but it didn't do much in the way of helping her find Colin. She tried in vain to remember anything else that might give her a clue about who or where he was. But it just wasn't there.

Her doctor said some of the memory loss may have been due to the concussion, or her mind's way of blocking out many of the things she'd seen during those three days. Horrific things. He said the memories could eventually come back, or be lost forever. Whatever the reason for the patchy amnesia, it frustrated Jacey daily. A sound, a smell, anything could bring a fleeting picture of those days to her mind, but only briefly. It was both exasperating and comforting. But what she remembered with clarity were strong arms around her during those horrifying nights, the muffled sobs from the children, the awful sound of animals in obvious distress, thunder that never seemed to stop, and her own frightening thoughts. She still suffered from nightmares now and then and the occasional panic attack, provoked by memories she couldn't find.

"Enough of that," she mumbled and drank the rest of Georgia's punch. Maybe she could find somebody to dance with too. She felt the slight stinging on her lips and knew in an instant she'd just made a mistake. There was pineapple in the punch. Thank God they had already taken pictures.

"Georgie!" she shouted across the room.

Georgia stopped in her tracks—as she danced with an obviously enamored groomsman—and shushed her. "You're so loud," she mouthed.

Jacey pointed at the cup. "There is pineapple in the punch," she said.

"Uh-oh," Georgia said, pushing the

grooms-man. He stumbled away but then hurried to her side. "Where's your EpiPen?"

"In my purth? I don't know," Jacey said. Great. Already. "Juth need benadwill."

"What?" Georgia said.

"Ben-a-dwill."

"I knew what you meant. I just wanted to hear you say *Benadryl* again." Georgia smiled.

Jacey swung at her but missed.

Georgia started to laugh. "Could this day get any funnier?"

Jacey tried to say, "Georgie" but it came out, "Thorthie!"

Georgia really started to laugh then. "I'm just sorry Willow and Colby already left. This is classic."

"Huwee!"

"Calm down," Georgia said. "It's just gonna make you talk funny for a while. Sit still and I'll go get the car. I'll be right back."

"Huwee!" she said again.

"I'll huwee. I pwa-mise," Georgia said over her shoulder.

Jacey rolled her eyes.

Georgia was, indeed, back quickly. "Come on. I found us a ride."

Jacey followed her through the crowd and into the parking lot, where a car sat waiting with the passenger door open.

"Get in," Georgia said.

"Whoth cah?" Jacey asked.

"Your car was blocked in," Georgia said. "I had to go with plan B."

"What pwan B?" Jacey got in the front and slammed the door as Georgia climbed into the back. Colin was in the driver's seat.

Jacey sucked in her breath and her mouth flew open.

"Thorthie!" she said and turned around.

"What?" Georgia said. "We need some benadwill. His car was available."

"Hello, Jacey," he said, smiling.

Jacey stared ahead. "Hewoe, Cowin."

Georgia cackled in the backseat.

"Jacey," Colin said, staring at her. "I . . . I don't know what to say."

"Me eva," Jacey said, finally looking at him.

"I've searched for you for months," he continued. "I've been all over Biloxi and half of Mississippi asking questions about you."

"I wiv in Baton Wooge," Jacey said.

"Here?" he said. "In Baton Rouge?"

"Uh, I hate to interrupt this little reunion," Georgia said from the backseat. "But in about five or ten minutes, her lips stop looking like a supermodel's and just get really gross. We might need to move this along a little. We need some benadwill. Pretty fast."

"Oh, yes, of course," Colin said and sped out of the parking lot. "To the . . . hospital?"

"No," Jacey said. "Thorthie's a nurth."

"What?" he asked.

"She said 'Georgie's a nurse,' but isn't that hysterical?" Georgia said. "No hospital. Go to the dollar store about a mile straight ahead. We need benadwill. She's only had a reaction to pineapple. Strawberries, however, will kill her—which is why she is *supposed* to keep her EpiPen and benadwill *with* her, but she never does."

Jacey shrugged. "I neva weememba."

"You need to weememba," Georgia said.

They pulled up to the store, and Georgia ran inside.

"Jacey . . . ," Colin said. "I . . . am . . . It's so good to see you. I thought I'd never see you again. I was so surprised today. I almost . . . I just can't believe it. Are you really all right? You sure you don't need to go to the hospital?"

"No," Jacey said. "No hothpital."

"I just can't believe it's you," he said again. He tried to take her hand, but she pulled it away.

"*You* can't beeweeve it?" Jacey said.

He moved his hand away from hers. "I was hoping . . . Well, I'm not sure what I was hoping."

"You a pweecha?" she asked.

"I'm a minister, yes," he said.

Jacey didn't answer.

"Does it make a difference?" he asked.

Once again, she didn't reply.

31

Georgia appeared with the Benadryl and opened the bottle. "Here, drink," she said. "All of it."

"The whole bottle?" Colin asked.

"It's children's Benadryl," Georgia said. "It won't hurt her, and the antihistamine will take care of the swelling. She'll be good as new after the two-hour nap she's about to take—whether she wants one or not. The antihistamine is gonna knock her on her . . . It's gonna knock her out."

"I can heah you," Jacey said.

"Yeah?" Georgia said. "Then hush up and keep chugging. Colin, do you mind taking us home?"

"Not at all," he said.

"Turn left on Bluebonnet," Georgia said, "then take a right on Highland."

They drove in silence for a few minutes while Georgia made sure Jacey was drinking the pink liquid.

Jacey was already becoming drowsy. "I need my cah," she said.

"For what?" Georgia asked. "You can't drive your cah. Flip that bottle around. See the 'do not operate heavy machinery' sentence? The car is what they're talking about."

"Ugh," Jacey said, then took another shot. She made a face. "Hawable."

By the time they arrived at home, Jacey was sleeping like a baby.

"Will you help me get her inside?" Georgia asked.

"Here," he said. "I'll do it."

Colin scooped her up easily into his arms and followed Georgia into the condo.

"Let's take her to her room," she said. "This way."

Colin laid Jacey gently on the bed and gazed down on her for a moment. He took the thick, creamy-white afghan from the cedar chest at the foot of her bed and spread it over her while Georgia watched. Then he gently touched her hand with his and turned to look at Georgia.

"I can't believe it's her," he whispered.

"Come on," she whispered back. "I'll fix you a cup of coffee."

Georgia quietly closed the bedroom door, and they walked down the hallway to the cheerful kitchen adorned with crawfish sketches and fleurs-de-lis.

Colin sat at the kitchen island and ran his hand absently over the smooth, silver-white granite while Georgia made coffee. "You have no idea how long I've searched for her."

"I think I do," Georgia said. She put the pod into the coffeemaker. "She's looked for you just that long." She pushed the power button and the Keurig sputtered to life.

He looked surprised. "Really? She didn't seem . . . happy to see me."

33

"I think she's still shocked," Georgia said. "About seeing you and, well, about that Bible-toting thing."

He shook his head. "I could've sworn I told her on the roof that I was studying to become a minister."

"Are you allowed to swear?" Georgia smiled.

He chuckled. "Touché."

"Exactly what kind of minister are you, if you don't mind me asking?" Georgia said. "I mean, since you were pinch-hitting for the Baptist guy, I'm assuming that's your team?"

He chuckled again. "Yep, that's my team."

Georgia handed him a cup of coffee.

"Already?" he asked. "Is that a bionic coffee-maker?"

Georgia shrugged. "Bionic? I'm not sure," she said. "It's a Keurig. Haven't you heard of them?"

"I guess not," he said.

"You don't get out much, do you, Rev?"

Colin chuckled. "I don't like technology."

Georgia raised a brow. "How do you survive in the year 2016 without it?"

"Quite well. You should try it."

"I'd rather eat dirt and worms for breakfast than be without my cell phone, thank you very much," Georgia said, pouring her own cup of coffee. She joined him at the island. "So . . . where were we? Oh, yeah, so you are a Baptist guy, and that's like . . . hellfire and brimstone, right?"

"A pretty good description of *some* of us." He smiled.

"So what else do you do?"

He took a sip of coffee and set the cup down. "Are you sure you're a nurse? Because you seem like a reporter."

Georgia laughed. "Nosy is what I am. Ask her." She gestured to Jacey's bedroom. "Nosy and curious."

"To answer your question," he said, "these days I'm a carpenter."

"Oh." Georgia nibbled a cookie. "Sorta like Jesus. Well . . . that's pretty good company, I guess."

He laughed. "I'm glad you approve."

"So, what do you build? Houses?"

"Mostly," he said. "Right now I'm working in Mississippi. Still rebuilding from the flood."

"Oh, that's cool. You have your own company?"

"I work with a company that rebuilds communities after natural disasters. It's a little like Habitat for Humanity."

"So it's charity work," Georgia said. "Commendable. I get it . . . So, who pays you?"

He raised a brow at her and smiled a little.

"Too many questions?"

"My turn," he said.

She shrugged. "Okay, shoot."

"What does she do?" he asked. "For a living, I mean. She's some sort of writer? I remember her saying she was a writer, but I've looked for books by Jacey Lang and can't find any."

"She is a writer, but she writes for magazines mostly," Georgia said. "She has contracts with a couple of big regional Southern magazines and does a lot of local stuff in Baton Rouge. But you probably didn't find her because she uses a pseudonym . . . a pen name. It keeps the phone from ringing off the hook."

"She's . . . famous?" he asked.

Georgia laughed and reached for the cookie jar again. She took out a couple of gingersnaps and shoved the jar toward Colin. "No, she's not famous, but her articles are really well-known around the South. She just likes the anonymity."

"I see," he said. He grabbed a few ginger-snaps and set them on the napkin Georgia handed him. "Is she seeing someone?" he asked.

Georgia sighed and weighed her response. She was always fiercely protective of her friends and even more so after Jacey's accident. She answered the question carefully. "Jacey doesn't have a boyfriend, if that's what you're asking."

Colin smiled. "That's what I was asking," he said. "Do you know why she never contacted me?"

Georgia paused. It was obvious Colin had no idea what happened to Jacey and the others. How would he have known? She hated to be the one to deliver the difficult news, but there was no way

36

around it. "Jacey was involved in an accident the day she got off the roof," Georgia began. "The motorboat that rescued her and the others collided with another one. It was nobody's fault, just a crazy stroke of bad luck. No one realized how bad the flood was at first, and most of it was in rural areas. After a couple of days, when word finally got out that people were stranded, they began to help. There were so many boats in the water looking for survivors. I guess you remember how the weather took a turn for the worse again during all these rescue efforts, and tornadoes were popping up everywhere. Everybody was trying to hurry out of the storm."

She paused and took a sip of coffee, then went to Jacey's bedroom door to check on her. She closed it gently and returned to the kitchen.

"It was a terrible accident," Georgia continued. "I really hate to tell you this, Colin, but the mother of those children and one of the boys were killed, along with two people in the boat they collided with. I'm so sorry."

Colin felt like he'd been punched in the gut. This was the last thing he'd expected to hear. He thought about Lillie, who was so brave and so protective of her children. He thought about the boys, whose faces were permanently etched in his brain, and how much the youngest one seemed to adore Jacey.

"To be honest, I'm surprised you didn't already know about it," Georgia said. "It was all over the news for a few days. Even here in Baton Rouge."

Colin stared at her blankly for a moment, still trying to digest the news she'd given him. When he found his voice again, he said, "I was on the roof another two days after they left. When I was finally rescued, I was . . . severely dehydrated. I had a cut on my leg and it became infected. Almost lost my leg. I was in the hospital for three weeks, in and out of consciousness for a few days, I'm told."

"I'm so sorry," Georgia said. "Is your leg okay now?"

"It's fine."

"You didn't read about any of this later?" Georgia asked. "I mean, after you got out of the hospital? It was online too. In fact, I worry all the time that Jacey's going to read about it while she's surfing the net. Maybe it's the memory thing, but she doesn't even know that people were killed in the accident. Or she just ignores it, which is what I suspect."

"I hate computers," Colin confessed. "I have a laptop and an e-mail address, but I rarely check it. I can barely use my iPhone. I can build you a house. I could build you a mansion if you asked me to, but the internet is still a mystery to me. I did manage to Google her name. I'm not even sure I spelled it right, but I searched for every

'Jacey Lang' and every variation of it I could think of. There were a few hits, but obviously none of them was a match. I don't remember her saying even once that she was from Louisiana."

"Really?" Georgia asked. "So, what did you talk about all that time?"

Colin shoved his cup away and reflected for a moment. "Surviving. We talked about the mom and her kids and how to help them. And what was really important to us."

"That makes sense," Georgia said.

"Tell me more about what happened after the accident," Colin pressed.

Georgia took their cups and rinsed them before putting them in the dishwasher. "They found Jacey in the water holding the boy who died. Apparently she had swum to him with a broken ankle and a head injury but wouldn't let go. She had a pretty serious concussion, and her ankle required plates and pins to repair. After the hospital stay, she went through months of rehab on her foot, had to keep it elevated in case of blood clots. Couldn't sleep. Didn't eat. Then a lot of post-traumatic stress that she still battles from time to time. It was really bad for a while. So . . . you see . . . she really couldn't contact you."

"I had no idea," he said. "No idea . . ."

He thought of what Jacey must've gone through those first few days and weeks, and how sorry he was not being able to help her. He thought about

39

the children who clung to their mother on top of that roof. They had been terrified, just as their mother and Jacey were. He had put them all in the boat, thinking they were rescued—and since there hadn't been room for all of them, he had stayed behind. He shook his head. He'd sent two of them to their death. He trusted God, but he'd never understand his ways.

"It was . . . more than the physical wounds, Colin," Georgia said. She brushed her dark curly hair from her face and pondered how to convey what he needed to know, without invading Jacey's privacy. "Jacey's a strong girl. Always has been—strong-willed and strong in body. She has days when she is totally and completely fine, but then there are days when she's preoccupied and moody. And that's never been who she is."

"Is this normal after a head injury?" Colin asked.

"Head injuries are strange ailments. The way the brain reacts to trauma is still somewhat a mystery. But I can tell you, she's had some . . . problems remembering. And when she *does* remember, she doesn't want to. She has never acknowledged the boy dying. And we don't talk about it. Her mind has pretty much blocked it. It's all very unsettling for her, to say the least."

He let that information sink in for a moment. "Do you think my being here will make it worse? In your professional opinion."

"I don't know. But I can tell you this," Georgia said. "She asked for you constantly in the hospital."

"I should've dug around more. I should've hired a private investigator," he said. "But I thought that maybe she didn't want me to find her. She had my contact information. Or at least I thought she did. I took her silence as rejection."

"Hey, Rev, it wasn't your fault. How could you have known? Especially since you were having a little issue yourself, you know?"

He shook his head. "Maybe I can come by tomorrow to see her?"

"I think that's a question for her." Georgia smiled. "Why don't you leave your number, and I'll give it to her."

He took a pen from his pocket, wrote something on the back of a business card, and gave it to Georgia.

She took the card and smiled. "I'm pretty sure we'll see you soon."

Chapter Three

Jacey stared at the card in her hand. "Colin Jennings. Construction. Builder of Houses. My Brother's Keeper." A cell number. And a Biloxi, Mississippi, address. She flipped the card over. "Promise I won't try to baptize you in the bathtub," he had written on the back of the card. It made her laugh.

"Well?" Georgia said, throwing an armload of warm towels at her. "Here, help me."

"Well, what?" Jacey said. She began absently folding.

"Are you going to call him?"

Jacey shrugged. "I don't know. Should I?"

Georgia sat down on the sofa. "Why wouldn't you?"

Jacey shrugged again. "You know, maybe it was just the circumstances that made the feelings so strong, and there's no point in pursuing it. Maybe it was all just this grand illusion I created in order to survive. That's possible, right?"

"I guess so," Georgia said. "But maybe it wasn't. You've talked about him for a solid year. He's here. Shouldn't you explore it?"

"I don't think I can be hooked up with a preacher, Georgie. That's just not gonna work for me."

"See, I don't understand that. He's still a *guy*. He's not a priest. It's okay for Baptist preachers to have girlfriends, wives, families. I was teasing when I said you were going to hell."

Jacey stood up. "Like I ever pay attention to what you say," she said. "And it isn't that."

"Then what is it?"

"I . . . I like to wear shorts," she said, moving the stack of towels from the sofa to the coffee table. "And cute little dresses. I like to go to parties. And although I rarely drink, when I get ready for a glass of wine . . . I want to drink it."

"So what you're saying is, you'd give up what you've described for a year as the perfect guy for a Marc Jacobs dress and a bottle of Cabernet?" Georgia said. "That makes you sound pretty shallow, but that's none of my business."

"Okay, point taken. Maybe it does sound a little shallow," Jacey said. "But what about you? Would you give up something for another person?"

"But we're not talking about me." Georgia laughed. "I'm not giving up anything for anybody. I've ridden that pony before, but my guy was a jerk. We're talking about you. And this guy . . . I don't know, Jacey. He seems like a pretty good fella. I get a good vibe from him. Besides . . . I haven't heard him ask you to give up anything."

Jacey shrugged but didn't answer.

"I've gotta go to work," Georgia said. "Listen, it ain't like the man has asked you to marry him. Just visit with him. This conversation is very premature. Maybe he took one look at you in that pile of orange taffeta yesterday and wondered what he'd been thinking these past few months too. Especially after you spit on him in the car with them big fat swollen lips."

43

Jacey laughed. "I guess you're right. Couldn't hurt to talk, huh?"

"You have chosen wisely, grasshopper." Georgia stood, grabbed her purse, then pressed her hands together. "Dear Lord, please help the people of this city behave tonight and not bring any hysteria, guns, or lawyers into my emergency room. Amen. See? I pray too."

Jacey laughed again. "Have a good shift."

"Good luck," Georgia called out as she shut the door behind her.

Jacey picked up Colin's card again. Then she closed her eyes and the memories came . . .

She was sitting in her car, looking at the bridge in front of her. The water rushed over the road, but it didn't look very high. Surely I can make it, she thought. She had the radio on the local channel, and they weren't reporting any road closures. If it was unsafe to drive over this bridge, they would report it, wouldn't they? The "Turn around, don't drown" commercials kept playing over and over in her mind, but this didn't look dangerous at all.

Besides, she needed to talk to these people. The article she was writing had the potential to shed some light on an element of the South that was largely forgotten. The downtrodden. The poor.

The uneducated. Many people subscribed to the theory that these people chose to stay in their current situation and live off of whatever the government would give them. But Jacey had spoken to too many of them to buy into that. They didn't want a handout. They wanted a hand up. She would do all she could to extend hers and make sure other folks around the South had the opportunity to do so as well.

She waited a few more minutes to see if any other vehicles were passing in either direction, but she saw none. The storm was getting more and more intense with every passing minute. Rain pounded the car so hard it was deafening. Wind bent trees in every direction and lightning popped right in front of her. She couldn't turn around: This country road was too narrow and had no shoulder, and she certainly couldn't back up. Her shortcuts had never been wise, and this one was shaping up to be the worst one ever. She made a decision and began driving . . . and for a moment, she thought she would make it . . .

She shivered and opened her eyes. "Stop it! Stop it!" she said aloud. "Don't relive it."

She looked at Colin's card again and picked

up her cell phone. She entered his number quickly before she could change her mind and texted.

"I'll be home this afternoon if you'd like to visit."

Before she could put the phone down, it vibrated.

"I'll see you at two."

Georgie's right, Jacey thought. *What could it hurt just to visit with him? I'm making a mountain out of a molehill, as my mama says.*

She went to her bathroom and got in the shower. *At least when he sees me this time I won't be covered in mud and muck—or orange tonfetti and fat lips.*

She grabbed a pair of white shorts, then decided against them. Should she wear shorts around a preacher? Then she put on a sundress with spaghetti straps and decided against that as well. Too much skin. She put on a pair of black yoga pants and a T-shirt that was a little oversized and was satisfied with that. But when she looked in the mirror, she saw what appeared to be a child dressed up in her mother's clothes.

"Ugh! This is ridiculous."

She finally grabbed a cool white cotton dress with no sleeves, very casual and comfortable. Not too short, yet not too grandmotherish. She slipped on a pair of brown leather sandals and put on a silver bracelet. Then she took it off. "You aren't going out to lunch," she chided herself. "Nobody wears bracelets around the house . . . or do they?" She put it back on, then took it back off.

She sat down at the vanity and applied a very thin coat of mascara to her already dark lashes and brushed her thick, shoulder-length hair. She put on a little lipstick, then rubbed it off with makeup remover. Too dark. She grabbed another shade and dabbed a little on, then rubbed it off too. She rolled her eyes. "He's not the pope or the Head Honcho and Bottle Washer of the Baptists," she said to the mirror. "He's just a guy." She settled for a clear gloss on her lips and went to the living room to wait for his arrival. And checked her appearance every two minutes until he arrived.

At exactly two o'clock, the doorbell rang.

She answered the door and smiled. "Hi," she said.

"Hi." He smiled back at her. "You look very pretty."

"Thank you." She felt her face flush a little. Great. Back to high school. "Please, come in." She stepped aside so he could enter the foyer.

Her memory had certainly gotten his features right. Over six feet tall, almost black hair, longer than most men wore it—but it worked on him. Piercing eyes so dark she could barely see where his pupils began.

She gestured toward the sofa. "Sit down. Can I get you anything?"

He sat on the sofa. "No, I'm fine."

Jacey sat down in the chair across from the sofa. "Listen, I want to apologize for yesterday. I was just so . . . stunned . . . when I looked up and saw you behind the pulpit."

"I was pretty stunned myself." He smiled. "The girl I'd been searching for all year turned out to be the prom queen."

Jacey laughed and relaxed a little. "I had some harsh words for the bride, I assure you."

"You look really good, Jacey."

"So do you," she said. "A lot better than the last time I saw you. On the roof, I mean."

"Georgia told me about . . . what happened. The accident," he said. "I'm so sorry."

Jacey was uncomfortable and stood up. "I'm gonna get a drink—you sure you don't want a drink? Oh . . . you don't drink, I guess. But I meant like some tea or something." She felt her face getting hotter.

Colin made a mental note not to bring up the accident again. "I'll drink some tea," he said. "And you can drink whatever you like. I'm a minister, not the liquor police." He smiled again.

She smiled back. "It's two in the afternoon. I wasn't going for the whiskey." She walked into the kitchen and fetched two glasses from the cabinet.

"This is Baton Rouge, right?" he asked. "I didn't think y'all put a time limit on the Jack Daniel's."

"Well, it isn't a game day." She grinned.

"Ah . . . she likes sports," he said. "A girl after my own heart."

That sentence gave her a little rush she wasn't expecting. She tried not to appear so pleased and searched her mind for a benign question.

"So, where are you staying while you're in town?" she asked. "At a hotel? With friends? A convent?"

"You do have a wicked little sense of humor, don't you? I think you've been around your friend too long."

Jacey laughed. "Could be."

"To answer your question, I have a travel trailer," he said. "I'm over at the Shady Palms trailer park, although I have seen no shade and no palms, for that matter."

"That's funny."

"Not a bad place," he said. "Interesting neighbors from time to time."

"I'll bet," Jacey said. "Listen, I meant what I said earlier. I truly am sorry about yesterday. The whole allergic reaction thing and . . . I guess I just don't know how to act around a preacher. I mean, of course I know how to act around a preacher . . . It's just, well . . . you know . . ."

"You're stammering again," he said. "You

know, you could act like you did the last time we were together. I'm the same guy I was then."

She took the pitcher from the fridge and filled up the tea glasses. "Not really," she said. "I mean, you know, I've never made out with a preacher. That makes me feel kind of . . . weird."

"I'm guessing you still haven't made out with a preacher. Unless you've been sneaking around the seminary. I wasn't ordained until recently."

Jacey laughed. "Then I guess you're right." She gave him his drink and sat back down in the chair.

"Do you have preacher problems?" he asked.

"I beg your pardon?"

"You seem a little hung up on the minister part. I thought maybe you collectively didn't care for pastors."

"Of course I like pastors, preachers, ministers, priests," she said. "I just . . . you know."

He smiled. "I don't know. Enlighten me."

Does he have to be so good-looking? she thought. *Preachers are old and soft and chunky. Not tall and dark and gorgeous. This isn't fair.* She glanced at his lips and quickly looked away. If the thoughts running through her head right now wouldn't send her to hell, she should at least have her ticket punched to purgatory for a century or so.

"I suppose I'm not sure what to say around you," she said finally. "On the roof, it didn't matter. We were . . . going to die. For a while I was sure of it. And you weren't a pastor at that time. You were just a guy. But the rules have changed now."

"Why do you say that?"

"Come on, Colin," she said. "Don't do that. You know what I mean. Things got . . . intense between us. We hid around the back of the roof and kissed and 'carried on,' as my late grandmother would've said. That's not something I would ordinarily do with a preacher or any other guy I'd only known for eight seconds. And we said things to each other. All kinds of things."

"What makes me different from the next guy?" he asked. "You're a beautiful woman. I'd have to be dead not to notice that. And by the way, I meant every word and every kiss."

Jacey put her tea on the coffee table and tried to find some graceful way to avoid telling him the truth. In the end, she gave up and spoke from her heart. "I meant it all too."

"Then if we both meant what we said, all we have lost is time," he said.

"This is real life, Colin," she argued. "We were knocking on heaven's door then. How could we possibly know it was real? We were under stress and duress and every other pressure word I can't think of right now. And, well . . . relationships that are based on intense experiences never work."

51

"Do you have an original argument or are you happy with quoting Bob Dylan and Sandra Bullock in the same sentence?"

Okay, he's not completely sheltered. He's listened to Dylan and watched movies. She laughed a little. "You weren't supposed to call me out on that."

"But I did," he said. "Look, maybe you're right. Maybe the circumstances led to the feelings. I don't know, but neither do you. I think we owe it to ourselves to find out. I've looked for you for an entire year, and to see you standing in front of me at a wedding I wasn't supposed to attend . . . well, I'd call that divine intervention. What would you call it?"

She shrugged. "Fate? Serendipity? Destiny? A coincidence?"

"Maybe," he said.

Jacey didn't reply.

"So how 'bout it?" he asked. "Want to go out with me tomorrow night?"

"Where would we go?" she asked. "I mean, what do you do when you go out?"

He leaned in close to her. "I'm gonna tell you a secret," he said. "Preachers eat at restaurants sometimes."

Jacey laughed. "Smart a—" she began, but cut herself off. Her face turned ten shades of red.

It was his turn to laugh then. "You were saying?"

"See?" she said. "I'll continuously have to watch my mouth."

Colin stood up. "You say that like it's a bad thing. But it's your mouth, so say whatever you want to say. I'm pretty sure I can handle it."

She smiled.

"Thank you for the tea. I'll pick you up around seven. And wear something casual. Preachers eat crawfish too."

She walked him to the door and held it open for him.

"See ya," he said, fixing his eyes on her lips for a brief moment.

The look wasn't lost on her, and she remembered just how good it felt to be kissed by this man. She put her hand on his chest and shoved him. "Get out of here," she said, laughing.

"One day soon you'll beg me to stay," he said as she closed the door.

"You wish!" she called after him, smiling from ear to ear. She heard his laughter outside.

Jacey leaned up against the closed door. The memories were rolling in like waves.

The car shifted in an instant. One second she was on the road and the next she could feel herself being swept away in the rain-swollen creek. Panic and paralysis struck. When she was finally able to move again, she grabbed her cell phone. She

53

tried to dial 911 but dropped the phone in the gush of water that came into the car. She yanked off the seat belt and searched the submerged floorboard for the phone. She finally found it, but it was already dead, waterlogged just that fast. Suddenly she realized the car was going to sink and she had to get out. She pressed the button to lower the window and shouted, "Come on, come on!" It had never moved so slowly. It finally stopped altogether before it reached the bottom. She squeezed herself out as the water poured over her face, as she coughed and sputtered. When she was free from the car, she tried to swim—but there was no swimming, only riding the current and grasping at the air for dear life because there was nothing else to reach for. Water, water everywhere . . .

Chapter Four

"I'm just curious," Jacey said as she discarded the fifth blouse. "Have I always dressed like a prostitute?"

Georgia lay on Jacey's bed and watched her dress and re-dress for half an hour.

"I'm curious myself. Do all the people in this city wait to do stupid stuff until I'm on duty, or am I just lucky like that?" Georgia asked.

"Georgie, focus. This isn't about you."

"Well, it should be," Georgia said.

Jacey glanced at her. "Are you eating chips in my bed again?"

"Only for the last thirty minutes." Georgia crunched the bag.

Jacey made a face. "Please sweep the crumbs out this time."

"I'm not leaving any," she said, swiping her hand over the floral comforter. "And I'm starving. There was no time for snacks last night. Can you believe there was a twelve-year-old who used super glue on her false eyelashes? And, oh, why is a twelve-year-old wearing false eyelashes? you ask. I don't know! Maybe we should ask her mother, who so generously told me if I wore a little more makeup and lost twenty

55

pounds, maybe I'd have a ring on my finger and a better attitude."

Jacey laughed. "Are you serious?"

"As a heart attack," Georgia said. "Then there was the twenty-year-old frat boy who thought stair surfing on a mattress was a good idea. Ten stitches under his chin for him, and a nice story for his grandchildren in the years to come. And of course, let's not forget the man having chest pains who actually entered the hallowed doors of my ER eating a chili dog. With jalapeños and extra onions."

"You need to go to a floor and get out of the emergency room," Jacey said.

"What? And miss all that?" Georgia said. "Yawn. It's too boring on the floor."

"Then stop whining and help me find something to wear."

"Seriously? The last fifteen things you've put on would've been fine. You're eating crawfish. Jeans, a T-shirt, and flip-flops would be appropriate."

"I know, but all of my T-shirts look . . . racy."

"Your T-shirts look racy?" Georgia said. "Frankly, you look like a preadolescent boy in your T-shirts."

"You're so funny," Jacey said. "It's so sad I can't shop for bras the same place you and Dolly Parton do."

Georgia glanced at her chest. "They do have their advantages."

"Focus!" Jacey said again.

"Fine." Georgia sat up and threw Jacey one of the discarded shirts from the bed. "Wear that and the jeans you have on. I'd run out and get you something new, but I have no idea where the Sisters of Aloysius shop for their habits."

"Eat your chips and shut up," Jacey said. "My T-shirts are tight. That's all I meant."

Georgia lay down again and stuck her hand in the chip bag. "They fit. Your T-shirts fit." She waited until Jacey looked in the mirror to quickly wipe the chip crumbs from the sheets.

"I hear you sweeping," Jacey said.

"Oops." Georgia smiled.

"When he gets here, you answer the door," Jacey said. "I don't want to look too eager."

"Wow," Georgia groaned. "I thought we were beyond high school, but okay."

"What are you doing tonight? Do you have a date? Because you need to have a date."

"I do have a date," Georgia said. "A date with Netflix and a cell phone whose battery has been removed. The perfect evening."

"I'm sure I won't be late," Jacey said. "You and I can hang out when I get home."

"You never know," Georgia said. "Preacher Man may have some tricks up his sleeve."

Jacey made a face. "I don't know how I could

ever kiss him without wondering if God was watching me."

"I don't know how to tell you this, but God was watching you last time you kissed him."

"I hate it when you make sense," Jacey said. "By the way, Buck called today. He left a message."

Georgia shrugged, but not before Jacey saw the hurt cross her face. "Color me so surprised. You can erase the message. I'm not going to listen to it."

"It's been a long time, Georgie," Jacey said. "Maybe you should hear him out and be done with it. Stop holding on to pain."

"There is no more pain," Georgia said, although Jacey doubted that was true. "There's just no point in rehashing it. It's done. He's sorry. He made a mistake. Blah, blah, blah . . . same old message. He needs some new material."

Jacey didn't respond. There was no need to argue about it. She'd tried that approach before. Georgia was still hurt from Buck's infidelity nearly two years after the fact. Jacey certainly didn't blame her, because she was mad at Buck too. But for Georgie's sake, she wished she could forgive him and let the whole thing go. Whether Georgia knew it or not, the hurt she still felt spilled over onto everything in her life.

"Okay then," Jacey said. "Makeup or no makeup?"

"Have you taken a recent turn for the Pentecostal?" Georgia asked.

"No." Jacey laughed.

"Then I would say put on some makeup. You know, you're making this a *lot* harder than it has to be," Georgia said. "Just go eat some good crawfish. Talk about whatever comes up. And don't worry about the Sermon on the Mount or the disciples or the Red Sea. Just have fun."

"You know an awful lot about the Bible."

Georgia made a face. "I'm not a barbarian."

Jacey laughed and went straight for the jab. "But you are a Catholic." She knew she would light a match, and Georgia didn't disappoint. There was a good-natured feud in part of Louisiana between Catholics and Baptists, and some folks on each side secretly thought they were just a little superior to the other. Jacey just liked to tease her friend. She personally didn't think God really cared what label you wore.

Georgia threw her hands up and hopped off Jacey's bed. "Why do people always assume Catholics don't know anything about the Bible?" She began folding the discarded T-shirts. "I went to catechism, which is the equivalent of Sunday school, for your information. The difference was, the nuns beat me into submission on a regular basis."

Jacey was laughing out loud now. She loved

59

stirring Georgia up about religion. "No they did not."

"Name the books of the Old Testament, Miss Bankston," Georgia mimicked. "Um . . . Genesis . . . Exodus . . . um, let's see . . . *Whop!* No, Sister Mary Pia, don't beat me! Come again? You want me to say a prayer? Dear Lord, don't let my parents find the cigarettes in my purse. *Whop!* No, Sister Mary Pia! Please!"

Jacey sat down on the bed, laughing at her friend. "Stop," she said. "You know it wasn't that bad."

Georgia made a face. "No, not really. But I did get my hand popped by Sister Mary Pia. *Every day.* But . . . they made sure I learned, and now I appreciate that. And I'll give them the benefit of the doubt. I was particularly hard to teach, I am sure." Georgia smiled. "You know . . . smart mouth."

"So hard for me to imagine you with a smart mouth," Jacey joked.

"I'm sure it is." Georgia laughed. "Anyway, the answer to your question is yes, you Protestant snob. I know my Bible."

"I won't question your biblical knowledge ever again."

"Thank you," Georgia said. "And in return, I'll send up a novena for you."

"You can send up a smoke signal for me if you think it'll work," Jacey said.

"There's an idea," Georgia said. She grabbed the empty chip bag and openly brushed her crumbs from the comforter as Jacey watched and groaned. "Now put some makeup on and get ready. I'll man the door."

"You are a sweetheart," Jacey said as Georgia left the room.

"Yeah, yeah, I hear you."

Colin arrived at seven sharp, and Jacey tiptoed to her bedroom door to hear his conversation with Georgia.

"Do come in, Rev."

"Nurse Georgia."

"She'll be out in a few minutes," Georgia said. "She's . . . doing something. Brushing her hair, trying to find the hat that matches her habit . . . I don't know."

Jacey rolled her eyes. She was going to kill her. But Colin laughed.

"So, where are y'all going and what are you doing tonight?" Georgia asked.

Colin glanced at his watch. "I think that's a record, Georgia. The interrogation started within eight seconds of entering this house."

"I must be slipping," she said.

"I think we'll go to over to Sammy's," he said. "They had good crawfish last time I ate there."

"Good call. I always enjoy crawfish at Sammy's," Georgia said. "So, what did you do today? Baptize any sinners?"

"Not today, but there's still time. You interested?"

"Me?" Georgia asked. "No. Thank you, though. I'm Catholic. I went ahead and did that at about three months."

"I have a good friend here in town who's the priest over at St. Aloysius," Colin said. "Wise man. I enjoy our talks."

"That's where I went to grade school," Georgia said. "I'm glad you like the current priest. Tell him I need to go to confession next time you see him."

"Is it going to make him blush?" Colin laughed.

"He may need oxygen," she said. "I'm glad you don't have a 'Catholic thing.' Sometimes other denominations do, you know."

"The Baptists haven't cornered the market on Jesus."

Georgia smiled. "You're a good guy, Colin."

"Could you tell her that?" He nodded toward Jacey's bedroom door.

"Tell her yourself," she said. "Jacey! The preacher's here!"

"Don't let her big mouth bother you, Colin," Jacey said, coming out of her bedroom. "She's all bark."

"I bite sometimes," Georgia said. "Ask Mr. Chili Dog from last night."

"You bit him?" Jacey asked, horrified.

Georgia laughed. "No, bonehead! I wanted to

bite the chili dog. But, yeah . . . that woulda been gross."

"You look exceptionally pretty tonight," Colin said.

"Thank you." Jacey smiled.

"I was actually talking to Georgia." Colin smiled and winked at her.

Jacey's mouth flew open. "You are awful!"

Georgia cackled. "Oh, I'm gonna like you," she said. "Say, Rev, you got any brothers? Matthew? Mark? Luke? John?"

"Let's *go,* Colin." Jacey grabbed his arm and led him to the door. "Go sew somebody up, Georgie."

"Is she always like that?" Colin laughed.

Jacey laughed with him. "Since the day I met her."

Springtime on the bayou meant something very important to most Louisiana folks. Besides the return of college baseball, it was crawfish season. The mudbugs were finally making their appearance much to the delight of . . . well, just about everyone in the state. Sammy's was a local favorite, and it was packed. Colin and Jacey would have to wait thirty minutes for an inside table, so they chose to sit on the side patio in the meantime.

Colin pulled out a black iron chair for her, and Jacey sat down. She waved at a couple sitting in the corner and spoke to a girl she knew from one of the magazines she contributed to now and then. The atmosphere tonight was vintage Baton Rouge, with a melting pot of people well represented—most of them loud and proud and representing the colors of their favorite teams, celebrating everything from birthdays to anniversaries to just being alive. Jacey often thought of Baton Rouge as New Orleans Junior. A zydeco band played inside the restaurant, just loud enough for Jacey and Colin to enjoy the music but still carry on a conversation.

"I'll say one thing for Baton Rouge," Colin said as he sat down. "Y'all sure know how to have a good time."

Jacey laughed. "It's a great place to live," she said. "I've been here nine years now, and I am always finding something new and different and exciting about this city and the surrounding areas."

"You aren't from Baton Rouge?" he asked.

"I'm from Shreveport," she said. "Well, Bossier City, to be exact."

"I know where Bossier City is. I worked on their port for a little while a few years ago. Back during my wandering days."

"There were wandering days?" she asked. "I'm intrigued. Do tell."

Colin smiled. "Boring and uneventful," he said. "I'd much rather hear about you and Bossier

City. What were you like growing up? Is your family still there? Any brothers or sisters?"

Jacey laughed. "You sound like Georgia," she said. "She's an interrogator too."

Colin smiled. "I'm sorry," he said. "I realized when I was searching for you this past year that we didn't cover these things on the roof, did we? We talked about . . . other things."

The smile faded from Jacey's face, and she fidgeted in her chair a bit. "Yes, I guess we did."

"Can I get you a beer?" said a pretty, perky college girl, breaking the spell at the table.

"Sweet tea for me," Colin said, seemingly oblivious to her batting eyelashes. "Jacey? Anything?"

"Tea's fine."

"Are you sure?" the waitress asked Colin, smiling broadly as she placed her hand on his shoulder. "The beer is ice-cold and flowing tonight."

"No thanks, tea is fine," Colin said politely.

"Okay, I will be right back," Perky Patty promised and sped away.

"I'm surprised she didn't sit in your lap to take your order," Jacey said.

"I'm sorry?" Colin said.

Jacey chuckled. "You didn't notice the sali- vating?"

Colin smiled. "Well, I *do* have that effect on

women. I guess it's my boyish good looks and Southern charm."

"You're so full of it," Jacey said.

Colin laughed out loud. "You got me, and no, I didn't notice. Besides, she was quite young, wasn't she?"

Jacey lifted her brow. "She seemed older than her years."

Perky Patty arrived as promised with their drinks. "If there is *anything* else I can get for you, my name is Susi with an *i*," she said to Colin. "And I'll be standing right over there." She pointed at the hostess podium just inside the door.

Jacey wanted to laugh but pursed her lips together.

"We thank you, Susi," Colin said, then turned back to Jacey.

Susi with an *i* hesitated a moment before she hurried off again.

"Does that happen to you a lot?" Jacey asked. She was slightly annoyed but mostly amused.

"As I said—" he began, but Jacey lifted her hand.

"I know, I know, the boyish charm thing. Whatever."

He winked. "It worked on you."

"It did not," she said. "Those were . . . trying times." Jacey took a sip of her tea. Too much sugar. She winced and poked her tongue out.

"You want something else?" he asked. "Wine? A beer?"

She studied him. "It's just a little sweet for my taste. And why are you trying to make me drink? Is this a ploy to get me tipsy and take advantage of me?"

Colin seemed surprised but grinned. "Miss Lang, there is nothing I'd like better than to seduce you, but I don't think my current status would allow me to feel good about it later."

Jacey smiled back. "Besides, wouldn't it bother you if I drank a beer?"

He shrugged. "I don't have a strong aversion to someone drinking a beer every now and then, or a glass of wine with a meal. Now, I'll admit I don't usually share that information with my fellow clergy because they would probably frown upon it." He smiled. "I personally don't drink anymore because my grandfather was an alcoholic. My father may be one—I really don't know. And I don't want to tempt fate."

Jacey nodded, wondering what he meant about not knowing if his father was an alcoholic. Since he offered no explanation, she didn't press it. "Probably a wise decision since alcoholism runs in families. But doesn't your opinion make for, I don't know, problems in your church? I mean, I've been Baptist all my life. I know drinking is, like you said, frowned upon."

"That's exactly why I don't share that opinion

with very many people," he said. "Also, I don't pastor a church. I prefer to do what I do: rebuild after disasters. There are lots of ways to reach people, and most of the ones I run across in those situations need not only financial but also spiritual help."

"So you just follow disasters around?" Jacey asked.

"I followed you, didn't I?"

She laughed. "An astute assessment, I assure you."

"To answer your question seriously," Colin said, "there are thousands of people out there who will never walk in a church for just that many reasons. Maybe they feel undeserving—as if God couldn't possibly love them because of things they've done. Maybe they feel like they'll be rejected by the members. Sometimes Christians are our own worst enemy," he said. "We act like we've cornered the market on forgiveness when we deny it to others. Of course, that does nothing but turn people off. Nobody wants to be looked down on. Church should be a hospital for sinners, not a gathering place for saints. And no, I didn't coin that phrase, but I agree with it 100 percent. It isn't always a popular stance. I prefer to be in the world, one-on-one. I don't want to watch over a congregation. I applaud the men and women who can, because the world needs them, but I'm not one of them."

Jacey was impressed, and her respect for him soared. "That makes perfect sense," she said.

"Now, we somehow got off the subject of you," he said. "Tell me about your family, about where you grew up."

Jacey shrugged. "There's not a lot to tell," she said. "I have one brother, Grayson, who is younger than me. He's at Texas A&M in his last year of college. He's studying to be a vet. In fact, he just got accepted at LSU's vet school, so he'll be here next year. My parents are great. My mom, Lisa, is a stay-at-home, and my dad is a financial adviser. That's why Georgia says I am so . . . let's see, 'cheap and frugal,' I believe." Jacey laughed. "I like to save my money."

"Nothing wrong with that," Colin said. "Where'd you go to school?"

"I went to high school at Captain Shreve," Jacey said. "Great school, loved it. I was a cheerleader and a swimmer. We lived in a nice subdivision in Bossier City, the kind where all the kids come out to play after school and on Saturday mornings. My parents still live there. And we had block parties too. I used to love block parties."

"So you kind of grew up in a perfect world?" he mused.

Jacey wasn't sure what to make of that statement. "I grew up in a secure world with my parents and brother," she said. "But we had our moments. Doesn't everybody?"

"Don't get your feathers ruffled," Colin said. "If I sounded . . . envious, I didn't mean to."

Jacey studied his face. "I'm guessing you didn't have the best childhood?"

"Let's just say it wasn't like yours," he offered.

Jacey didn't reply. If she'd learned one thing this past year, it was that pressuring people into talking about something they didn't care to talk about didn't usually yield a positive result.

Susi with an *i* appeared to tell them their table was ready, and Colin grabbed Jacey's hand when she stood up. Susi deflated a little and Jacey smiled.

The crawfish were excellent, hot and spicy, the tails tender and juicy and fresh from the ponds. The corn and potatoes took on all the right flavors from the boiling pot, adding another texture to a meal fit for the King of Mardi Gras. Food just didn't get any better than this. Neither Jacey nor Colin had eaten any this season, and the first batch was always the best crawfish you ever had. These did not disappoint.

"I can't eat another bite," Jacey finally said, pushing the platter away.

"I ain't quittin' yet," he said.

"Ugh," she said. "I feel like a cow."

He smiled. "But you still look like a lovely little heifer."

"Such blatant flirtation from a man of the

cloth!" She laughed. "Be careful not to sweep me off my feet."

"I already did that," he said. "Last spring."

"Last spring," she repeated, gazing out the window.

> And just like that, she was racing through the rushing waters, grabbing for anything that would slow her down. She slammed into limbs and other debris and groped blindly for a firm hold. The water pulled her under, then spit her out again, ten, twenty times. She sputtered and gagged and tried to scream for help, but the water was a vortex—spinning and swirling with raging force. She couldn't stay above it long enough to cry out. She was surely going to die. No one could survive this. Finally, she managed to clutch a limb as the water continued to gush in torrents. She held on for dear life.

"Jacey?" Colin said.

She looked at him, taking a moment to register where she was.

"Are you okay?"

She shook her head. "Uh-huh."

He wiped his hands and stood up, then threw some cash on the table. Susi with an *i* was there in an instant.

"Can I get you any dessert?" she began.

"That'll do it for us," he said to her and pulled Jacey's chair back. "Thank you."

"What about your change?" Susi asked.

"You keep it," he said. "Are you ready, Jacey?"

"It's okay," Jacey said. "I'm fine, really."

"Come back to see us!" Susi called after them.

Colin grabbed Jacey's hand as they walked to the car. When they got in, he looked at her.

"Do you want to talk about it?" he asked.

"I do not," she said.

They rode in silence all the way back home.

Chapter Five

"I'm sorry, Colin," Jacey said, breaking the silence as Colin parked in front of her condo. "I've been . . . Lately I get these . . . unwanted and unprovoked images in my mind. Memories. I don't know why and I don't know how to stop them. I'm not sure I want to stop them. But they terrify me." She didn't know how to explain it to him without sounding as crazy as she sometimes felt.

He took her hand. "Don't worry about it," he said. "You've had a lot to deal with. If you want to talk about it, I'll listen. If you don't, we'll just talk about something else. I just like being here with you."

She closed her eyes and leaned her head back against the seat. He made her feel so comfortable and so safe. Maybe she *did* want to talk about it, but she wasn't sure how to begin. There was no rhyme or reason to the memories when they came, and no easy way to explain how they felt. What she did remember was sketchy and fragmented at best.

And what difference did it make anyway? It almost made her mad at this point. Why didn't the images just stop showing up? The flood was over, done, finished. She should be able to shake it off, as the rest of the world apparently had. She just wanted to carry on with her life. Jacey had asked to see Lillie and her boys, but the doctors had told her they were taken to another hospital, treated, and released—so that was good, a relief. But something about that night of the rescue still nagged at her. Troubled and uneasy feelings still flooded over her at the oddest times. Like tonight at Sammy's, when Colin had mentioned something about springtime. She had glanced past him and through the window and seen the magnolia tree outside—huge and old and loaded with big white flowers—and the memory of the turbulent water had almost taken her breath away. She saw it as clearly as a photograph: She was holding on to a magnolia limb, full of blooms, sweet and fragrant, while the water swept her away.

She opened her eyes. "It was a magnolia limb," she said.

"A magnolia limb?"

"When I was in the water, before I made it to the roof, I was holding on to a magnolia limb. It was huge. The tree must've fallen in the storm," she said. "And tonight, when I saw the tree outside . . ."

"You remembered," he said. "And you're right, it *was* a magnolia limb. It was still on the roof when we left."

"Is that good? It's good that I remembered that, isn't it?"

Colin took her other hand and held them both close to his face. "I would think it's good to remember, but I'm not a psychologist," he said carefully.

"You think I need a psychologist?" she asked, alarmed.

"I don't know," he said. "But if you do, there's certainly no shame in it. That's what psychologists do, Jacey. They help you."

She pulled her hands away and leaned against the seat again. "But what could I even tell him? I see little bits of things I don't understand? It's so frustrating to remember a little bit at a time. And the memories aren't always sequential. I remember pieces of things, little morsels, and sometimes they make no sense at all. Like, there's this memory I have of a gold necklace—a locket, of all things. I have no idea why."

"Don't try to force it," he said. "Let it come to you. And when it does, don't fight it. Whatever you are remembering isn't happening again. It's just a memory."

"I try to tell myself that all the time," she said. "When I start to feel panicky, I remind myself it only happened once. Sometimes it works. Sometimes it doesn't."

"You will remember it all one day," Colin said softly, "but not until your mind is ready. That's okay. Don't force it to happen." He touched her face gently with the back of his hand.

She looked at him silently, trying to decide if she should say what she was thinking. The old Jacey would never even consider it. She was cautious and careful. But After the Flood Jacey thought, *Why not?* She guided his hand back to the side of her face. "The only thing I remember clearly and quite vividly . . . is you."

Colin pulled her closer. "I remember you clearly, too, and I've remembered you every day and night since," he said. Then he lowered his lips to hers.

He kissed her, his lips gentle and undemanding. Then he pulled away quickly.

Jacey looked at him for a moment, then pulled his head back toward hers. This was what she'd been missing. No other kiss had measured up. Colin's kiss became more intense, and this time it was Jacey who pulled away.

"Not bad for a preacher," she said, trying to lighten the moment even though her heart raced.

He chuckled. "Yeah? We have tongues just like regular guys."

She laughed. "And apparently you know how to use it."

He smiled. "Can I see you tomorrow?"

"I'd like that," she said, opening the car door.

When he started to get out, too, she held up a hand. "No, stay. I think I want to be alone for a while."

"Okay," he said. "I'll call you tomorrow."

"Good night," she said.

"Good night."

Colin sat in the car and watched Jacey walk up the sidewalk and disappear inside her house. He felt like jelly inside. No one had ever made him feel the way Jacey did. He'd felt it a year ago when she was on the roof with him, covered in mud and cuts and scrapes and bruises. It wasn't just the situation that made his feelings so intense, as she had suggested. It was her—the way she carried herself with grace and confidence, even when in dire straits. He was attracted to her spirit and strength. He watched her compassion for those children and their mother, the way Jacey gathered the youngest boy in her arms and held him, told him stories, sang to him. The way she encouraged the obviously poverty-stricken mother and tried to help her plan for a better life after they were rescued. Amid a hopeless situation, she gave that family reassurance, and her cheerfulness never subsided. In Jacey he glimpsed a woman who was selfless and loving instead of one obsessed with money and prestige and appearances. It had been a long time since he'd met someone like that. He thought then that he was falling in love with her after only two days on a poorly shingled rooftop in the middle of a muddy sea. If he was falling then, he was plummeting now.

Jacey fixed herself a cup of tea and went to the patio. She sat on the chaise and looked at the stars. She absently traced her mouth with her fingertips where Colin's lips had been. The man sure could kiss, but she'd known that long before tonight. She'd dreamed of those kisses for a year. No one else's kisses stood a chance. She knew because she'd kissed a lot of frogs in the last few months . . . and that's exactly what they had felt like. Frog kisses.

She could remember every physical second of being on the roof with Colin—every touch, every gesture. Why couldn't she remember anything else? She closed her eyes and drank in the night air. She could smell the jasmine that climbed the garden wall near the fountain. And charcoal. One of her neighbors must have barbequed today. And of course she could smell magnolias. Magnolias had a distinct aroma, sweet and lemony. The south was full of magnolias, and they were in full bloom. Their shady street was lined with them. She tried to concentrate only on the clean, citrusy smell of the huge white flower because maybe it would take her back again. In a few short moments, she was back in the water.

The current had slowed a bit, and she no longer struggled for air. She was still moving quickly, but at least she wasn't being tossed around like a rag doll. She could see her surroundings, even though the rain came down in sheets. But the lightning was terrifying, and she needed to get to land . . . if only there was land. She saw only water and trees in every direction. No landmarks to lead her, no familiar sights. She had no idea where she was or how far from the road the water had taken her. Her arms fastened around the magnolia limb and she relaxed her legs. It wasn't like kicking them would help anyway. The undercurrent was way too strong. Even though the water had slowed, it still moved her into trees, debris, and other things she could feel beneath the surface but couldn't see. The slimy things she felt in the water made her scream with terror.

She looked for a tree with branches low enough to climb, but she could never position herself close enough to one. The current was still too strong for that. It would be dark in a little while, and she'd still be in this water. She could feel the first wave of panic beginning to creep into her mind. She had to get out of this swirling death trap before dark.

And then . . . she heard it. Children? Children crying? She whipped her head around every which way to find the sound, and finally she saw them. Straight ahead. A woman and four children on top of a roof, maybe fifty yards away. The woman was motioning to her, and the children were shouting to her. She repositioned her grasp on the limb and held on. She was headed directly toward them, thank God.

The top of the roof was surrounded by more trees, so it must have been in the woods. If they hadn't screamed to her, she might have never seen them. The water was moving faster now and she struggled to hold on, but her limb slammed into a tree. The branches slapped her in the face, but she barely noticed, and after she lost her grip on the limb she began swimming for the roof. Twenty feet away. Ten. They reached for her, all of them. She dragged herself up as they tugged her clothes and arms. She finally lay flat on the broken shingles, panting and bleeding from a deep cut above her right eye.

"Are you all right?" the woman asked. "Are you hurt?"

Jacey lay on the edge of the roof and

panted, trying to catch her breath. As the family gathered around her, a sudden rush of water carried her magnolia limb onto the roof beside her. One of the boys pulled the branch farther up on the roof, then leaned over her. "We'll keep it just in case we have to ride it out of here," he said.

"Hello! Jacey, are you here?"

Jacey opened her eyes, expecting to find herself lying atop black shingles. But Georgia was sliding the patio door open.

"It's early," Georgia said. "Why are you already back?"

It took Jacey a moment to collect herself. "What?"

Georgia's brows furrowed. "Are you all right?"

Jacey sat up straighter. "I'm fine."

"You sure?"

"Yep, all good," Jacey said, fully back in the present.

"Where is the good reverend?" Georgia sat down in a patio chair across from Jacey's chaise.

"I sent him home," Jacey said.

"Oh?" Georgia said. "He try to sprinkle you with holy water?"

Jacey smiled. "No, he was quite the gentleman."

Georgia looked deflated. "Oh. How . . . boring."

"He *did* kiss me," Jacey said.

"Ohhh . . . better, much better. Tell me more."

"Nothing more to tell," Jacey said. "Were you here when I came in?"

"No, I had to run to work for a little while," Georgia said. "So much for my Netflix date."

"I'm sorry. I know how close you and Netflix are."

Georgia laughed. "I'm still about to binge. I just covered for another chick so she could go to a ball game or something. I didn't really ask. If you ask questions, they'll tell you, then you have to act interested, and then they think you're friends. Blah, blah, blah."

Jacey shook her head. "You are an awful human," she said.

"I know. But it sort of balances out your sickening sweetness, which is nice."

Jacey smiled. "Again . . . you are an awful human."

"Agreed," Georgia said. "So, what are you doing out here all alone?"

Jacey shook her head. "I'm just trying to remember. And it's driving me crazy."

Georgia looked at her and sighed. It was hard to watch her friend struggle, but she knew these were demons Jacey had to face by herself. She couldn't tell her about the boy or about his mother. Jacey needed to remember it in her own time. There was nothing she could do about it now, and forcing the memories on Jacey could cause more harm than good. As a trauma nurse, Georgia knew not to push the mind's limits when it had seen things it just couldn't accept. Jacey would find her way out of the darkness. The best Georgia could do was to be there, without questions or judgment, and without urging. She leaned back into the chair. "I'll just hang out here with you for a while."

Jacey smiled at her again. "You aren't really an awful human."

Georgia smiled back. "I know."

Chapter Six

Colin drove away from Jacey's condo with a frown on his face. Jacey's state of mind worried him. In fact, he wasn't entirely sure his presence was beneficial to her. As much as he wanted to be here with her, if he thought it was harmful, he'd leave and never return. Maybe he could help her spiritually. It was his job to help her spiritually, but his feelings for her clouded his own judgment. It was easy to advise people when you only had their best interests at heart. But with Jacey, it was different. It had everything to do with her ending up in his arms. All he wanted to do was wrap her up close to him and shield her from every bad thing in the world, including the memories that tormented her . . . the very memories that Jacey wanted to flee and embrace at once.

The cell phone rang and he smiled, hoping it was her. But when he looked at the screen, he saw the name. *Jasper Jennings*. He immediately felt the anger stir inside him. What did his father want this time?

"Hello?" Colin said.

"Well," Jasper said. "I'm surprised you answered."

"I'm surprised you called," Colin said.

"I'm going to cut to the chase and offer you the reins of this company one more time."

Colin clenched his jaw. "I don't want to do this with you again, Dad," he said. "I'm not interested. Sell the company."

"Colin, you can still be—what did you call it?—a 'good man' and run this company."

"Like you are?" Colin asked, immediately regretting the words. He had to forgive this man—if not for his father's sake, then for his own.

Jasper drew in a sharp breath. "Contrary to what you believe, I have a good reputation in this city."

"I don't know what bothers me more," Colin said, resigned to the fact that forgiveness was not coming tonight. "The fact that you care about what other people think, or that you couldn't care less about what I think."

"You have the same blood running through your veins as I do, son," Jasper said in a low and cautionary voice. "You may hate it, but it's true. Eventually, the Jennings will come out. This is your company, and I won't have a stranger sitting at the helm."

"Are you done?"

"One more month," Jasper said. "I'll give you one more month to come to your senses. Then I want your answer. If I have to sell this company, I will cut you off from the money and from this family. Not that you'd mind the latter. Don't be a fool, Colin."

Colin cut the connection and dropped the phone on the seat beside him. He shook his head. It was just like his father to threaten him with money. That's all the man knew—all he'd *ever* known how to do. He sent Colin a ten-thousand-dollar check every month and assumed Colin used it to live on. He had no idea his son lived in a travel trailer that he pulled around behind his truck, or that he only used the Jennings money to buy materials for rebuilding homes. In fact, his father didn't know much of anything about him and never had. His mother and the hired help raised him in a Biloxi mansion that Jasper Jennings rarely graced with his presence. He was always at work. Or in another city. Or in the arms of another woman. Or God only knows where else. When he did come home, he had very little to do with anyone in the house—especially his only child. Colin had spent his lifetime wondering why his own father resented him. He certainly wanted no part of the multimillion-dollar Jennings Construction . . . or what his mother had so appropriately dubbed "Jennings Destruction."

He thought about his mother. Ava McKinna Jennings was the consummate long-suffering Southern belle. Always a lady, ever aware of the outside world watching and waiting for the make-believe castle to crumble. The women of the society page weren't always as kind and gentle as they looked. Their tongues were sometimes more deadly than swords. Sadly, his mother was included in that clique. She called it survival. She could be kind and tender, especially with Colin, but he'd seen her cut other women to the quick with her words, and he'd seen them do the same to her. Colin loved his mother but didn't understand her. He'd never understood why she allowed herself to be sucked in by this life of pretend marriages, where prestige equaled material things and children were mostly trophies. He pitied her and could not comprehend why she stayed in a loveless and emotionally abusive marriage. Several times in the past he'd asked her why she didn't divorce his father. Most of the time he got no answer at all. If he did get one, it was always the same: "You should try to reach out to your father, Colin. He isn't as bad as he seems." Colin couldn't comprehend why she always defended the man.

Growing up, he'd played the part of a child of privilege. Mostly for her, but he hated it. He loathed boarding schools and country clubs and the brand of clingy Southern belles who were groomed to marry well and do little else. He had very few close friends, and most of them felt the same way he did . . . even if they *did* accept their fates in their father's offices, or the reins of companies they never wanted. They were heirs apparent to the thrones that were thrust in their paths. Only Colin and his lifelong friend, Joshua Aaron, took different roads. And both of those roads enraged their fathers.

Joshua was Colin's best friend and had been since they were in grade school. Joshua had been groomed since childhood to take over his father's medical practice, a highly regarded and successful orthopedic clinic that catered to athletes. But Joshua wanted to be a football coach, a far cry from the prestige he could acquire by joining the family practice. He and his father had debated, fought, slammed doors, and disowned each other many times after Joshua announced his intent to forgo the medical practice for coaching. It had taken many years before Dr. Aaron forgave him, but eventually he had. The difference in the Jennings household was Colin and his father had never shared the same relationship as Joshua and Dr. Aaron. In fact, they hadn't shared a relationship at all.

Colin drove up in front of his travel trailer in the Shady Palms trailer park and turned off the ignition. He let his thoughts turn to Jacey. Just thinking about her made him smile, and the unpleasant conversation with Jasper was temporarily forgotten. He knew Jacey had been jealous of the little waitress earlier. He saw the girl flirting with him, but didn't want to encourage her or let on to Jacey that he'd noticed. Jacey's reaction had delighted him. He wondered what she was doing in that moment, and hoped the memories would leave her alone tonight and let her rest.

The little boy whimpered in Jacey's arms. She whispered in his ear, "It's okay, buddy. It's okay." But no amount of soothing helped. The fretting soon turned into sobs, and she held him on her shoulder and rocked him. She began singing the first song that popped into her head. The words of Van Morrison's "Into the Mystic" filled the stillness of the night. The rain had mercifully stopped for now, and the only sounds were Jacey's voice and the water lapping at the roof. The boy, Demarcus, grew still in her arms while she sang, and she felt an overwhelming sense of peace as she gently swayed him back and forth. Then, suddenly and without warning, he was ripped away from her.

Jacey sat up in bed and screamed. Georgia was by her side in seconds.

"Another dream?" Georgia asked.

Jacey wiped the sweat from her face. "Somebody jerked him out of my arms," she said. "It was dark . . . I couldn't see who it was. But they took him." She was shaking and close to tears.

Georgia turned on the lamp by Jacey's bed. "It's okay," she said. "It was just a dream."

"But that's just it," Jacey said. "I don't think it was."

Georgia remained quiet. She offered no hints. "You want some water? You want to get up for a while?"

"I want to get up," Jacey said. "But you go back to bed. I'm fine. I promise. You have to work tomorrow."

They walked into the living room, and Jacey sat down on the oversized sofa. "You can go back to bed, Georgie. I'm fine, really."

"I've worked on less sleep than this," Georgia said. "I'll stay up with you awhile."

"This is happening more frequently now, isn't it?" Jacey asked.

"What do you mean?" Georgia asked. She went into the kitchen to fill the kettle with water.

"It just seems like these dreams and little snippets are coming fast and furious now," Jacey said.

"Maybe it's your mind telling you that you're ready to remember all of it," Georgia said.

Jacey remained silent and thoughtful for a few moments. "I think it has something to do with Colin showing up. What do you think?"

"I think sometimes a person, or a song, or a

smell even, can trigger . . . all sorts of things," Georgia said. "Even if we wish it wouldn't."

Jacey glanced at Georgia dipping tea bags in and out of their cups on the kitchen island. She knew Georgia was thinking about Buck, but she'd never admit it.

"Here," Georgia said, offering Jacey the steaming cup. "Let's see if this sleepytime tea is a marketing ploy or the real thing."

"That sounds great," Jacey said.

Jacey was still shaken by the dream, but she wasn't afraid this time. She wasn't frantic, which was new. Usually when she remembered something or had a nightmare about the flood, it frightened her and she tried to stop the memory. Tonight she was filled with curiosity for the first time since the accident. Instead of pushing the thoughts away, she embraced them. "I want to find the family," Jacey said. "I want to see them."

Georgia snapped her head around. She'd known this moment was coming. Jacey had never mentioned wanting to see the mother or the children after the flood. Georgia figured it was her mind protecting her again, or maybe the doctors and nurses had satisfied Jacey's curiosity. Part of that was true. Georgia knew that deep down, Jacey knew something tragic had happened—but her subconscious was keeping her from pursuing the answers to her questions.

"Did you hear me?" Jacey asked.

"I did hear you," Georgia said. "We'll see what we can do." Georgia made a mental note to go straight to Jacey's neurologist's office as soon as she got to work in a few hours to see what he thought about this new development. She liked Dr. Plauche. He was always very forthcoming and helpful when she asked questions about Jacey, while being careful at the same time to guard doctor/patient privacy.

Jacey sipped from her cup of tea. "Where should I start?"

"I'm not sure."

"I feel different tonight, Georgie," Jacey said. "I don't know why I haven't thought of this before. I should've reached out to them a long time ago. Maybe I'll make some calls tomorrow."

"Hmm," Georgia mused, not entirely sure what advice to offer. "Maybe Colin can help? Biloxi is his neck of the woods."

"That's a great idea," Jacey said. "I'm sure he will at least know where I should begin."

"Right now, let's focus on getting sleepy again," Georgia said. She wanted to at least talk with Dr. Plauche before Jacey went full-fledged investigative reporter on her. "I have to be at work in four hours."

"You're right. I'm sorry," Jacey said. "I'm keeping you up. Go to bed. We'll talk about it tomorrow."

"Only if you go back to bed too."

Jacey stood up. "Good night," she said and headed to her bedroom.

Georgia smiled. "See you in the morning. You sure you're okay?"

"I'm fine," Jacey said. "I promise. I actually feel better than I have, emotionally, in a long time."

Georgia retreated to her room. Jacey watched her close the bedroom door, then sat down at the desk in the living room and turned on the computer. She could get a jump start on locating Lillian and her children right now. She put her hand on the chair at the desk and stood there before pulling it back. A few times before she had sat at this same keyboard to search for answers about the flood, but for some reason, she always changed her mind. Something always kept her from plugging in the information. She knew even then, of course, that her subconscious was keeping her from looking—but she always justified it some other way. She told herself she was in a big hurry, or she reasoned she didn't know the full names of the family on the roof—anything to keep herself from actually looking. She defended all those obstructions in her mind, knowing full well the journalist in her could have figured it out anytime she wanted. The difference was, tonight she was ready.

She looked at the desktop computer, slowly pulled back the chair, and sat down. There would be many stories online about a mother and four children who had been stranded on a roof for days in a flood. There would be pictures, articles, opinions, and human interest stories. Maybe even an interview with some of her fellow roof tenants.

Jacey looked at the search bar and pondered what to type. Finally, she wrote, "Mother and children stranded in flood, Biloxi, Mississippi." The images popped up immediately. She recognized them! Picture after picture of the sweet family she'd shared that harrowing experience with filled up the computer screen. She looked at the sweet faces of the children and the captions underneath. Dewayne Jackson, nine years old; Derek Jackson, six years old; Devin Jackson, five years old; and Demarcus Jackson, three years old. Their mother, Lillian, age thirty, smiled down on them. Jacey saw the gold locket around Lillian's neck and recognized it at once. It was the same locket she sometimes dreamed about. Of course it belonged to Lillian Jackson. They were beautiful children, and Jacey grinned at the picture. So happy, cheesing it up for the camera. Demarcus was smiling so big you could see his precious dimples. Colin had told Demarcus his dimples were so deep he needed a Q-tip to clean them. That had made the older boys and

Lillian laugh. For some reason, looking at his face on the computer screen made Jacey want to cry.

Jacey scrolled down to find the story that accompanied the photograph. And then she saw it. The headline: "Mother and son die in boat crash after flood." What? What was this? She slapped at the scroll bar with a shaky hand.

> **Thirty-year-old Lillian Jackson and her three-year-old son, Demarcus, were killed Saturday when their rescue boat collided with another. Also killed in the crash were . . .**

Jacey stopped reading. Her heart hammered in her chest. "No," she whispered. "No, no, no, no . . . ," she repeated over and over, hoping the black-and-white words blaring on the screen would somehow rearrange themselves. But they didn't change, and she read them again and again. She felt tears stinging her eyes, and she blinked as they blurred her vision.

> **The mother and son were being rescued from a three-day stint on their roof in rural Harrison County. They were passengers in a boat when they collided with another rescue boat on the rain-swollen river. The remaining children**

are being treated at a local hospital. No word on their conditions. An additional survivor is listed in serious but stable condition. Her identity hasn't been released.

Jacey gripped the sides of the chair until her knuckles turned white. As she stared at the computer screen, the memories started to flood over her again. Things that had been hidden in the corners of her mind for so long suddenly leapt at her from every angle. Images, smells, sounds were as real to her on this night as they had been that evening. She closed her eyes and clung tightly to the chair. She could almost taste the murky water.

The men—no, the angels—who had come to rescue them said there were tornado warnings out, and two had already touched down nearby. "Jimmy," Jacey whispered out loud. His name was Jimmy, and the other one was Dan. The men moved them carefully off the roof and into an aluminum boat with a small motor. They had to move quickly. The rain had started again, and it brought the crackling lightning and deafening thunder with it. The wind was picking up with every passing minute. Jacey wanted off of the roof, but she didn't want to leave Colin.

"There's no room, Jacey. I can't go," Colin said. "But you have to go now. I'll be all right. They will call someone for me. It's okay. I promise. You have to go now."

"I don't want to leave you," she said.

"I know, but you have to," Colin said, shoving her from the roof into the boat. "Go. I'll be fine. I promise."

She kissed him, hard and fierce and fast. "You find me," she said. "Swear."

He crushed her against his chest. "You have all my numbers. Don't lose them. Jacey . . . I . . ." He stopped talking, but his face said it all.

She smiled. "Me too," she said, feeling everything he felt and more. She held on to his hand until she couldn't.

As they sped away, Jacey gathered Demarcus into her arms and watched Colin until the roof faded from sight. She tried to face forward, but they were moving too fast. Her eyes teared, and she couldn't see anything except water and trees anyway. She kept Demarcus close to her as they bumped into floating trees and God only knew what else in the swirling water that seemed to stretch forever.

She smiled at Lillian and the other boys.

"We're gonna make it!" she shouted over the motor. "Didn't I tell you that?"

They grinned at her, and Lillian smiled almost serenely, one hand holding the locket around her neck and the other gripping Devin. "Thank you," Lillian mouthed.

Jacey smiled at Lillian, and in the next instant she heard Jim shouting, "Look out!"

She saw the other boat, but only for a split second. Flying, weightless, splashing, sputtering, pain, darkness meshed into one feeling and then, nothing.

Jacey remained in the chair, her hands still gripping the arms and her heart racing as fast as it had on that boat a year ago. Demarcus had flown out of her arms in an instant—she hadn't held him tight enough, she *couldn't* hold him tight enough. Something stronger than her had ripped him from her arms, and she never had a chance against it. Neither did he. She felt the tears rolling down her cheeks even though her eyes remained tightly closed. For the first time in a year, she remembered Demarcus with perfect precision. Sweet boy, with his dimpled cheeks and Elmo giggle. He loved toy cars and

Pop-Tarts. He talked about wanting Pop-Tarts for three straight days. Jacey had promised him they would buy a sackful as soon as they set foot on dry land. He loved his mother and his brothers ferociously. When he sat in Jacey's lap, he had twirled her hair in his fingers. And when one of his brothers got close, he'd shove him away and say, "No! My Jacey!" That made Jacey smile.

She opened her eyes and looked at his picture on the screen. Then she sobbed. She sobbed with months' worth of pent-up frustration, from being held prisoner by her own mind . . . and with the fresh pain of grief for a child she'd known only briefly, but whose loss left her heartbroken.

Chapter Seven

Colin was startled out of a deep and dreamless sleep by the banging on his trailer door. He looked out the window, then grabbed his jeans, which were lying across the chair.

What? Jacey? What was she doing here in the middle of the night?

He pulled on his jeans and opened the door. Without a word, Jacey flung herself into his arms.

Colin held her against him. She wasn't crying, but she was visibly upset. He pulled her inside without breaking the embrace and closed the door behind them.

After a minute, she whispered, "I remember. All of it."

He held her tighter. "I'm so sorry, Jacey. I'm so sorry."

She gently shoved herself away and looked at him. "I couldn't hold him, Colin. It happened so fast. He was in my arms and then he was just . . . gone."

Colin's heart ached for her as he looked down at her face. Her eyes were swollen. Her hair was a mess. She wore yoga pants and a T-shirt and wasn't even wearing shoes. He led her over to the sofa.

"Look at me," he said. "Are you all right?"

She shook her head slowly. "I am. I'm just really, really sad." Her voice broke slightly, and he reached for her again but she stopped him. "I know I look a mess, and showing up here in the middle of the night is just awful. I'm not a stalker. But I just needed . . . I wanted . . ."

"Sh . . . ," he said and pulled her back into his arms. This time she relented. "You can stalk me anytime."

"I didn't know where else to go," she said.

"You came to the right place."

She began to cry again. "How can my heart hurt so bad for a child I knew only three days?" she asked. "He wasn't even mine."

"That's not true," Colin said. "He shared something with you that was life-threatening for all of us. Of course he had an impact on your life. You could've known him for fifteen minutes or fifteen years. The result is the same . . . You feel a loss. You're supposed to feel a loss."

Jacey cried against him for a long time, remembering everything about the precious little boy who was so happy even amid a disaster. Demarcus didn't care. Even as the rain pounded around him, he played and giggled and teased his brothers. It wasn't fair. His whole life had been in front of him.

Jacey's tears finally subsided, and she nestled herself into Colin's chest. "I don't understand why God lets things like this happen."

Colin stroked her hair. "I don't either," he said. "I know that's not the answer you were looking for, but it's the only one I can give you. I may be an ordained minister, but I'm just a man. I would never presume to know the mind of God."

"At least you're being honest with me. But I want to know why Demarcus had to die."

"So do I," Colin said. "But I can't explain childhood cancer or accidents or any other tragedy. And I can't explain why Demarcus is gone. It hurts me too."

"He was precious," Jacey said. "So sweet and trusting and happy. Even under the circumstances he was happy."

"I know," Colin said.

Jacey sat up suddenly and looked at Colin. "What do you think happened to the other kids?" she asked.

"I don't know. Did they ever talk about their father? Maybe he has them."

"He wasn't in the picture. Does the state step in during a situation like that?"

"What do you mean he wasn't in the picture?" Colin said, puzzled. "Not at all? Were they divorced?"

"Something Lillian said to me . . . ," Jacey said. "When Lillian was still pregnant with Demarcus, he left. She hadn't heard from him since, but I don't know where he went. We had that discussion before you showed up."

Colin thought for a moment. "I guess the State of Mississippi would step in under those circumstances. I imagine the boys are in foster care."

Jacey didn't like the way that sounded at all. "Do you think we could find out?"

"We could try," Colin said. "What do you have in mind?"

Jacey shrugged. "I don't know . . . I'd just like to see them. At least make sure they are okay after the accident. Make sure somebody is seeing to their needs. Those boys were abandoned by their father, and now their mother is gone. Can you imagine what they must be feeling?"

Colin smiled and pulled her to him again. Her heart was as big as the moon. He loved her.

There. He had acknowledged it.

"We'll start looking for them tomorrow," he said. "I promise."

"Thank you, Colin." She put her arm around him and rested her head on his chest again. "I really need to go back home," she murmured sleepily.

"Not a chance," Colin said. "Close your eyes. Sleep."

Colin woke up much later to the sound of his cell phone vibrating on the table beside the sofa. He picked it up, then glanced at Jacey, still sleeping in his arms. The text was from Georgia.

"Please tell me you know where Jacey is. I woke up to go to work, and she isn't here. And if she isn't there, don't scold me for losing her."

Colin chuckled. He texted back:

"Asleep in my arms."

The reply came seconds later.

"I knew it! Don't call me when the hellfire and brimstone starts falling on you two sinners."

Colin shook his head.

"It wasn't like that," he wrote. "She needed me."

"And I need Blake Shelton, but we see how that's working out. I'm going to work. I'll be stopping by St. Aloysius to pray for you both. Maybe the priest will give me some holy water to sprinkle on you. I hope it doesn't sizzle. I'll pick up a new rosary for good measure."

Colin chuckled, then replied:

"Knock yourself out. I'll take any prayer I can get. By the way, I want you to meet a friend of mine."

"Did you find one of them?"

"Aaron."

"What does he do?" she asked.

"He's a football coach."

"Hmm . . . interesting. I'll think about it."

Colin placed the phone back on the table and smoothed the hair away from Jacey's face. Her eyes were swollen. She had a bit of sleep drool on her lips, and she was snoring slightly. He'd never seen a more beautiful woman. He wanted to pull her against him and kiss her until she begged him to stop, morning breath and all.

Jacey opened her eyes, and for a moment had no idea where she was. But she knew without a doubt the arms that enfolded her belonged to Colin Jennings. She looked up. "Good morning," she said.

"Good morning." He smiled.

She tried to sit up, but he held her next to him.

"I need to go home," she said. "I am so sorry I showed up here in the middle of the night. I assure you I don't normally do this."

"I didn't assume that you did," he said.

"I should've at least called you first. I am so embarrassed."

"Why would you be embarrassed?" he asked. "This was exactly where you should've come. To me."

She didn't answer right away.

"Let me ask you this," he said. "Did you feel safe here? Do you feel safe now?"

"Yes," she said.

"Is there another place you wish you'd gone?"

She answered truthfully, "No."

"There's your answer."

She relaxed against him. "Colin, do you think there really is . . . something between us?"

"You should be glad there are clothes between us," he said.

She smiled. "That's not what I meant."

"I know," he said. He pushed her away from him so he could see her face. He crooked his finger under her chin. "Look at me, Jacey."

She looked at his dark tousled hair and bare chest and tried to think about anything besides how incredibly good he looked this morning.

"What's between us is real," he said. "It was real on the roof, and it's real today. But I have to tell you something . . ." He paused before he continued.

"I think I'm falling for you," he said. "I knew it a year ago. It's because of your courage and compassion and your heart. You can call it crazy, and you can say it's too soon. But I'm falling for you harder and faster than I ever thought possible."

Jacey stared at him. Frankly, he could've sung the ABCs after saying he was falling for her because she didn't hear the rest of it. The ringing in her ears prevented it.

"I need to go," she said, getting up from the sofa. "Do you know where I left my shoes?"

Colin stayed on the sofa. "You didn't wear any," he said.

"You know what? I didn't," Jacey said, nervously moving all over the travel trailer in quick bursts, looking for things she didn't even bring with her last night. "Then I guess I just need my keys."

"I put them on top of the refrigerator," Colin said.

She walked quickly to the kitchen area and tried to reach the top of the fridge, but didn't even come close. She saw a box on the floor, dragged it over, and stepped on top—but she fell straight through.

Colin chuckled and stood up. "Empty," he said.

Jacey smiled and stepped out of the cardboard. "Sorry," she said. "If you could just reach my keys, I will get out of your hair. No point in hanging around. I've taken up too much of your time anyway, and I need to . . ." She watched him walk slowly toward her. *That chest. That wavy, messy hair. That body.* She cringed. Georgia was right. Jacey *was* going to hell.

"You need to what?" he asked.

"Touch . . . I mean go. Um, I need to go," she said.

Colin reached toward the top of the fridge, fetched her keys, and dropped them into her hand. Then he lowered his face closer to hers.

"Okay then," she said, pointing toward the door. "I'll just go ahead and go now."

He smiled and let her pass by without reaching for her.

"Bye, now," she said, practically jogging to the door.

"Bye."

Jacey slammed the door of the travel trailer and ran through the grass, wet with morning dew. She could not get out of there fast enough. Falling for her? Why did he say that? He'd said it *out loud*. Was he insane? Clearly there was something wrong with the man, and she'd just spent most of the night at his house. What if he was a serial killer posing as a preacher? He could be an escaped convict. Or mean to dogs. What if he liked cats? A man didn't just go around telling women he didn't know that he was falling for them. It was crazy, and *he* was crazy too.

She glanced at the clock in her car and drove straight to the hospital where Georgia worked, ten minutes away. When she got to the emergency room parking lot, she texted Georgia.

"Come outside ASAP."

She put down the phone and closed her eyes. Her thoughts turned back to Demarcus and Lillian. Her heart ached as she thought about that sweet boy who never got a chance to live, and the thought brought fresh tears to her eyes. She pictured him twirling her hair and singing nursery rhymes in her lap. And telling her about his cars and trucks. She felt sick each time she remembered the force that ripped him away from her, knowing she had been powerless to stop it. But she was determined to find the other three boys and make sure their lives turned out to be something special—for their mother and their brother.

Georgia opened her car door and startled her.

"Good morning, you brazen harlot," she said. "Please tell me all about it. Don't leave out a single detail."

"I remembered, Georgie. I remembered what happened after the flood. All of it."

Georgia's demeanor changed immediately. "Oh, Jacey, honey, I am so sorry. Are you all right?" she asked. "Do you want to come in and see if we can find Dr. Plauche? He's probably making rounds."

Jacey sighed. "No," she said. "I'm okay. I promise. In fact, I feel much better now that I can remember it."

Georgia grabbed Jacey's hand and squeezed it. "I wish I could've told you," she said. "We just didn't think it was a good idea. Dr. Plauche thought it would be better for you to remember it on your own. Did it just come back to you?"

"Well, not entirely," Jacey said. "After you went back to bed last night, I starting snooping around online. It only took one search."

Georgia shook her head.

"I don't think I really wanted to know Not until lately," Jacey said.

"Because of Colin?"

"Probably," Jacey said. "Seeing him has sped up the flashbacks. Before he came, they happened every now and then. But when he showed up . . . boom. I could almost summon them. I couldn't take it anymore. It made me feel so anxious. I think last night I just decided it was time to know, and I knew exactly how to find out."

"And you're sure you're okay?"

"I am, really. I've decided I'm going to find the other boys. I want to make sure they're all right and being taken care of."

"I think that is a fabulous idea," Georgia said. "I'm in too. Now . . . about last night . . ."

Jacey rolled her eyes. "Nothing happened."

"Don't even try to sell me that. He's a preacher, not a dead man. And I am quite sure preachers have sex. How else do they get all nine hundred and ninety-nine of them kids they all have?"

"You are so depraved."

"Oh, I know. What's that got to do with anything?"

Jacey looked at her friend. "He told me he thought he was falling for me."

Georgia's mouth flew open. "Really? How exciting! What did you say?"

"I got my keys and left," Jacey said, her voice indignant.

"How . . . mature of you," Georgia said.

"What was I supposed to do? He doesn't even know me."

"I don't think that's entirely accurate," Georgia said. "I think he got to know you pretty dang well on that roof. I think for each day you spent together there, it was like . . . three months in dog years."

"Be serious, Georgie."

"I am serious," Georgia said. "I think the man knows exactly what he wants, probably always did. He found it, lost it, and found it again. He was probably afraid *not* to tell you. Think about it."

Jacey didn't answer.

"Let me guess," Georgia said. "Your overactive writer's imagination has turned him into some dangerous criminal, probably a member of ISIS, and you've decided you should stay away from him."

Jacey made a face. "Serial killer," she murmured.

Georgia's eyebrow shot up. "Oh, even better," she said. "Let me ask you this: How does he make you *feel?*"

Jacey smiled a little bit thinking about waking up in his arms, strong and protective.

"See?" Georgia said, reading her face.

"Still, it's . . . I don't know . . . *soon.*"

"My grandparents got married four days after they met and stayed married sixty-four years," Georgia said. "Next argument?"

Jacey didn't have one and was suddenly a little ashamed of herself for running out of his trailer so quickly. She looked at Georgia. "He sure can kiss."

Georgia smiled. "Looks like it," she said. "And I'll tell you something else. You need to get honest with yourself."

Jacey frowned. "What do you mean by that?"

"You need to examine your feelings for him. I think they run a lot deeper than you realize."

Jacey brushed her off. "No," she said. "I know you're cheering for the fairy tale, but there ain't one going on here."

"You sure about that?" Georgia asked. "By the way, I want you to pull the rearview mirror down and take a good look at yourself. Surely he meant what he said. I can't even look at you right now."

Jacey pulled the mirror down and looked at her reflection. She looked horrible. Swollen eyes complete with evidence of the sandman's visit. Mascara all over her face, hair a hot mess, and some kind of nose debris stuck on her cheek. She made a disgusted face. "Ugh."

"Not a pretty sight, is it?" Georgia asked. "Go home and do something about it before you venture out into the world today." She opened the car door and put one foot out. "I'd like to stay and chat, but a nice gentleman with a power saw removed one of his thumbs this morning. I'm thinking that's a wee bit more important than all this self-created drama."

Georgia shut the door and left Jacey staring at her reflection.

Chapter Eight

Colin stirred the scrambled eggs and smiled. *Could she have gotten out of here any faster?* When she had fallen through the box, it was all he could do not to laugh out loud—but she was already like a doe in headlights, so he'd held it in check. She was a beautiful mess, and he loved everything about her. He was glad he'd told her he was falling for her, even if it did send her running out the front door. Keeping the words to himself had felt like a weight around his neck. She was falling for him too—he was sure of it. It was just going to take her longer to figure it out. That was fine with Colin. He had nothing but time. In fact, he was going to let her stew in her juices for a while.

He checked his watch. He had an appointment with Reverend Willis this morning across town. Then he was going back to Biloxi for a couple of days for business. One of his houses was nearly finished, and he wanted to make sure the work was done and done right. He trusted the men he hired, but he always liked to be there for the final inspection.

More than anything, though, he really wanted to go back because this was the best part. He liked to watch a family when they held the keys to their new house for the first time. There wasn't another feeling like it in the world. Being a part of that moment kept him going. Even when the money ran out, even when he couldn't find any help, even when his father tried to stop him, seeing the faces of a homeless family walking into a house that was *theirs* made all the struggles worthwhile. His father called it "wasting money," but Colin called it "investing in people." And the battle raged on.

He knew he'd eventually have to talk face-to-face with his father and stop the phone calls. Jasper wasn't the type to conduct family business over the phone. He wanted his son in front of him so he could hammer and hammer and hammer until he chiseled him into resolve. But Jasper had no idea who he was dealing with. The only reason Colin had avoided another man-to-man talk was because it never ended well. He already knew what Jasper would do: First he'd try to make him feel guilty. Tell him how hard he'd worked all his life to pass the company along to his only son. When that didn't work, there would be more threats of being cut off from the money. Colin had tried time and time again to tell him he didn't want the money, that he could make his own way in the world. That sounded a lot better than saying, "I could never steer this company because I don't respect the man at the helm. I may be your biological son, but I have no idea who you are."

Colin pushed the plate away and drank the last swallow of coffee. Maybe this week was a good time to have the final showdown with his father and cut ties with Biloxi altogether. He liked Baton Rouge. He thought about Jacey sleeping in his arms this morning. And he sure liked the scenery.

He picked up the phone and dialed the numbers.

"Hello?"

"Aaron?" Colin said.

"Hey, buddy," Aaron replied. "Where you been, man?"

"Baton Rouge," Colin said. "Taking care of a little business."

"That sounds right," Aaron said. "What else is going on?"

"I'm headed back to Biloxi for a few days and need a place to crash."

"Door's always open for you, brother," Aaron said.

"Thanks, man, I owe you. Hey, speaking of owing you . . . Remember when you said you wanted to find a good Catholic girl with her own mind, her own job, and a sense of humor?"

"Had I been drinking?"

"I was at Mass with you." Colin laughed. "I think you'd only had communion."

Aaron laughed. "I remember."

"Well," Colin said. "Have I got a girl for you."

∙ ∙ ∙

Jacey stood in the shower and alternately thought about Colin, Demarcus, Lillian, and the other boys. Her heart ached with the loss and her tears fell silently, washed away with the water that swirled down the drain. But it wasn't just sorrow she felt. Something else began to rise inside her and fought for her attention. So many conflicting feelings . . . sorrow and hope, anxiety and exhilaration, regret and contentment. This wasn't over yet—the flood, the death of Lillian and Demarcus, her own injuries wouldn't end in sorrow. Jacey wouldn't allow it.

She wanted to begin the process of finding the surviving boys today. It broke her heart to think about them all alone in the world, no mother or father, and a little brother they adored, gone. She prayed they were together and happy, regardless of where they were. Maybe a family had adopted them all, or maybe they were in a foster home awaiting placement. Whatever the case, she was determined to find them and see for herself. She would make it her mission to see that those boys had a fair chance at a good life. It was the least she could do.

"I'm falling for you," Colin had said. Those little words took up a minuscule amount of space on a piece of paper, yet they had the power to change someone's entire world. The words had scared her out of her mind this morning, made

her run out of his house like a kid caught stealing bubble gum. Why had she done that? It seemed childish and immature to her now, but earlier it had been her natural reaction. She'd heard those words before from another man she'd dated for a nearly a year, but they didn't scare her then. In fact, she was ashamed to say she hadn't really felt anything at all. Except maybe a little guilt because she hadn't felt the same way. But they certainly hadn't made her run. So why did she run out of the house at Mach 5 with her hair on fire this morning? She had to go back to the trailer and apologize to Colin for acting like a child. Besides, she thought what scared her most of all was that she felt the exact same way he did. She wondered if she was falling for him too.

Jacey turned off the water and hurriedly dried her body. She wrapped a towel around her hair, put on her robe, and went to the kitchen. She would try some of that sleepytime tea this morning. Surely it would knock her out. Maybe she *wasn't* falling in love with Colin Jennings: She just needed some sleep, and that was all. She had learned and remembered some disturbing news last night, and she wasn't thinking clearly. That was understandable.

She would've run out the door regardless of what he said. The man was half-naked and gorgeous. *Really* gorgeous. And those lips . . .

she didn't need to be there. Of course she ran. It was absolutely the normal response any self-respecting Southern girl would've had. Probably. Maybe. Sort of. Not really. She put the kettle on the burner. Then the realization punched her in the face.

"You're an idiot," she said out loud. "A walking, breathing idiot. You *are* falling in love with him."

Somehow saying the words out loud made her reaction crystal clear. Colin's words hadn't scared her to death: Her own feelings had. She'd never been in love before, so she didn't know exactly how it was supposed to feel. But *overwhelmed* was a good word to start with, followed closely by *excited, apprehensive,* and for some reason, *liberated.* She felt alarmingly and deliciously aware of another human being. How about just plain old *freaked out?* So this was how it felt to fall in love . . . She decided she liked it.

She turned off the burner and grabbed her phone. She had to tell him, *needed* to tell him. How could she keep this information to herself? No wonder he had told her. He'd recognized the truth and wanted to share it with her.

She dialed Colin's number, but it went to voicemail. Forget it. She'd drive over there and tell him herself. Wasn't that the proper protocol for saying, "I may be falling in love with you"? In person? Maybe. She didn't know. But nothing sounded sweeter to her than being near him again.

She rushed to her room to dry her hair and get herself ready. She was on a mission that had to be completed today. Right now. Yesterday would have been even better.

Fifteen minutes later she was in the car, headed for the Promised Land. The scenarios played through her mind . . . Should she just blurt it out as soon as he opened the door? Should she wait a few minutes? Throw herself into his arms on sight? They all seemed like excellent choices, as long as she got the words out of her mouth. She'd waited all her life to fall in love, and now that she was headed in that direction, she wanted to shout it from the proverbial rooftop.

She drove up in front of his trailer but didn't see his truck, and her natural high deflated a bit. Where was he? Had he said he was going somewhere today? She couldn't remember, probably because of the Olympic gold medal for sprinting she'd won when she left earlier. She parked the car and looked at her watch. She'd give it a little while and see if he came back soon. If not, she'd surely see him tonight.

Colin backed out of the driveway of Reverend Willis's office and steered his truck toward Interstate 10. He was headed to Biloxi, but an odd sadness washed over him. It was strange when you no longer looked forward to going home. He didn't really have a home to go to anyway. The travel trailer was home to him now, and he could park it anywhere.

Reverend Willis had certainly given him a lot to think about. Colin had made it clear to the man once before he wasn't interested in serving as the pastor of any church—that instead he preferred to minister to the outside world. But Jim Willis had another idea. He wanted Colin to be the pastor of their new outreach program. They wanted someone who would minister to the needs of people in dire straits, and not your average Sunday-morning pew-sitter. Reverend Willis said he already had a church full of pew-sitters, but he wanted to extend a hand to the less fortunate and needed help to do it. Colin's title would be associate pastor, but he wouldn't always work within the walls of the church. Reverend Willis assured him he would still be able to build homes for the needy and rebuild for people who had lost their property in disasters, and he hoped Colin could even find some new volunteers to help him among the members. Colin agreed to think about it.

He did give it serious thought as he drove toward Biloxi. An associate pastor of a church the size of this one meant a good salary and benefits to go with it. He had to start thinking about the future. Especially if he wanted to invite Jacey into it. The money his grandfather left him was almost gone, which was okay with him. He always thought it felt dirty, like he was using mafia money or, at best, ill-gotten money. His grandfather wasn't really one of the good guys. He had started Jennings Construction years ago, and Colin was embarrassed by all the rumors about how crooked his grandfather was in business. One thing he could say for Jasper: When he took over the company, their reputation was improved trifold. Too bad Jasper couldn't factor that same respectful behavior into his personal life.

Colin used a little of the money from his grandfather to buy his truck and trailer, but most of it went to rebuilding homes. But now he had to be practical. If he wanted to continue doing what he loved, he would have to find another way to finance it. Jasper Jennings was about to cut him off. He figured his father had given him the money out of guilt for never being around, but it felt worse than taking money from a crook.

In the way they had so many times over the past year, his thoughts turned to Jacey. He smiled, wondering if she'd figured it out yet. She was a smart girl, so it shouldn't take her too long. He'd seen that look on a couple of other faces in his thirty years. In the meantime, it would do her good to wonder where he was for a few days.

Playing games wasn't his style anymore, but what Jacey needed was some space and time to think. She'd gotten an awful lot of information thrown at her at all at once. He knew expressing his feelings would scare her, but there was no sense in waiting. He'd seen too much in his life to worry with protocol. Her life had nearly ended ten minutes after he put her in a boat that day, and other lives had. No one was promised tomorrow. All the more reason to tell her today.

Jacey waited for nearly an hour before she decided to go home. Where was he? Didn't he know she was about to burst with this new-found affection for him? Shouldn't he be waiting around to see if she were going to come back? *Who does that?* she thought. *You basically tell someone you're in love with them and then go to the grocery store?*

She drove home and crawled onto the sofa. She was truly exhausted . . . too many emotions last night, too much information today, added to very little sleep. She put her cell phone on her chest so she'd be sure to hear it ring, then closed her eyes. *Only for a moment,* she thought. *I'll just lie here and rest my eyes.* She was asleep inside two minutes.

"Hello?"

Jacey stirred on the sofa. "Is it already four?" she asked.

"If it isn't, the ER is missing a nurse," Georgia said. "Have you been asleep all day?"

"Only since about noon, I think." Jacey looked at her phone. Still nothing from Colin.

Georgia put down her bag and sat in the chair beside her. "Well?" she said. "Any more developments in the case?"

Jacey smiled. "I'm falling in love with him, Georgie. I am." She spoke as if she was revealing a big secret.

"Duh," Georgia said. "I could've told you that last year."

"Whatever." Jacey laughed. "You didn't know."

"Willow and I both knew. You're the bonehead who had no clue. You walked around here all down in the dumps, dating every guy who walked by. You spent an entire week in and out of consciousness asking for Colin. It wasn't hard to figure out."

Jacey laughed again.

"So? Did you tell him?" Georgia asked.

"I went over there to tell him, but he wasn't home. And I have no idea where he is. I thought he would've called by now."

"Probably still stinging from that eloquent reaction and how lovely you looked this morning," Georgia said. "I would've caught the first bus out of town."

"Ha-ha, you're so funny," Jacey said.

"Oh, I know, but that's not the issue here,"

Georgia said. "By the way, I am officially off until next Thursday."

"That's right," Jacey said. "Thursday till Thursday. I had forgotten your vacation was coming up. What are you going to do with your freedom for seven entire days?" Jacey asked.

Georgia leaned her head back. "I may spend them all in this chair. Has it always been this comfortable?"

"You say that every time you sit there," Jacey said. "And I agree. It was our best purchase ever."

"When you marry Colin, I get custody of this chair."

"I can't even get him to call me back. I think you're counting your chickens."

"We'll see," Georgia said.

Jacey threw a pillow at her. "I'm cooking tonight. Tacos and margaritas."

"My dream supper," Georgia said. "If he won't marry you, I will."

Chapter Nine

Colin woke up early the next morning and headed out to the deck of Joshua Aaron's beachfront home. He was glad Joshua had kept the house after his parents moved to Florida when his dad retired. This house was one of Colin's favorite places. He felt a deep sense of peace when he was here. Probably because he'd always found refuge here.

He took a deep breath and exhaled slowly. He missed the Gulf when he was away, even if there was very little else he missed in Biloxi. He missed the sound of the waves rolling onto shore early in the mornings when it was still silent everywhere else in the city. He grew up listening to the Gulf every morning and every night. As he looked down the deserted beach, he could see the majestic mansion on the bluff nearly a mile away where he'd grown up and where his mother and father still lived. He'd like to say he missed his childhood home, but the truth was, he didn't. It wasn't his home anymore.

He took a sip of coffee and continued to stare at the lonesome stretch of beach between his youth and the man he was today. Fifteen years ago he'd run down that beach all the way to this very house with a duffel bag full of clothes, forty-six dollars in cash, and his pride. He'd swallowed that pride and gone home the next day when Jasper had found him. Colin probably should've planned that escapade better than he had, but at sixteen, it was the best he could do. Since then, running away from Jasper Jennings had become the thesis statement of his life. But no more. It was time to put an end to the constant turmoil that had defined his relationship with his father for as long as he could remember. He realized long ago he'd have to forgive his father for being inattentive while he was growing up, even if calling him "inattentive" was generous. There had been no playing catch in the backyard, no fishing expeditions on Saturday mornings, no tucking in at bedtime, and no camping out under the stars when Colin was a boy. In fact, his father was so absent it used to surprise Colin to catch a glimpse of Jasper at the house.

For many years, Colin used his father's absence as an excuse to do anything he wanted. It was his favorite crutch. He had learned exactly how to hold Jasper hostage, thus beginning the four years of his life when he punished his father. He agreed to go to college if Jasper agreed to leave him alone. The older Colin got, the more Jasper wanted to permeate his life with his suggestions, but Colin couldn't believe it. Jasper had never had a thing to do with his son—then all of a sudden when it came time for college he wanted to be his buddy? Colin wanted no part of it and didn't even realize he was shoving away the very thing he'd craved all his life. All he knew was that it seemed to hurt his father when he didn't want to be near him, so the games continued.

College was a four-year nonstop festival that Jasper financed without question. An endless parade of frat parties, women, and alcohol. Colin maintained a C average by the skin of his teeth. Most of the time he was in a bar with his buddies. It was in one of these bars that his life would change.

Jasper showed up unannounced a week before Christmas during Colin's senior year. Colin was shocked when he opened the door of his apartment one day and Jasper walked straight in.

"What are you doing here?" Colin asked.

"I came to help you pack," Jasper said.

"What?"

"Your mother wants you to come home for Christmas, and I'm here to see that you do as she wishes," Jasper said.

"I'm afraid you wasted a trip." Colin almost laughed. "Since when did you start caring about my mother's feelings?"

Jasper's face turned red, but he didn't reply to the insult. "Where are your suitcases?"

"Dad," Colin said, forcefully this time. "I am not coming home for Christmas. I am going on a ski trip with my . . . a girl. It's already planned.

I'm not ten years old. You don't get to choose for me anymore."

Jasper sat down on the sofa, and for the first time in Colin's life, he saw defeat on his father's face. He thought witnessing Jasper's pain would bring satisfaction, and he waited for the euphoria that should accompany it . . . but it never came.

"Colin, this isn't about me," Jasper said. "It's about your mother. She is very upset that you have chosen a trip over coming home, and frankly, I am too. You should—"

"Just stop it, Dad," Colin said. "I'm sorry you drove up here, but I don't believe you came for Mother. It isn't your style to go to bat for somebody else, not even my mother. I'm not buying it." He'd never moved away from the front door and he opened it. "You need to go home."

Jasper didn't say a word, just picked up his hat and walked out the door without looking back.

Colin waited exactly five minutes before driving to Trinidad's, a nearby bar. He began drinking early in the afternoon, and his buddies soon joined him and they stayed well into the evening. He'd managed to numb his feelings with Scotch, but his father's voice still echoed in his ears. And for some reason, the look he'd seen on Jasper's face was bothering him.

He didn't particularly want to be in this bar, but he couldn't go back to his apartment. If he did, that girl would call or come over and she'd stay. What was her name? He kept forgetting it, even though she'd made it a point to be at his place much more than he wanted her to be. He'd only met her a couple of weeks before, so he had no idea why he'd agreed to go to Vail with her other than his love for skiing and the fact that her parents owned a house there. It certainly had nothing to do with her. She was exactly the kind of girl he was expected to date and eventually marry, but she bored him out of his mind. He realized he was using her—for all kinds of things—and that realization didn't make him feel any better.

His friends had long since gone home, but Colin stayed at a little corner table, alone with his thoughts and his Scotch. It was nearly one a.m. Closing time. He moved camp from the table to the dark mahogany bar and asked the waitress to pour him another round.

She wiped the bar in front of him. "I'm no expert," she said, "but I'm pretty sure you've had enough tonight."

"I'm no expert either," Colin said, "but I don't think a . . . twenty-five-year-old barmaid can tell me what I need or don't need. Besides . . . I don't wanna go home."

"I'm sorry to hear that," she said. "The good news is, you don't have to go home . . . but you can't stay here."

"Does the owner know how you treat your patrons?" Colin asked, only half-joking.

"He does."

"I just need a nightcap," Colin said.

"Can't do it, buddy. I'm closing in fifteen minutes. But I'll call you a cab."

"Got my car outside."

"Not on my watch," she said, grabbing his keys off the bar.

"Hey," Colin said. "You can't take my keys."

"I just did."

He shrugged. "Just like my father, always taking," he muttered. "Story of my life."

She stopped wiping the counter and leaned against it. "Aw, what's wrong, poor little rich boy? Daddy take the trust fund away?"

Colin didn't answer.

"I struck a chord," she said. She picked up a phone on the bar and dialed a number. "Hey, it's Julie at Trinidad's. Can you send me a cab, please?"

"They know you?" Colin asked.

"Not the first time I've had to call," Julie said.

"Do you enjoy your job . . . Uh, what's your . . ."

"Julie," she said.

"Julie. You are very attractive, Julie. Do you enjoy your job?"

"Not really," she answered. "Why?"

He shrugged. "No reason." He didn't know why he had asked. He really just wanted to talk to her. "You're very perceptive, Julie. I'm a little drunk because my father has never been there for me. You don't know what that's like, do you? It makes me mad. Is that so bad? Does that make me a poor little rich boy?"

Julie looked at him for a moment, then began wiping the bar again without answering.

"Answer me, Julie," he said, a little too loud.

She looked down the bar at the bouncer. He was about to get up from his stool, but she waved him off.

"What's your name?" she asked.

"Jasper Collingsworth Jennings the fourth," he said. "But you can call me Colin."

"How old are you, Colin?"

"Twenty-three," he said. "How old are you?"

She ignored the question. "So what are you doing here all by yourself on a Thursday night?"

"I'm trying to hustle a barmaid," he said. "Do you want to go home with me? You're pretty and I'm a good catch."

She chuckled. "I appreciate the offer, but no. I don't want to go home with you."

"Why not?" he asked. "I'd think a girl like you would jump at the chance to bed down with a guy like me."

She stopped cleaning again and looked at him. "A girl like me?"

He shrugged. "You know," he said. "You're a . . . bar girl."

"Lord, give me patience, because if you give me strength I'm gonna need bail money too."

The burly bouncer laughed but kept his seat.

"Colin, you are spoiled, entitled, and drunk, and your words are offensive," Julie said. "I don't find any of those things endearing."

"You can't talk to me like that. You don't even know me."

"And you don't know me either," Julie said. "Yet you were quick to decide my life would magically get better if I slept with you."

"It couldn't get any worse." He snickered.

She sighed. "I'm going to tell you this because there is an outside chance it will help you. Then my friend Shorty down there at the end of the bar is going to escort you outside to wait on your cab."

Colin glanced at Shorty, who was huge. *Oops.* "Okay," he said.

"I am twenty-two years old," Julie began. "I have a four-year-old daughter at home with my grandmother, because one night I fell for a line from a boy just like you. Never heard from him again, and that hurt me very much. So you know what I did? Instead of going to a bar every night and drowning my sorrows in alcohol, I picked myself up, dusted myself off, and got a night job at a bar so I could go to school during the day and make life better for me and my little girl. Your daddy's ignoring you? Boo-hoo. How sad.

I have no idea who my daddy is. So before you come back in here with another lame sob story, you might want to find out the circumstances of the person you're whining to first. Good night, rich boy. You can come get your keys tomorrow."

Colin stared at her. She was amazing. And whatever she was eating, reading, snorting, or drinking to get that way, he wanted some of it.

"Time for you to go home, Colin," she said. He saw Shorty approaching him and he stood up. He wasn't drunk enough to think he could do anything to this guy. They headed toward the door. Then Colin turned around.

"Julie?" he said.

She turned around behind the bar and looked at him. "What?"

"What do you do?"

"What do you mean?" she said.

"When it falls apart around you?"

She smiled a little. "I pray, Colin."

I pray. Those two words changed his life and the way he treated people. It didn't happen overnight, but those words set the wheels in motion.

Chapter Ten

"Wake up, Georgie."

Georgia didn't move.

Jacey shook her friend. "Come on," she said. "I have to be rattling your teeth by now. Get up."

"What do you want?" Georgia flipped over quickly, her face inches from Jacey's.

Jacey moved back. "Your breath is atrocious."

"So is your timing," Georgia said. "I told you I was sleeping twenty-four hours straight."

"It's been ten, which is enough," Jacey said. "Get up. Pack a bag. We're going to Biloxi."

Georgia made a face. "Why?"

"I've done some research, and I know where to start looking for the kids," Jacey said. "I want to get there before the office closes. Get up."

"Why don't you just call Colin?"

"Because Colin isn't answering his phone," Jacey said. "Anyway, I'm mad at him."

Georgia yawned. "Why? For not catering to your every whim?"

"No, certainly not," Jacey said. "Okay, yes! Where is he?"

"Probably at the library checking out a book on how to deal with neurotic women," Georgia said.

"Do you ever get tired of being a smart a—"

Georgia cut her off. "No, no," she said. "Watch your mouth. You're a preacher's wife now."

"You make me want to punch you in the face," Jacey said.

"Before or after you force me from my slumber to go on a wild goose chase with you to Biloxi?"

Jacey sighed. "After."

"Out of my way," Georgia said, throwing back the bedcovers. "I'll shower and pack three bikinis. Then I'll be ready."

"It's not a vacation," Jacey told her.

"Wanna bet?" Georgia smiled.

An hour later they were packed and on their way to Biloxi. Jacey hadn't been back to Mississippi since the accident, and she wasn't sure if the trip would stir up the anxious feelings she'd grown accustomed to. But the two-hour drive from Baton Rouge to Biloxi proved anything but stressful. The only angst she felt was about finding the boys . . . and a little bit of fear as Georgia weaved her beloved Corvette in and out of traffic. She sighed with relief and settled back into the seat after Georgia whizzed by a tractor trailer.

Jacey looked at the marsh through the car window and felt a deep and satisfying peace. She hadn't felt that way in a long time. The sadness from learning the truth about Lillian and Demarcus remained, but finally remembering the accident had set her on a path of action and taken much of her anxiety with it. She was, at least, better than she'd been before she remembered. More than that, the hope she'd found difficult to reach for the past few months had resurfaced.

While she was recovering, Jacey had spent many, many hours thinking about her life before the flood. It was, for lack of better words, *vanilla. Benign. Uneventful.* She was the oldest child, the big sister, the one who always followed the rules and didn't make waves. While all of those traits were surely admirable, she began to think she was . . . well, boring. There had to be something missing from her life, something she had overlooked in her quest for perfection, a purpose to fulfill. Living—*surviving*—on a roof for three days had started the wheels of motion. At one of the worst parts of the storm, and before Colin had arrived, she had wrapped Demarcus up in her arms and huddled with Lillian and the other boys while the weather exploded around them. She knew they were going to die, that they would either be swept away from this unstable roof or be struck by lightning. She wondered during those fifteen minutes of terror what she'd be remembered for. Good grades? Beautifully worded stories? Perfectly ironed clothes? It was almost as horrifying as the storm. She vowed then and there if she ever made it off this roof alive, she'd do something worthwhile. It didn't have to be great, it didn't have to be applauded or recognized . . . but it had to be meaningful.

"So, your big stud wants me to meet his friend," Georgia said, snapping Jacey back to the present.

"What?"

"The morning you were all cozied up next to Colin, I texted him to see if you were there," Georgia said. "While we were texting, he mentioned he wanted me to meet his friend. So . . . what do you know about him?"

Jacey threw her hands up. "Nothing. See?" she said. "I don't know anything about his friend, but I'm supposedly falling in love with the man? Shouldn't I know something about the friend? Does this make any sense to you?"

"Don't start that again," Georgia said. She screamed at the car in front of her, "This is the passing lane, moron!" She turned back to Jacey. "Anyway, don't go off the deep end. I thought we'd already settled that."

"Oh, I know how I feel," Jacey said, white-knuckling the dash. "I just can't believe it. Nothing ever happens like this—you aren't supposed to fall in love this fast. I keep thinking I'm breaking all the rules."

"I'm sorry," Georgia said. "I feel like that virtually *all* the time, and I rather enjoy it."

Jacey laughed. "Well, it's new to me, but I intend to embrace it. As soon as I figure out how that works."

"If nobody broke the rules, or amended them at least, nothing would ever get accomplished," Georgia said. "Take me, for instance. If this car in front of me doesn't stop going *forty miles an hour* in the *passing lane,* I'm probably going to push her with my car. That is breaking the rules, yet I'd be providing a quality service to everyone else on the road."

Jacey rolled her eyes. "Tell me about the friend Colin wants you to meet."

"All I know is he's a football coach," Georgia said. "And that's already one gold star. Let's hope he's at least as handsome as the Rev, and that will be two gold stars."

"Is this still a five-star system?" Jacey asked.

"Of course," Georgia said. "I invented the five-star system, so why would I change it? Is there another system being used that I am unaware of?"

"I used the frog-kissing system this past year," Jacey said.

"How'd that work out for you?"

"You win," Jacey said.

The first stop of the journey was in Gulfport to visit the Harrison County Department of Child Welfare. They would surely know where the boys were placed after they left the hospital last year. Jacey was excited to find the boys and bounded into the office with high hopes. But her optimism was short-lived after she began

138

asking questions and explaining the situation to the beleaguered woman at the front desk. Her name was Mrs. Ellis, and though Jacey found her most friendly and helpful about some things, that's as far as it went. She couldn't give Jacey any real information about the boys, she said. It was against the law. She couldn't even tell her if they were still in the state of Mississippi. Jacey thanked her for her time and turned to leave the building. This time she looked around before she left. Amid her boundless optimism upon arrival, she had completely missed the atmosphere of the office. It was a dismal and gloomy place. The waiting area was packed, and none of the patrons looked happy. The phones rang nonstop, and Jacey suddenly felt very sorry for Mrs. Ellis and anybody else who worked here. *It must be awful to deal with this kind of thing day in and day out,* she thought.

She got in the car and looked at Georgia. "No dice," she said. "They can't give me any information."

"I was afraid of that," Georgia said. "But don't get discouraged."

"I'm not," Jacey said. "In fact, I already have another idea."

"What?"

"I'm not telling you till tomorrow," Jacey said. "In case you try to talk me out of it."

"When have I ever talked you *out* of some-

139

thing?" Georgia asked. "I'm always talking you *into* something."

Jacey laughed.

Georgia sped toward the coast of Biloxi. "Okay, Jacey. Let's find a place to sleep."

"Where do you want to stay?" Jacey asked, scanning her phone for hotels.

"Preferably something on the beach," Georgia said. "And when I say 'on the beach,' I don't mean across the street."

"Here we go," Jacey said, punching a few buttons on her phone. "Reservations made. All we have to do is get the key from the front desk."

Fifteen minutes later they arrived at the Belle Ame. It was a beautiful twenty-six-floor hotel, reopened in 2006—a year after the first four floors were destroyed by Katrina's storm surge. Mother Nature knew no addresses, so both rich and poor sometimes suffered at her hands. But the hotel and casino had come back strong, a favorite among locals and tourist alike. The Belle Ame boasted a couple of four-star restaurants and was located on the beach. Georgia was quite pleased.

She pulled into the hotel and put the Corvette in park, then handed the keys to the young valet who looked thrilled about the car he was lucky enough to park. "She'll do eighty in five seconds and she corners like she's on rails," Georgia said, eyeing the boy warily. "I told you that so you wouldn't wonder about it and decide it was a good idea to check it out for yourself. This car in my child. I will kill someone over it." She narrowed her gaze and handed the teenager a folded twenty. "You have a nice day!"

"Was that really necessary?" Jacey asked as they walked to the entrance. "You probably scared him to death."

"Betty doesn't like being driven by someone she doesn't know," Georgia said.

"You name your vehicles, yet I'm the one that had to go to therapy," Jacey said.

The bellman led them to their third-floor room after Jacey grabbed the key cards from the front desk. Jacey had stepped outside the box and booked a suite that did not disappoint. A living room area and kitchen provided all the comforts of home, complete with a minbar and a basket of snacks on the small dining table. The bedroom was spacious and decorated with ornate antique furniture that reminded Jacey of her grandmother's house. It was both elegant and comforting: two of Jacey's favorite things. She lay back on the king bed for a moment and breathed a contented sigh. It was good to be here.

Jacey jumped up to enjoy the view from the balcony with Georgia, who had gone straight for the French doors as soon as they entered the room. When her phone beeped, Jacey quickly retrieved it from her purse, hoping it was Colin.

Instead, there were two voice messages from her mom and one from her brother—whose voicemail entreated her to call their mother back before she "spazzed out." Jacey chuckled. Still nothing from Colin.

She called her mom and listened to her recount her adventures in gardening over the past week—how she still couldn't get Jacey's dad to help her weed the daylily beds and how pleased she was that her daughter sounded so happy. Jacey failed to mention that she was in Biloxi or that she'd finally remembered the details of that dreadful day. It would only worry her mother, who'd either insist Jacey come home or show up in Biloxi herself. That was the last thing Jacey needed on this mission. Her mother was a worrier and a fixer, and while Jacey loved and respected her, this was something Jacey needed to do. She knew her mother would try to talk her out of it, not because she didn't want her child to find the children, but because she'd be afraid of her daughter getting hurt in the process.

Georgia's excited voice came from the balcony. "Jacey, come see!"

Jacey put her hand over the phone and shushed Georgia. She pointed at the phone and mouthed, "Mama."

"You *have* to come see!" Georgia said again, louder this time.

"Uh . . . I gotta go, Mama. Georgie needs me.

Call you tomorrow, love you." She hit the end button and ran to the balcony. "What is the matter with you? I was telling you to shut up, not speak up."

"Look!" Georgia said, pointing downward and to the right. "What do you see?"

"What are you talking about?" Jacey asked, looking all around from their balcony.

Georgia grabbed her shoulders. "Look!" she said again. "That house, right there. *Who* do you see?"

Wait—was that Colin? Why was Colin on that deck? And who was that girl with him? And *why* did he have his arm around her?

She looked at Georgia. "I'm going to kill him."

"And I'm going to help," Georgia said.

Chapter Eleven

"It's really good to see you, Julie," Colin said. "How's Dani?"

"Dani is a teenager," Julie told him. "Just turned thirteen. Can you believe it?"

"Are you kidding me?"

"I wish I was," Julie said. "She's trying to get that little teenager attitude too. I'm keeping a tight rein on that. How are you?"

Colin gestured to a chair, and they sat down across the patio table from each other. "Well . . . I think I'm in love," he said with a lopsided grin.

Julie's hands flew to her mouth. "What? Are you serious? Oh, Colin, I am so happy to hear this! Who is she? Where's she from? Is she here?"

He smiled even bigger. "I knew you'd be happy to hear that," he said. "She's from Baton Rouge. She's the girl I was on the roof with during the flood. Jacey. Her name is Jacey."

Julie looked surprised. "I thought you couldn't find her. We just talked about this, what—two or three months ago?"

"It was the craziest thing," he said. "I went to Baton Rouge to do some work for a church, some interim stuff. While I was there, I performed a wedding and she was a bridesmaid. I couldn't believe it myself."

Julie shook her head in amazement. "His mysterious ways," she said. "I told you a long time ago to trust the plan even when you couldn't see it, didn't I?"

He smiled. "You changed my life, Julie. I'll never be able to repay you for that."

"I didn't change your life. All I did was give you the formula." Julie smiled in return.

"You put me in my place."

"You asked for it." She laughed. "Listen, it has been great seeing you, but I really have to go. Dani and her little friends are probably driving Mike insane by now."

"How is Mike?" Colin asked.

"He's great. After six years of marriage, I still feel like I need to thank you for introducing us every morning when I wake up."

Colin laughed. "I'm just glad it worked out."

"We're solid," Julie said. "If our little teenager doesn't kill us both."

"Dani's a good kid. Just testing her independence a little. Come on. I'll walk you out."

"No, stay here," Julie said. "I'm going to walk down the beach back to the hotel." They both stood, and she reached out to hug him. "I can't believe you are actually in grown-up love. And I can see it in your eyes."

Colin embraced his friend. "I want you to meet her. Soon."

She pulled away. "I can't wait to meet the

woman who gave you that goofy look in your eyes."

Julie stepped out of the gate on the deck, then turned back around. "Wait," she said. "Does she love you back?"

"Of course she does," Colin said. "She just doesn't know it yet."

Julie laughed. "I'm sure you'll find a way," she said, waving as she walked away.

Colin watched her until she made it to the hotel property next door. Julie Hargis was a true friend. The night after she read him the riot act in the bar, Colin went back to apologize and fetch his keys. Apologizing was a first for him. He usually said whatever he wanted and let the chips fall where they may. It didn't always make him popular, but he didn't care. Looking back, that wasn't a trait he was proud of. Julie made him realize, in his drunken stupor, what a jerk he was.

That night he walked to the edge of the bar and asked if he could talk to her.

"You again?" she said in a monotone voice. "I'm working."

"I'll wait," he said.

She shrugged. "Suit yourself." She looked at him for a moment. "Are you going to order something? Let me guess. Scotch?"

"Uh, water's fine," he said.

"Good choice," she said, then disappeared. She

was back shortly with a tall glass of ice water and lemon. "I'll be back when I can."

The bar was packed most of the night, and many of the patrons were friends or acquaintances of Colin's. That included the girl he was supposed to go on a ski trip with in a few days. Chandler was her name . . . Chandler something, maybe Miller. The fact that he didn't even know her last name wasn't lost on him either. His life had become a series of short-term relationships, if you could even call them that. *Alliances* was probably a better word. He used everyone he knew for all sorts of reasons. He used Chandler for sex, and he used the guys as wingmen. He used his father for money. And he did it all with no passion, no feeling, and no guilt. For maybe the first time in years, he was ashamed of himself. Maybe the shame he should have felt had been buried beneath all the anger he used to keep warm at night. Whatever the case, it was coming to a head.

His buddies asked him to join them at their table, but he declined. Chandler hung around with him for a while at the bar, but Colin finally asked her to leave him alone.

"I'm just not good company right now, Chandler," he said. "And look, I'm sorry, but I can't go on this ski trip with you either. It isn't about you . . . It's me."

"Are you kidding me?" she said, her eyes flashing.

"I'm sorry, Chandler. I really am," he said. "I'm sorry about everything. Trust me when I tell you, you are way better off without me."

"Fine. Good-bye, Colin." She stormed off to join the party in the back of the bar.

Great. Another casualty of the USS *Colin*. He felt bad about it, but he couldn't fake it with her anymore. It was time for him to get honest with everyone, starting with himself.

Long after his friends and most everyone else had gone home, he was still sitting on the barstool waiting for Julie. Whatever she had tapped inside of him, he wanted more of it. He had thought of nothing else today except her words last night. One paragraph from a tiny woman with a dish towel thrown over her shoulder had caused him to reassess his entire life. He needed to hear more of what she had to say, because he knew there was a wealth of information inside her. She had *lived* her pain, dealt with it, and moved on. Colin bathed in his. He needed the formula, and she could give it to him.

Finally, after the doors were locked and the last customer was gone, Julie poured herself a glass of water and joined him.

"So, Colin," she said, sitting on a stool behind the bar. "What's going on?"

He stared at the girl and didn't really know where to begin. She met his gaze without blinking.

"Are you afraid to be in here alone with me?" he asked.

"Are you a rapist or a murderer?" she said.

"Right now I seem to be satisfied with hurting myself," he said.

"That's a pretty good observation," she said. "A critical first step."

"I need to know what you know," he said.

"I'm sorry?" Julie's brows furrowed.

"You seem . . . happy," he said. "In spite of your circumstances. How do you do that?"

"You don't know any happy people?"

Colin thought about his family, then his friends. With the exception of Joshua, the answer was no.

"Not really," he said. "There's a formula you use, whether you realize it or not. I wanna know what it is."

Julie moved around on her stool, reached under the bar, and pulled out a book. "Here's my formula."

She shoved the book across the bar to him.

"This is a Bible," he said.

"You're very smart, Colin. Ivy League?"

He chuckled. "You have a very quick wit."

She smiled at him. "Survival 101. If you can't fix it, laugh at it."

"So you read the Bible," he mused. "You do realize you work in a bar."

"And?"

Colin held up his hand. "I'm not being

disrespectful," he said, wary of another tongue-lashing. "I just meant . . . Is a bar the best place for a Bible?"

"Can you think of a better place for a Bible?" she asked.

Colin shrugged. "I see your point," he said. "But how many times have you actually used this Bible in here?"

"Counting tonight?" She thought for a moment, then smiled. "Once."

He continued to stare at the book in front of him. "Tell me," he said finally.

Julie leaned back until she was against the wooden column behind her. "If you're asking me to tell you how I got to this point, it's a long story." She sighed. "Are you sure you want to hear it?"

"I am," Colin said. "It's what I came here for. That, and to apologize for being such a jerk last night."

"You think you're the first jerk I've had to deal with in here?"

"Probably not, but I'd like to think I'm the first one to apologize."

Julie told him a story that night that he thought about many times over the years. About a girl who was raised mostly by her grandmother because her mother was a drug addict, in and out of jail and in and out of her life. Julie's grandmother was a staunch believer and attended church

150

on a regular basis, but she taught Julie much more than what it meant to be inside a church. She taught Julie how to *practice* Christianity, and how to accept her mother for who she was without carrying a torch of anger over who Julie wanted her to be. "I'm not saying you love her behavior. I'm saying you love your mama," her grandmother told her. "Anger and grudges won't hold anyone hostage except you. And when you feel like pointing out others' mistakes, remember that you're going to make a few of your own. We all do." Her grandmother was right, of course.

One night Julie drank a little too much and went home with a boy, and the alcohol coupled with his charm led to his bed. That was the last time she'd seen or heard from him, and a couple of months later she realized she was pregnant. Julie said it would've been easy to become bitter, but when she looked at her baby, she knew God had given her a blessing. She could never consider her daughter a mistake, so she chose to see the joy in the situation instead of the pain. She went to a junior college during the day, worked at the bar at night, and tried to spend any spare time she had with her child. She focused on the things to be thankful for and not the things that tested her.

"As far as a formula," Julie said, "I don't know what to tell you. Focus on the good instead of the bad? Maybe that's it. Forgive people even if they aren't sorry? I don't know, Colin, but it works for me. I don't know if it will work for you. You have to figure that out yourself."

"So you're saying God is your magic formula," Colin said, completely missing her point.

Julie laughed. "No," she said. "He's not a big magician sitting in the sky with a magic wand. But he's not sitting up there with a flyswatter either, just waiting for one of his flawed humans to screw something up. You have to find your own way. My way happened to begin with a Bible and a really cool grandmother. This is what works for my life. Maybe you'll need to hang upside down from a tree and chant. I don't know . . . I've never been the kind of person to push my belief system on somebody else. I can only describe the view from my standpoint."

Colin's life had begun to feel so empty and meaningless to him that anything she had to offer was worth a try. That night Colin began a journey with Julie, who led him by the hand—but only because he asked her to. He began to attend church with her, her grandmother, and Dani. While it took him many months to really comprehend the words of the pastor, Colin dug in. He studied the Bible every second he could. He had long talks with Julie's grandmother and the pastor of the church. Slowly, Colin began to change. The anger he'd harbored toward his father for so many years faded somewhat. It didn't disappear, but he wasn't defined by it anymore. But it wasn't until he joined a team of men at the church who built houses around the country for the homeless that he really "got it." Colin had found his calling, and he saw it as an opportunity to mend fences with his father.

He went home to Biloxi in March of that year, right before Easter. He drove straight to Jasper's office without telling him he was coming. He had played out every scenario in his head on the drive down from college, and they all ended the same way: with Jasper embracing his son and telling him how wrong he'd been.

He skipped the elevator and bounded up the stairs to his father's second-floor office. His secretary, Nancy, tried to flag him down, asked him to stop, but Colin didn't want to wait. He wanted to start this reunion now.

"Dad," he said, flinging open the office doors, "I'm sor—" What he saw stopped him in his tracks. Jasper was in a passionate embrace with a woman whose face he couldn't see, but it was not his mother. He turned around and left . . . and never again set foot inside Jennings Construction.

Chapter Twelve

"Who is she?" Jacey asked from her knees on the balcony. She was hiding behind a huge potted plant.

Georgia, on the other hand, was leaning so far over the rails that Jacey feared she would fall.

"I don't know who she is, Crouching Jacey, Hidden Moron," Georgia said. "She just went inside the hotel. Shall we investigate?"

"No," Jacey said. "I don't care who she is."

"Nice try. Come on, let's go look at her up close."

"Why is he even at that house?" Jacey asked. "And why won't he answer my calls?"

"Both valid questions . . . that we can't answer from this balcony. Come on, get up. You look ridiculous."

Jacey stood up reluctantly and looked at the deck next door. Colin was still standing there, the same place he'd stood to watch the woman walk into the hotel. She felt an urge to throw something and yell. She didn't like the unfamiliar feeling. Then it dawned on her: She was jealous. *Great,* she thought. *Another feeling to add to the hodgepodge of emotions already swirling around.*

"Put on your sunglasses and let's go." Georgia urged her to the door.

Jacey allowed herself to be shoved even though she knew the idea was absurd. "What are we going to do? Knock on every door in this hotel?"

"If necessary," Georgia said. "But we can start at the pool area."

They got off the elevator on the first floor, and Georgia pulled Jacey through the lobby toward the back of the hotel grounds.

"Slow down," Jacey said. "I can't see anything in here with these shades on."

"The early bird gets the worm," Georgia said. "Haven't you ever heard that?"

They got outside and saw the woman almost immediately. Jacey stopped in her tracks and stared. Georgia shoved her so hard she fell against a chair that skidded across the concrete and made everyone look. Including the nameless woman.

"Oh no!" Georgia said, grabbing the chair. "Sit down . . . just sit down like we're just . . . sitting down."

Jacey was fixated on the woman two tables over, who sat by herself and faced the pool. She was quite pretty, very well-dressed, and had just hugged the man on whom Jacey had staked her claim. Jacey wanted to run up to the table and say, "Who are you and how do you know Colin?" But instead, she had to settle for sitting and staring. She turned to Georgia.

"What exactly are we doing?"

"Recon," Georgia said. "We're doing recon."

"And after we gather the recon, what will we do with it?"

"We'll . . . have it gathered. I don't know, just shut up," Georgia said. "And keep watching her. I'm going to do a walk by."

"A what?" Jacey asked.

"I'm gonna walk by her table," Georgia said, exasperated.

"Be careful," Jacey whispered.

Georgia stopped and looked at her. "Yes, I'll be careful. If she points her sunscreen at me, be sure to call 911.'"

"Why do I let you talk me into things?" Jacey asked.

"Because I get stuff done."

Jacey couldn't argue the point. She watched in horror as Georgia stopped at the woman's table and said something to her. Georgia smiled and walked slowly back to Jacey.

"What did you say?" Jacey whispered.

"I asked her what time it was," Georgia said.

"You have a watch on your wrist and your phone in your hand," Jacey said.

Georgia shrugged. "Doesn't mean they work."

"What did she say?" Jacey asked.

"She said it's six thirty," Georgia whispered.

Jacey sat up. "That's it?"

"That's all I asked."

"So we know nothing more than we knew on the balcony, right?" Jacey stood up.

"Where are you going?" Georgia asked.

"Back to the room," Jacey said.

"No!" Georgia grabbed her hand. "Plan B in full effect, starting now."

"Dare I ask?" Jacey said.

"We're going to walk on the beach," Georgia said, pointing to the right. "Thataway."

Jacey pulled away from her. "Oh, no we're not," she said. "I've already stalked him one time this week. If I show up in Mississippi, what's he going to think?"

"I don't care what he thinks," Georgia said. "He owes me an explanation."

"He owes *you* an explanation?" Jacey said.

"You know what I mean," Georgia said. "Just come on."

Jacey followed Georgia down the wooden plank that headed to the beach. When she looked over at the deck next door, Colin was gone.

"He's not there anymore," Jacey said. "Let's go back in."

Georgia stopped. "We can go knock on the door," she said.

"No, really, I'm sure there's an explanation," Jacey told her. "And besides, we didn't see him doing anything wrong. He hugged a woman. She could be anybody. She could be his sister."

Georgia raised her brow. "I thought you said he was an only child."

"Okay," Jacey said. "She could be his cousin. Whoever she is, it's none of my business. Not really."

Georgia shrugged. "Whatever you want to do is fine with me."

"Fine, let's go back in." Jacey turned back to the hotel.

"I'm just saying . . . if it were me, I'd wanna know who that woman was."

Jacey finally got it. She turned to look at her friend. "Not everybody cheats, Georgie. And besides that, it isn't like he and I are . . . dating."

"Oh, but he almost said he was in love with you, and you almost said you were in love with him. See, that sort of superseded dating for y'all. It's like you walked before you crawled." Georgia paused. "And I am aware that not everyone cheats. Just everyone I know."

Jacey stopped and looked at Georgia. She knew where her words were coming from. "Listen, I know it still bothers you, so stop pretending it doesn't." Jacey put her hand on Georgia's shoulder. "Let's just go back to the room, order room service, watch a movie, and forget about it. I'm in Biloxi on a different kind of mission. He'll call me when he's ready."

Georgia sighed. "Can we at least get something terribly unhealthy like fried oysters and pecan pie?"

"That sounds perfect," Jacey said. She didn't

even glance at the woman as they strolled past her again on their way upstairs.

Jacey did try to forget about all of it when she lay down to sleep, but the truth was, it really did bother her. She hated this new feeling surging around in her body. Jealousy, they called it. That ugly feeling was pouring itself into every thought she had. Jacey had never had a serious boyfriend, so jealousy over a man was unfamiliar territory. She had dated a lot, but never seemed to find the one guy who made her want to be around him for more than two months. She always assumed that there was something wrong with her. When she discussed it with her mother one day, her mom had just laughed and assured her there was nothing abnormal about her. "When he shows up, you'll know it," she had said. But for years, her friends had been getting married or at least engaged at the speed of light, and she was still looking for Mr. Right. All she'd ever found was Mr. Right Now. Until she got slammed onto a roof in Mississippi. After that, everything changed.

The woman from Colin's deck may be a perfectly lovely person, Jacey told herself. But all she could see was another woman's arms around the man she loved. It didn't conjure up any pleasant feelings. After ordering room service, she had eaten her fried oysters emotionally—too fast and too many. Now she was sitting up in bed wishing room service delivered antacids too.

She wanted to appear cheerful to keep Georgia at bay. There was no way she was going to mention these particular feelings to her. She'd have them scaling the wall over the balcony on knotted-up sheets. Georgia clung to her bitterness over her ex—so much, in fact, that there wasn't a man in the country she trusted. She always joked that if she ever got into another relationship, she'd be eighty years old in the nursing home, making sure the man had one foot on a banana peel and the other in the grave. Only Jacey wasn't sure it was really a joke.

Jacey didn't believe Colin was the type of man to tell her he was falling for her, only to run back to Mississippi to be with another woman. But whoever the woman was, Jacey could tell Colin was very close to her. She could tell from their body language that they were familiar. Just how familiar, she had no idea. Maybe living with Georgia so long had made Jacey suspicious of everybody. It certainly wouldn't be that far-fetched. Georgia was steeped in suspicion.

She closed her eyes and thought about the boys instead. She wondered where they were tonight, if they were being taken care of, if they were in a good home with good people. It broke her heart to imagine them out there in the world without their mother or father. No child deserved that.

Surely she would find some answers tomorrow.

Surprisingly, Jacey slept well. She woke to the sound of Gulf waves and seagulls. She stretched, rolled over, and saw Georgia sitting on the balcony with the doors open.

"Hey," she said.

"I was trying to be quiet," Georgia said. "Did I wake you up?"

"No. Have you been up long?"

"For a little while." Georgia stood and walked back into the room. "No sign of Colin this morning, by the way."

Jacey smiled. "More recon?"

"Something like that." Georgia smiled. "I've actually been sitting out there thinking about what you said yesterday. You know, the 'not everybody cheats' thing."

Jacey sat up in bed and pulled her covers up around her. "Georgia, I know how hurt you were . . . I didn't mean to minimize—"

Georgia stopped her. "No, you're right," she said. "I picked a bad apple. And I knew it for a long time, even in high school. I just didn't want to admit it."

Jacey started to speak, but Georgia shushed her again.

"I felt so . . . *betrayed*," she said. "That was the worst part of it. I lost my best friend, the man I was going to marry, the man I thought would love and protect me for the rest of my life.

161

Then . . . when I found out about *that* girl, and all the *other* girls . . . it was as though I had been living a lie. For *years*. Everything I believed in was an illusion. None of it was real. Ever. That was the hardest part."

Jacey reached out and grabbed her hand. "I'm so sorry," she said.

Georgia squeezed her hand and let it go. "I've just been sitting out there this morning thinking about Colin," she said. "He's not the same kind of guy, Jacey—and I'm not saying that because he's a preacher. He's a good guy with a good heart, and he's solid. Don't let what we saw yesterday and my paranoia cloud your feelings for him. Eventually I will get over my distrust of the entire male population. I'd like to start with Colin."

Jacey smiled. "It's gonna be okay," she said. "You'll find the right guy. And when you do, he'll be everything you always wanted and will never give you a reason to doubt him."

"Well . . . I'm not going that far, but I'm willing to cut your guy some slack." Georgia smiled.

"You know what?" Jacey said. "I'm curious about who that woman was. And I think I'm jealous, too, which sucks . . . but I am keeping an open mind."

"Jealous?" Georgia said. "That must be a new one for you."

"It is. And I don't like it," Jacey said. "It made

me want to slap the woman, punch Colin, and throw things."

"Yep. That's jealousy."

Jacey hopped out of bed. "Come on, girl, we've got places to go and people to see. I call shower." She sped into the bathroom and slammed the door before Georgia could beat her there.

Chapter Thirteen

Georgia carefully maneuvered the Corvette over the blacktop road, complaining all the way.

"Where are we?" she asked. "This road is a pig trail. The first wild goose chase was better than this one."

Jacey studied her surroundings. They were definitely on the right road this time. "This is the one. I'm sure of it."

"Why in the world were you down here in the first place?" Georgia asked. "I mean, were you planning on being kidnapped?"

"I told you I was writing that story about rural Southern life. It was for a regional magazine, not just Baton Rouge. I was just trying to find some people to talk to."

"Why didn't you just call somebody?"

"Because you need to see things for yourself before you can fully translate them onto paper," Jacey said. "At least, I need to. I don't imagine it's the same for Stephen King."

"Thank God," Georgia said. "He is my absolute favorite writer, you know."

"I know," Jacey said. "Why do you think I used him as an example? Wait . . . stop the car. Stop."

Georgia slowed the car to a stop and put it into park.

"This is it," Jacey said, her heartbeat stepping up a pace. "This is the bridge." She opened the door and got out. Georgia followed her.

Jacey stood at the foot of the bridge and stared.

"Are you okay? Are you freaked out?" Georgia asked.

Jacey shook her head. "I'm good." She looked at the newly constructed bridge, still adorned by orange Men Working signs. It hadn't been too long since they'd repaired it. Seeing it now was surreal. It looked so . . . ordinary, so non-threatening. It didn't give the slightest hint of danger or foreboding, yet this was the very place where fate and water had swept her away into another life. Everything about her had changed in this very spot. This bridge and this site didn't bring back any welcome feelings.

"Come on, let's go," she told Georgia.

They continued to drive down the winding road for another couple of miles while Jacey stared at the river that ran alongside it. The river that almost swallowed her.

"We've been too far. There's nothing down here. Are you *sure* that was the bridge?" Georgia asked. "You could be confused."

"I'm not confused. I am absolutely sure that was the bridge," Jacey said.

Nearly three miles after Jacey began driving, they saw the first house.

"Finally," Georgia said. "Who would want to live back here, cut off from civilization?"

"I think it's wonderful," Jacey said. "Just smell that air."

Georgia wrinkled her nose. "I think that's cow manure or chicken poop."

"You are so cynical," Jacey said, secretly thankful that Georgia was taking her mind off the angst she felt after seeing the bridge. "Come on, let's go see if anyone's home."

"I think I hear banjos," Georgia said. "I'm staying in the car."

"I know you're afraid of the chickens, Georgie," Jacey said, laughing. "It's okay. You can stay inside."

"Look at them," Georgia said. "Necks all stretched out, sharp little noses just waiting to peck my eyes out, weird eyes on each side of their heads. I mean, how do they see? East and west at the same time? There literally is not enough money in the world to make me get out of this car."

Jacey laughed at Georgia powering up the window and pulling her T-shirt up around her face. "Suit yourself, but if I find somebody to talk to, I may be awhile."

"Take your time," Georgia said. "I'll just be here. In the car. With both my eyes intact."

Jacey walked gingerly around the chickens pecking the ground near her feet. She called out, "Hello? Anybody home?"

"In the back," came the voice from behind the house.

Jacey walked around the house until she saw an old woman picking berries from a vine on the fence.

"Hello?" Jacey said again.

"Well, hello there," the woman said. "Are you lost?"

"No, ma'am," Jacey said. "Well, I don't really know where I am, but I'm not lost either."

The woman wiped her hands on her apron and laughed. "Well, now you have my attention." She bent over slowly to pick up her berry bucket, and Jacey rushed over to her side.

"Here," Jacey said. "Let me help." She picked up the bucket and matched the woman's measured steps. "My name is Jacey Lang," she said. "I'm hoping you can help me find a house around here."

"Nice to meet you, Jacey," she said. "My name is Mrs. Ernestine Harrison. Whose house are you looking for?"

"It's nice to meet you, Mrs. Harrison," Jacey said. "But that's just it . . . I'm not sure whose house I'm looking for. Well, I am, but I don't know who lives there now. Or if the house is even still standing."

"I see," she said. "And Ernestine will do just fine."

Jacey smiled. "Okay, Mrs. Ernestine."

"Well, somebody raised you right," she said. "Young folks these days have no respect for old folk."

"My mama would skin me alive if I didn't respect my elders," Jacey told her.

"Then somebody raised your mama right too." Ernestine patted her hand.

They reached the back porch, and Jacey held out her hand to help the woman climb the wooden stairs.

"Whew," Ernestine said as she sat down in the rocker. "That gets harder every year," she said. "But I sure don't want the berries to waste. My Ebben used to love a berry cobbler. He been gone near about ten years now, and every spring I make at least one berry pie just so he knows I still think about him. Some folks probably think that's kinda crazy. But I sure do miss him." She took the corner of her apron and dabbed her eyes.

"I'm so sorry," Jacey said. "Was Ebben your husband?"

"For sixty-five years," she said. "Every night I think, *The Lord gonna take me tonight and I'll see my Ebben again.* But every morning I keep waking up." She laughed—cackled, really. "But I guess the Lord knows what he doing."

Jacey smiled.

"That's enough about me. I'm just an old woman," Ernestine said. "Now tell me about this house you're looking for."

"Well," Jacey said, "I don't know if you remember this or even if you knew about it, but there was a flood last year, right around here. And I thought maybe—"

"Did I know about it?" Ernestine interrupted. "Like to killed us all! Water came right up to this porch, it did. I was scared to death. So much loss . . ." She looked out across her yard. "Nothin' like that had ever happened around here. That sweet little girl just down the road died in that flood. The water just swept that house away. She always took care of me, brought those boys to visit. The big one mowed my grass and the little ones loved to gather eggs . . ." She dabbed her eyes with her apron again.

Jacey felt her own eyes fill with tears. She was talking about Lillian and her boys. She knew it even before she asked. Her hands began to shake.

"That baby boy died with his mother," Mrs. Ernestine continued. "Almost broke my heart in two, I tell you. I've been so worried about those boys I don't know what to do. I tried to take them, but you know those State folks don't want no old woman raising kids."

Jacey took Mrs. Ernestine's hand in hers. "That's why I'm here," she said. "I'm trying to find the boys. I was on the roof with them."

169

Mrs. Ernestine's hands covered her mouth. "It was you?" she asked. "It was you?"

"Yes, ma'am. It was me. I'm looking for the boys. I'd like to see them."

"Those babies asked for you," she said. "Jacey, you said? Yes, that's it! I got my good friend at the sheriff's office to take me down to the hospital to see them, and they told me about you. They asked me to 'find Jacey.' Lord, this is a miracle as sure as I'm sitting here!"

Jacey was crying by now, too, her heart aching for the boys and for this woman. "Are you sure it was me they asked for?" she said. "Do you know where they are? How I can find them?"

"Oh, I'm sure," she said. "They wanted *you*. And I know just where they are. I make my friend check on them every week. But those boys aren't happy, I can tell you that." She leaned forward and put her hand on the side of Jacey's face. "This is a miracle, Jacey," she said again. "How did you find an old woman in the woods?"

Jacey put her hand on top of Mrs. Ernestine's, still resting on her face. "I'm not sure." She smiled, although she was still crying. "Somehow I . . . knew where to go. Is the house still there? Can I go look at it?"

"Weren't nothing left of it," Mrs. Ernestine said. "It broke apart in the floodwater and washed away. Weren't nothing more than a shack anyway."

Jacey was disappointed. She had wanted to see the house, her refuge in the storm, thinking it might bring the closure she still needed. But it wasn't meant to be.

"You just thank the good Lord you were all off that roof before the house fell apart," Mrs. Ernestine said. "I don't think nary a one of you would've survived it."

"Yes, ma'am," Jacey said. "You are probably right."

They heard screaming, and both turned their heads to see Georgia running up the back steps, chickens nipping at her heels.

"These freaking chickens are trying to kill me!" she said, a short but piercing scream escaping her lips every few seconds.

Mrs. Ernestine looked at Jacey. "Does she belong to you?"

"Yes, ma'am." Jacey laughed.

"God help you."

Chapter Fourteen

Colin sat in the kitchen of the home he grew up in and watched his mother prepare tea.

He checked his watch again. He wanted to be done with all things Jennings Construction, and he had no idea why his father insisted on dragging it out. Jasper seemed to thrive on pointless drama, but this time Colin decided enough was enough. He'd called his father and requested this meeting. This time he would tell him face-to-face and be done with it. Starting a new life in Baton Rouge was becoming more and more appealing to him. He found himself actually looking forward to this appointment with his father, a first for him. As soon as it was over, he could be on his way.

Jasper was late, of course. Anything to exercise power over his son made Jasper happy, even if it was something as insignificant as making him wait. Colin drummed his fingers on the smooth marble counter while he waited.

His mother poured herself a cup of tea and joined him at the kitchen island. "Are you sure I can't get you anything?" she asked. "Evie is here. Maybe some of her scones? I know how you enjoy them. I can get her to make some for you."

Colin smiled. "No, thank you, Mother," he said.

"I just want to get this over with." He looked around the kitchen, stark white, sparkling and devoid of life. Much like his parents' marriage. The comparison wasn't lost on him. He almost said the words to her but caught himself. No sense in hurting her for no reason. Besides, it wasn't as though anything was going to change this late in the game.

"Colin, I am worried about you," she said. "I have no idea where you live, how you live . . . You don't come home, and you seldom call. Are you all right?"

"I'm fine," he said, patting her hand. Despite their differences, he loved his mother and didn't want her to worry about him. "I promise."

"Where are you living?" she continued. "Is it safe?"

He chuckled. "I'm living in my travel trailer," he said. "It's safe. Unless a hurricane comes, which might be a problem."

"Don't joke about that," she said. "I do worry about you, and I wish you'd come home. This house is enormous, and your father would barely even know you were here."

"But I would know it," he said. "Being kept by another person may work for you, but he isn't going to own me."

As soon as the words left his mouth he saw the hurt cross her face.

"Mother," he said, feeling very real shame,

173

"that was a terrible thing for me to say. I didn't mean it. Please forgive me." He put his hand over hers, but she pulled away.

"I know what you think about me, Colin," she said.

"Mom, I am so sorry—"

"No, let me finish," she said.

Colin remained silent but felt horrible about his callous comment. Sometimes, even now, his anger and resentment reared its ugly head. The last thing he wanted was to direct it toward his mother.

"As I said," she began, "I know what you think about me. But in my defense, I am more than what you see. I do more than host a bridge club on Tuesdays. I don't spend all my time on the phone chatting about this week's gossip. I don't just throw dinner parties and bridal showers." She took a sip of tea and gently placed the cup back in the saucer. "I sit on two boards whose only function is to support cancer research and displaced children. There is no glamour in that, I assure you. It is real work and it is difficult. I do not earn a salary from either, nor would I take one if it were offered. So while I may have a luxurious life that you dislike, I do have a few redeeming qualities."

She paused for a moment and looked out the huge window behind the kitchen table. Finally, she turned back to Colin. "Perhaps I made mistakes while raising you. Children don't come with instruction manuals, and someday, hopefully, you'll find that out. But I did the best I could. Not only that, I did what I *thought* was best for you. If I failed, it wasn't out of indifference. It was out of love. The anger you've harbored for so long . . . I thought it would dissolve when you became a member of the clergy, but I can see there is still much of it there. You are supposed to be a beacon for forgiveness, but maybe you should rethink your career decision. Or at least rethink what it really means to be a minister. I don't know how you can help anyone else when you can't even help yourself."

She got her cup and saucer and left the room, with Colin staring after her.

Her words were like a slap to his face. Even though she'd said the words quietly, Colin knew she was infuriated. So was he. Not only infuriated, but hurt. He clenched his jaw. He could take most anything from his father, but his mother's words cut him like a knife. Maybe because on some level, he knew they were true.

He really did feel like a fraud sometimes when he counseled other people. He felt it in the pit of his stomach when he told other people about the importance of forgiveness. Somehow he couldn't take his own advice. He had never fully let go of the anger toward his father and certainly hadn't let go of the resentment. During the first few months of going to church with Julie, he thought he had a handle on his fury . . . until the day he stepped into his father's office and saw him with that woman. There had been rumors of other women as far back as he could remember, but that day he saw it for himself.

The truth was, Colin held on to his disappointment and wrath from that day, fused it with his childhood frustrations, and used it as fuel and motive. He grimaced at the conflict churning inside him. Yes, his feelings were wrong, but weren't they justified? At least in his mind they were. Besides, forgiveness didn't always mean repairing the relationship. It just meant one's actions and thoughts weren't driven by the offense anymore. Right? Even so, Colin couldn't say with any certainty that was true for him. He rubbed his forehead with his palms. Maybe his mother was absolutely right. He was not only an imposter, but the worst kind of imposter for using God as an excuse.

He looked at his watch again. Forty-five minutes late. He couldn't stop the irritation he felt, though only moments before he had chastised himself for feeling it. It was this kind of blatant disregard Jasper had for anyone else's feelings that powered Colin's rage. How busy could the man be? He didn't lift a finger anymore. Somebody else did the work while he sat at his desk and gazed down on his empire from above.

Colin got up, walked to the sink, and looked outside. The Gulf tossed and roiled much like the thoughts in his head. Should he go after his mother? Tell her on some level she was exactly right about him? He couldn't just ignore what she'd said, not when it had knocked the breath out of him and visibly upset her.

He turned and walked from the kitchen to the dining room searching for her. Regardless of how he felt, he didn't want his relationship with his mother to turn into the same bitter chaos he shared with Jasper. He had to apologize to her.

"Mother?" he called.

She didn't answer.

"Mother?"

He walked into the foyer, thinking maybe she had gone outside. Just as he opened the door, Jasper appeared.

"Finally decided to show up?" Colin asked.

"Some things can't be avoided," Jasper said, hanging his hat on the hall tree.

"Yeah? Blonde or brunette?" Colin asked. He peered out the front door, still looking for his mother.

Jasper ignored the jab. "Your mother isn't outside," he said.

"I'll find her." Colin closed the heavy stained glass door.

"I thought you wanted to talk," Jasper said.

"I need to talk to Mom first," he said as he climbed the stairs. "I'll be right back."

Colin went to her bedroom and knocked on the door. "Mom?" When she didn't answer he knocked again. "Mom?"

Finally, he opened the door slowly and saw her teacup and saucer on the floor. He swung the door open and saw her on the floor too.

He rushed to her side. "Mom? Mom?" he said frantically. "Dad, call 911!" he shouted.

He grabbed her wrist and felt for a pulse. She was alive, but her heartbeat was very slow. And she wasn't responding to his voice. He heard Jasper running up the stairs.

"What? What happened? What did you do?" Jasper crouched down to his wife's side.

"What did *I* do?" Colin said.

"Did you upset her? What did you say?" Jasper rocked his unconscious wife back and forth in his arms.

"Did you call 911?" Colin asked, ignoring the question.

"Yes," Jasper said in a sharp tone. *"Colin, what did you say to her?"* he demanded again.

"I don't remember . . . We were just talking," Colin said, feeling much like the small child who'd carelessly broken the window in this very room with a baseball years ago.

"She has a heart condition," Jasper said, still

gently rocking back and forth. "She didn't want you to know."

"What? Since when? Why didn't she want me to know? I would've—"

"You would've what?"

Colin didn't answer. The hot shame he felt slowly permeated his body. Had he caused this?

"What can I do?" Colin said, feeling helpless as he stared at his mother, still and pale.

"Aren't you a praying man?" Jasper asked, his voice cracking.

Colin nodded his head.

"Then pray."

Chapter Fifteen

Ernestine Harrison meant what she said. The "friend" she had at the sheriff's office was the sheriff himself.

Harrison County Sheriff Roger Jefferson was at Mrs. Ernestine's home exactly one hour after she called him. Before he arrived, Mrs. Ernestine told Jacey and Georgia all about Roger and how the two of them had become close friends.

"Roger was a little snot-nosed boy who grew up right down this road." She laughed. "Always into something. His daddy, Cephus, worked for my husband. We used to own close to three hundred acres of land around here. We raised cattle, you know. When Ebben got sick, we had to sell it off piece by piece until all that was left was this old house place. Anyway, Roger's daddy was a good, hard worker. Could fix just about anything from a tractor to a refrigerator." She laughed again. "That Roger tried to fix things too. He just made a bigger mess. He was real smart in school, though. Always made good grades, played a lot of sports. He went to college on a scholarship. I don't think I have ever seen a daddy any prouder than his was. Cephus got to see Roger graduate before he passed away. I was so glad of that. Roger went on to become the first black sheriff of Harrison County. I sure wish Cephus could've seen that too. Roger has never forgotten the old lady who made him cookies and Kool-Aid every day. Comes to visit me once a week, even though he's got other things to do. Me and Ebben never had no kids, and I 'spect Roger was the closest thing we had to one of our own. He sure is a good boy."

Soon after, Roger Jefferson, a big man with a warm smile, walked into Mrs. Ernestine's house with an armload of groceries and a bouquet of spring flowers.

"How's my favorite girl?"

"How many times do I have to tell you to stop spoiling me?" she said. "But I'm sure glad you still don't listen."

Roger laughed and gave her a hug. "Now, Mama Ernestine, you know I always listened to you."

Mrs. Ernestine introduced the girls to Roger. "Y'all need to sit down at the table and have a talk." She excused herself and went outside to tend to the chickens.

Roger shook hands with each of them and sat down at the table. "Mama Ernestine told me about you on the phone, Jacey. You don't remember me, do you?"

"No, sir, I don't," Jacey said, a little confused. "Should I?"

"I helped pull you out of the water," he said.

Jacey swallowed. "Thank you," she said, her chest suddenly tight. "I don't know how I could ever thank any of you enough."

"No need for that," he said. "We were just doing our jobs. It sure is good to see you healthy and well. I understand you are trying to find the boys."

"Yes, sir," she said. "I'd really like to see them."

He leaned back in his chair. "Those boys were the light of Lillian's life," he said. "She didn't have much of an education and never had more than a minimum wage job here and there, but she would've done anything for those boys." He turned and looked outside at Mrs. Ernestine feeding the chickens. "Mama Ernestine helped keep all of them fed, but she'd never tell you that.

"Lillian was a good girl, but she got messed up with the wrong man. Followed that trash down here from Atlanta," Roger continued. "He's doing life in Angola now. Drugs do terrible things to a person, and they make you do terrible things to other people. The boys never really knew him, and that was a blessing. He came in and out of Lillian's life, and she always let him. I guess she really didn't know any better."

"Did Lillian know he was in prison?" Jacey asked.

"No," Roger said. "I doubt it. He killed a man in New Orleans a couple of months before the

182

flood. Went to jail the same night. The only reason he would've called her is if he thought she could bail him out. And he knew better."

"What an awful story," Georgia said quietly.

"It is," Roger said. "Unfortunately, it isn't an uncommon story when drugs are involved. But, to answer your questions about the boys . . . Yes, they are in foster care here in Biloxi."

"What about their grandparents?" Jacey asked. "Doesn't anybody want them?" She felt a fresh surge of compassion for the boys. This entire story was heartbreaking.

"We finally got in touch with a sister of Lillian's after the flood," Roger said. "She wasn't concerned at all, I hate to say. Lillian's parents are both in a nursing home in Atlanta. The sister has children of her own and is in no better shape financially than Lillian was. I took it they weren't on the best of terms in the first place. Her sister said—and I quote—'Hell no, don't bring me no more kids.' The boys' father renounced his parental rights soon after the last boy was born. I'm sure that was to get out of paying child support, which he never paid anyway."

"So they're just out there in limbo now?" Jacey asked. "Does the family they're with want to adopt them?"

Roger shook his head. "They don't seem to be doing too well with this family," he said. "You know, I'm not making any judgment calls, but some folks really care about these kids and some folks just take them in for the check." He remained silent but looked at Jacey.

She caught on immediately. "We gotta get them out of there," she said. "Now."

"Easier said than done," Roger said. "We're dealing with the state and child services. That's a whole lot of red tape."

"Well, let's get the scissors," Georgia said, apparently completely on board.

"Can I at least see them?" Jacey asked.

"I'll see what I can do," Roger said, standing up. "You know, I'd take all three of them myself if I weren't sixty-eight years old. But this was my last election and I'm tired. I wouldn't be good for a houseful of rowdy boys trying to play sports and go to school. But . . . maybe some young folks would be just what they needed."

The seed Roger Jefferson planted wasn't lost on Jacey. In a quick flash she imagined herself cheering at a baseball game as "her boy" slid into home. She smiled broadly at Roger. "Thank you so much."

"Thank *you*," he said. "I'll be in touch." Roger walked into the yard and stopped to talk to Mrs. Ernestine on his way.

"No, Jacey," Georgia said as soon as Roger closed the door.

"What do you mean?"

"You know what I mean. I see that look on your

face, and I was sitting here for the conversation. You can't adopt three children."

"Why not?" Jacey asked.

"Because you're twenty-five years old!" Georgia said. "Because you haven't the slightest idea how to raise a kid. Because you, I don't know . . . because . . . you just can't be adopting kids."

"Don't you think we are counting our chickens before they've hatched?"

"Don't you dare bring those chickens into this," Georgia said. "You need to think about all of this."

Jacey smiled. "Speaketh the woman who has always said, 'When something is right, you just know it.' Remember?"

Georgia rolled her eyes. "I know that look," she said. "You are about to pursue this with everything you've got, aren't you?"

"Let me think about that," Jacey said. "Yes, I am."

"Okay. If I can't change your mind between now and when you see them, I'll get on board."

"Thank you," Jacey said.

"But there's just one thing. I'm not going back through Colonel Sanders's playground unless I can ride you piggyback to the car."

Jacey laughed. "Hop on."

Chapter Sixteen

The waiting room was a pale and tranquil blue, theoretically designed to calm the nerves and make people forget where they were. But that antiseptic smell . . .

Colin hated hospitals, and he'd spent weeks in this very one after the flood. He looked over at Jasper, his face wan and expressionless. What was Jasper thinking? Had Colin actually heard his father's voice break as he held Colin's mother in his arms? Colin had spent years thinking Jasper didn't care about Ava. Nothing seemed further from the truth today.

"Has this happened before?" Colin asked, cutting through the silence that hung between him and his father.

Jasper looked at him as if he didn't understand the question. "What did you say?"

"I asked you if this has ever happened before."

Jasper looked down the hall and avoided Colin's gaze. "A couple of times," Jasper said.

"When?" Colin pressed.

"Just a couple of times in the past," Jasper said. "What did you want to talk to me about?"

"Huh?"

"You came to the house to talk to me today," Jasper said. "What did you want?"

Colin paused, then shook his head. "Nothing," he said. "It was nothing really."

He watched his father get up and walk down the hall. Colin was doused in guilt. He was the last person to talk to his mother before this "episode," as Jasper called it. Had his careless words brought this on? The cardiologist called it some sort of twelve-syllable disease, but all Colin heard was "life-threatening." When Colin asked, Dr. Seiler cautiously affirmed that what happened today could have been brought on by stress, but he went on the say that with heart disease, no one was to blame. That was of little comfort to Colin. He'd said something very hurtful and offensive to his mother, and the next thing he knew, she was on her bedroom floor unconscious. Heart disease may have been the culprit, but he'd been the catalyst.

Jasper appeared with two cups of coffee and offered one to Colin.

Colin accepted the cup. "Thank you," he said.

Jasper didn't reply.

The uncomfortable hush was broken when the nurse informed them that Ava was in a room and they could go up and see her. Colin and Jasper rode the elevator without speaking. When they got to the room, Jasper turned to him.

"I'd like to see her alone," he said. "Just for a few minutes."

Colin started to protest but decided he'd caused

enough problems today. He stepped away from the door and let his father go in.

Colin leaned up against the wall and pulled out his phone. He turned it on for the first time in twenty-four hours. It felt like it had been months since he'd talked to Jacey. He needed to hear her voice, to hold her, to tell her about the chaos in his family. He should've told her already, but he wanted to fix it first. Now it seemed all he'd done was make the situation worse.

He listened to Jacey's cheerful message. "So, I thought I'd let you know I have thought about what you said to me, and I think . . . well, I think I need to talk to you in person. And I'm sorry about the box I broke. Something crunched under my feet, so I hope it wasn't important. Also, I looked in the mirror after I left and I'd like to apologize for how bad I looked too. Anyway, I'm about to run out of time to leave this message so call me. Bye."

Colin smiled. She was beautiful to him, in every way. He put the phone back in his pocket and leaned his head against the wall. He may want her and need her, but she didn't need this. He'd overstepped his bounds with Jacey. He never should've told her he was falling for her . . . at least not now. Jacey didn't need another line item on her trauma-filled résumé. She was just getting her life back together, and she shouldn't have to deal with crazy family drama and Colin's most obvious shortcomings. Maybe the best thing to do was to take a step back. He'd expected to make a flying trip to Biloxi for a few days, cut ties with his father, visit with his mother, and head back to Baton Rouge to the girl he was sure he was in love with. He heard his mother's words again, chastising him for calling himself something he just wasn't . . . and she was right. He wasn't fit to call himself a man of God, or even a good son. Why did he think he'd be a good partner for Jacey? What kind of son didn't even know when his mother was sick?

He took his phone out of his pocket and impulsively sent Jacey a text.

"I am sorry about this, Jacey, but I have to take a step back from you and me. I am not the man you think I am or the man I presented myself to be. I hope you find the boys and bring them the same joy you brought me. Please take care of yourself."

He pushed the send button before he changed his mind and put his phone away.

Jasper came out of the room and closed the door gently behind him.

Colin stepped toward his mother's room, but his father touched him on the arm.

"Let's go over here and talk first," Jasper said.

Colin followed him to a small and vacant waiting area. "What's going on?" he asked.

Jasper motioned for him to sit down.

Jasper sat across from him and leaned forward in the chair. "Colin," he began, "your mother has been ill for quite some time."

Colin started to ask a question, but Jasper waved him off.

"I know you may be angry that you weren't made aware of this . . . among other things. But I won't have you blaming your mother. I could've told you she was sick myself, but I respected her wishes. Don't go into her room half-cocked and demanding answers."

Colin bristled but didn't respond. This was no time to get into another altercation with his father. He would respect Jasper's wishes, for Ava's sake. "I understand," he said.

"Good," Jasper replied. "Dr. Seiler is still in the room with her discussing options. The heart disease has gotten much worse in the last few months. There are three blockages, and one is 100 percent. We are most likely looking at open-heart surgery sometime this week. Maybe as early as tomorrow."

Colin was stunned by this news. "I thought it was something controllable," he said.

"As I said, her condition has worsened. For a while, she responded quite well to medicine. But the last few months . . ." His voice trailed off and he leaned back in the chair.

Colin sat in silence. Stress *was* a factor in heart disease, wasn't it? If he hadn't caused the stress himself, he'd certainly contributed to it. He thought back on recent months and the few times he actually talked to his mother. She asked him repeatedly to visit, but he said he didn't want to see Jasper. She even offered to come to him, but he said he was too busy. Today his words had caused her to become so angry that she'd walked away from him. And God only knew what happened to her internally after she climbed the stairs.

"Can I see her now?" he asked his father.

Jasper nodded toward the door of her room.

Colin opened the door slowly and peered inside.

"Mom?" he said.

Ava was propped up in bed, her eyes closed. She opened them when she heard his voice and stretched her arm to offer her hand.

He grabbed her hand. "I'm so sorry, Mama," he said. "I didn't mean to—"

"Stop," she said. "You didn't cause any of this."

"I should have been here for you," he said. "I didn't know you were sick. I would've dropped everything."

"That's exactly why I didn't want you to know," she said. "I'm going to be fine. There will be plenty of time to repair . . . a lot of things. Okay?"

Colin shook his head. "What can I do for you?"

She squeezed his hand. "You can stay here with me and tell me all about your life."

Colin sat down in the chair beside her.

"What do you want to know?" he asked.

"Well," Ava said, "let's start with your love life. Anybody special?"

Colin thought about Jacey and the text message he'd sent her earlier. He shook his head. "No, ma'am," he said. "Not really." The words pierced his heart.

Chapter Seventeen

Jacey stared at the sunset on the Gulf from the balcony of their room. Life was perfect right about now. She had the best friends anyone could ever ask for, a job that gave her all the freedom she wanted, and finally a man to love. She had tried to deny it, but she couldn't. What she felt for Colin was completely different from any other feeling she'd felt in high school, and he was unlike any man she'd dated since then. It felt good to give in to the emotion and everything that went along with it. All the sappy, saccharine clichés she'd always heard but never understood had become crystal clear to her. She didn't know whether to gag or laugh.

She glanced down at the deck of the house next door. Whoever that woman was, and whatever she was doing with Colin, it didn't bother Jacey so much anymore. He would never disrespect her by being with another woman. She had faith in Colin, and that was all she needed. She had trusted him with her life once before, and she could trust him again. So what if their romance hadn't happened amid candles and roses and the traditional frills? It had happened with moonlight and magnolias, and that was even better. She and Colin had already proven they could withstand the tough times. Wasn't that half the battle?

She leaned back onto the chaise and smiled. Soon she would see the boys again . . . and who knew what would happen after that? Before the flood, a scenario like this would've scared her to death. A situation she couldn't control? An outcome she couldn't predict? No, thanks. But now, even while mourning for Lillian and Demarcus, she felt liberated somehow. No longer tied to the weight of order and routine. She was absolutely open to anything this journey had to offer. If her time on the roof had taught her anything, it was that life was uncertain. If she could adopt these boys, it would be a beautiful and unexpected gift.

Georgia, however, had spent every second of the trip back from Mrs. Ernestine's house naming all the reasons Jacey couldn't seriously consider adopting three boys she barely knew. She was too young, too naïve, and too unmarried to raise three kids. That made Jacey laugh out loud.

"This is not who you are, Jacey," Georgia said. "Your clothes are arranged in color order in your closet. You line up your shoes like little soldiers ready for battle. You pay your bills the day you get them, and you save money like a miser. Your life is a bouquet of order. Children are messy."

"You have told me since the day we met to be more spontaneous," Jacey argued.

"But I was talking about eating raw oysters and

bungee jumping, not having three kids all at one time," Georgia said. "Have you lost your mind? They didn't even come out of your personal uterus."

"Look, I know it sounds crazy, but doesn't it seem like all this is happening for a reason? Colin shows up—then I just happen to remember the accident all of a sudden? We happen to find Mrs. Ernestine, who in turn happened to know the sheriff? And they *both* knew Lillian and the boys? Come on, Georgie. It's fate. It's serendipity."

"We found Mrs. Ernestine because we drove down a road that was an insult to roads. My car will never recover," Georgia said. "That was a . . . fluke. Not a sign from God."

"How do you know, Georgie?" Jacey asked. "Have you ever gotten a sign from God?"

"Not unless you count the trampy underwear I found in the console of my fiancé's truck last year."

Jacey laughed again. "Something tells me God didn't have anything to do with that."

"My point is, this is too much," Georgia continued.

"Why?" Jacey asked. "Why is it too much? I am young. I have a career that's going well. I could buy my own place with a yard and maybe some land and animals . . ." Her voice trailed off as she thought about it.

"Will you listen to yourself?" Georgia nearly

195

shouted. "You can't keep a cactus alive, and now you want a farm? And children?"

Jacey shushed her. "Calm down. I'm just dreaming out loud."

"Well, you need to dream about new clothes or shoes or something. This is the craziest thing I've ever heard. Adopting kids at twenty-five? You just learned how to cook macaroni and cheese last week. Didn't know how to make French toast till a month ago. Turned all the white clothes pink 'cause you put a freaking red shirt in the washer with them. Three days ago you asked me if white meat chicken and dark meat chicken came off the same chicken! And you want a kid? Not just a kid, but three of them?" Georgia threw her hands up.

"Watch the road, Georgie!" Jacey said. "You took your hands off the wheel."

"You took your brains out of your head," Georgia said, launching into another speech. "Fine. Even if I could overlook the abnormal way you want things to be neat and tidy, what are you going to do about feeding three kids? Buy a place across from McDonald's? By the way, that stuff will kill you."

Jacey finally stopped answering Georgia and let her ramble. Georgia was notorious for being all bark and very little bite. She flew off the handle in a second, but if she had time to really think about something, she would usually come around. Besides, if adopting these boys became an option, Jacey was going to pursue it—no matter what Georgia or anybody else said. From now on, she was following her heart . . . even if it got hung out to dry.

When they got back to the hotel room, Georgia finally gave up the fight. "I don't know why I'm talking," she said. "I know you aren't listening. Am I right?"

Jacey smiled. "That's right."

"Fine," Georgia said. "I'm going to take a shower and wash the chicken off of me. You stay out here and think about what I've said. Which you won't, but you need to. Ugh . . . chicken hands. This is disgusting."

Jacey laughed at Georgia, then walked over to open the French doors. She leaned over the balcony railing and looked into the pool below. She studied mothers and their children while they interacted. Though she knew parenting was maybe the most challenging job on the planet, she could learn how to be a good parent. How hard could it be to love children? No matter whose body they came from? That should come naturally from anyone. They were children: little clean slates. All children really needed was a home where they could feel safe and secure, adults who loved them unconditionally, and arms to hold them when they were scared. She could figure everything else out later.

She thought about her own parents and how she and her brother never had to wonder if they were loved or supported. *It must be terrifying for those boys right now to not feel that anymore,* she thought. How could she *not* offer herself to them? She had been through the most dangerous and challenging thing in her life with them by her side. She couldn't desert them now, the way everyone else had. Of course, Lillian hadn't chosen to leave them, but it didn't make her any less gone. They deserved someone to fight for them, and she was the only one left who could. She wasn't going to let them down.

Jacey stepped back into the hotel room when her phone beeped. She looked at it and felt her heart quicken. It was from Colin. *Finally.* She was so excited she couldn't retrieve the message quick enough.

She read the short paragraph, then reread it. What was he saying? Surely she was not comprehending this properly. This had to be his idea of a joke. She sat down on the edge of the bed and read it again.

"I am not the man you think I am . . ."

What did that even mean? A "step back"? She stared at the phone, not believing the words she'd just read. Was he telling her good-bye? Had he lied when he said he was falling for her? She immediately thought about the woman on the deck. Was this because of her?

Jacey read the message again and again. This didn't make any sense. She felt a slight wave of panic, and the tears began to pool in her eyes. Why would he say these things to her? And what was he doing? Just . . . dismissing her? Through a text message? As if she didn't even deserve to hear it face-to-face?

She remembered waking up in his arms and how good and safe she'd felt. She'd never felt anything close to that before. It was so intense it had scared her to death, but she had trusted him, dropped her guard, and let him in. Now he was taking it all back? Had she done something wrong? She tried to remember exactly what she'd said on the voicemail she left for him. She played everything over and over in her mind and came up with absolutely nothing. How could it be something she said or did? She hadn't even seen him since that morning.

She held the phone tightly in her hand. Five minutes ago her world had been as close to perfect as it could get . . . and now it was crashing down on top of her. The tears that filled her eyes were now dripping off of her chin, and she swiped at them. She felt betrayed and abandoned. Was this what a broken heart felt like?

"I've been thinking," Georgia said, stepping out of the bathroom, her hair wrapped in a towel. "Maybe it's not such a bad . . ." She looked at

Jacey sitting on the bed, clutching her phone. "What is it? What's wrong?"

Jacey didn't speak but handed the cell phone to Georgia.

Georgia read the message. "Are you kidding me? This is it? There's no more to it?"

"No," Jacey muttered.

"Of all the low-down . . . No, I'm not having this." Georgia began flinging clothes out of her suitcase. "I'm fixing to go next door and find out what's going on, because somebody over there knows. He's not going to do this to you. Not on my watch."

Jacey jumped off the bed. "No! Don't you dare!"

Georgia yanked the towel off of her head. "Why not? He can't just send a text message and not explain it. Who does something like that? I'm about to get some answers."

"I'm asking you not to," Jacey said again. "Please. It doesn't matter."

"What do you mean it doesn't matter? Of course it matters. He doesn't get to do this. Not this way."

Jacey stood up and wiped her eyes with Georgia's discarded towel. "It's my fault," she said. "I should've known better. Nobody falls in love in three days, goes missing for an entire year, and then rekindles it in a week. That just doesn't happen. It's my own fault."

Georgia sat down on the bed. "It is *not* your fault."

Jacey rolled her eyes. "Come on, Georgie. Let's be serious. I bought into the whole thing, the star-crossed lovers, 'Oh, I'll never forget you, God brought us back together' farce. It was all one . . . big . . . lie. And I fell for it. You know, you're right. I'm not grown-up enough to raise a kid. And three of them? I'd probably mess them up much worse than they already are. You know why? Because I'll fall for anything. I'm not smart enough to be anybody's parent."

"Stop it," Georgia said. "You're hurt and you're mad. I get it. But this is about *him,* not you. This is selfishness and immaturity at its finest. Trust me. I recognize it."

Jacey sat down on the bed again. "I just can't believe it," she said. "He seemed so . . . different from anybody else. So . . . real and up-front and honest. He made me feel . . . special."

Georgia smirked. "You can buy a minister's license online," she said. "Frankly, I'm a little disappointed in myself. I can usually get a pretty good read on people. I gotta tell you, Jacey, I had a good feeling about him."

Jacey sighed. "*You* did? I fell in love with him."

"Oh, honey, I know you did. But listen. I don't want to hear you say you can't be anybody's parent. You are perfect for those boys. Forget

201

Colin. You are here on a mission, and it has nothing to do with a lying, cheating, wannabe preacher."

Jacey stared at her. "You spent an hour telling me all the reasons I shouldn't pursue this."

Georgia shrugged. "You know how selfish I am," she said. "I just didn't want you to love somebody more than you love me."

Jacey smiled halfheartedly. Then she shook her head. "I don't know. It seems like a crazy idea now."

"Why? Because some preacher selling snake oil went back on his word? What do you need him for anyway? Look, I know your heart is broken, and I remember exactly what that feels like. But I'm not going to let you wallow around in it as long as I did. In the immortal words of Taylor Swift, shake it off."

Much easier said than done. Jacey felt like she was sitting on the bed with her heart outside her body, totally exposed and vulnerable. "It feels different now," she said.

"Take Colin completely out of the equation," Georgia said. "Would you still want to help those boys? Of course you would, because that's who you are. Don't let what one jerk did to you keep you from giving something beautiful to someone else. I can't think of another person more qualified for the job than you. You are the most unselfish person I know, and it would be a shame to deny that to a bunch of kids who really need it right now."

Jacey smiled. Georgia always knew what to say. Even though she still felt the injuries from her first boxing match, she was determined not to let them sideline her. She could nurse her wounds and help heal someone else's at the same time.

"You're right," Jacey said. "I came here for one reason and one reason only. I don't need Colin to help me with it or fix it for me. I can deal with this . . . broken heart business later. Right now we have things to do."

She picked up her phone up and erased the message from Colin. She never wanted to see those words again.

Chapter Eighteen

Colin insisted on staying the night with his mother, much to Jasper's dismay. Jasper tried to argue there was no way a fold-out hospital chair could comfortably fit Colin's frame, but Colin had already deferred to his father too many times today. There was no talking him out of it. Jasper had reluctantly left around eight p.m. at Ava's prodding. Together Colin and his mother watched the late news and shared some truly terrible hospital food.

"Why don't you go and get yourself some decent food?" Ava asked him.

"I'm good," Colin said. "I'm not really hungry anyway."

"Since when?"

Colin chuckled. "I don't think I'm a growing boy anymore," he said.

Ava smiled and patted his hand. "You sure aren't my little boy anymore. I have missed you, son."

That felt like a punch to the gut. "I'm sorry," he said for what felt like the hundredth time today. "I should've checked on you. I should've—"

"Please don't start that again," Ava said. "I wasn't trying to make you apologize. I was simply stating a fact. I missed you."

"I missed you too."

"See?" she said. "Was that so hard?"

"No, ma'am." He smiled.

"I do need to apologize to you, however," his mother said. "What I said to you today, I . . . I shouldn't have said it. You are a grown man, and you don't need me to tell you how to run your life or your career. I had no business meddling, and I'm sorry."

"No," he said. "That's not true. I've disrespected you, I've asked questions that were none of my business, and I've accused you of things I knew nothing about. You had every right to say whatever you wanted to me and more. I haven't been a good son."

Ava took his hand and squeezed it. "I only want what's best for you," she said. "You do know that, don't you?"

"Yes," he said. "I know that. I just . . . I don't know . . ."

"What?" Ava prompted when Colin fell silent.

"I'm not sure I know who I am anymore," he confessed. "If I'm not hating Jasper Jennings, I don't think I have an identity at all." It gave him no joy to say it out loud. In fact, he was ashamed of himself. But he needed to say it to his mother. He needed her to hear it. "And no, I'm no man of God. I've made a mockery out of the title."

Ava sighed. "You've been hard on yourself since you were a child. You always had to do everything perfectly. If your building blocks fell, you cried. Not because they fell, but because you hadn't arranged them so they wouldn't."

Colin chuckled. He could barely remember that, but she was right.

"You have always had a heart for the underdog," Ava continued, "and you still do. It's evident by what you do for flood and hurricane victims. But what you refuse to do is forgive your father. Or yourself."

Colin was uncomfortable with her words, but there was very little he could do about it. He couldn't storm out, leaving her sitting in her hospital bed, even if that was his first instinct. And he knew it was the wrong one.

"Let's not do this, Mom," he said. "Not right now."

"Can you think of a better time?"

Colin didn't answer.

"You don't even have to talk," Ava continued. "I'll do all the talking. But this time you're going to have to sit there and listen."

"I'm listening," he said.

"I want you to hear me out before you comment. Can you do that?"

He nodded his head.

"When your father and I married, things were much different between us," Ava said. "We were so young and so in love. He was everything I ever wanted. Warm, compassionate, caring."

Colin was having a hard time imagining that, but she had his attention.

"Your father wanted to be a veterinarian," Ava said. "Did I ever tell you that?"

"No," Colin said, surprised. But then he suddenly remembered, years ago when he was maybe eight or nine, bringing home a stray dog. Just a homeless mutt that had followed him up to the house from the beach one day. He was sure his father was going to make him get rid of it, but the opposite had happened. Jasper had helped him bathe the dog and even fixed a place for him to sleep by Colin's bed. They named him Hobo. That dog became his faithful companion and for years made every step Colin made. He was always a gentle and unassuming pet—an old soul, his mother called him. One day when Colin was a senior in high school, his mother met him at the door when he got home and told him Hobo had died, probably of old age. Colin cried like a child as he dug the grave to bury him, and he remembered his father coming outside, putting his hand on his shoulder, and taking the shovel from him to finish the job. It was a good memory of his father. One of the few he had.

"Your father talked about it all the time," Ava continued. "He wanted to finish his under-graduate degree, then apply to vet school. But your grandfather was grooming Jasper to take over the construction company. Jasper hated the very thought of it. He had to work summers for Collingsworth, and it wasn't a pleasant atmosphere for him or anyone else. You don't remember much about your grandfather, do you?"

Colin shrugged. "Not too much," he agreed. "I remember him being at our house a few times. He always looked mad, and I remember him telling me one day not to be a pansy after I cut my finger on a can and cried."

Ava shook her head. "I remember that day too," she said. "You needed four stitches in your finger. And I had some harsh words for your grandfather."

Colin smiled. "I might remember a little of that too."

"Your father endured a lot of abuse at the hands of Collingsworth," Ava said. "And I don't mean just mentally." She looked at Colin to see if he understood.

"He . . . hit him?"

"More like beat him," Ava said. "Back in those days no one raised an eyebrow when a father 'disciplined' his son. There was no number to call or shelter to go to. It is one of the reasons I have been so involved in children's advocacy. Your father had a terrible childhood, Colin."

Colin took a moment to process that and actually felt sorry for his father—an emotion he'd never even considered when it came to Jasper.

"He didn't tell me about any of this until after you were born," Ava said. "He became very sullen when I was expecting you and standoffish with both of us after you were born. I finally confronted him. After much coaxing and, well, begging, he told me about his youth. But as much as I tried to tell him he could break the cycle of abuse, he wouldn't believe me. In the end, he was right. He *did* abuse you, but instead of physically abusing you, he did it emotionally. Sadly enough, I think he thought he was doing you a favor."

Colin stared at her, not sure what to make of her words. "So you're saying he avoided me all my life because he was afraid he would hurt me?"

"I'm saying he did not want to perpetuate the cycle. Your grandfather tried to strangle your grandmother when your father was eight years old because she'd smiled at the milkman. He did it in front of Jasper. She left him the next day and left Jasper with him. She told your grandfather he could keep Jasper because she wasn't going to raise a monster just like him. And your father heard her say it. How's that for a legacy?"

Colin sank back into the chair. He tried to imagine what it must've felt like to hear those words coming from your mother as an eight-year-old child. He thought about Ava and how gentle she had always been with him . . . how comforting it was to be hugged by her when he was a kid, how she always smelled like lemon and verbena, how her soothing words could fix anything in his young world.

"Why didn't you ever tell me this?" Colin asked.

Ava sighed and leaned back into her pillow. "When you were young, it wasn't appropriate. And when you were older, I tried to tell you," she said. "Many, many times. Once when you were sixteen, you screamed back at me, 'I don't want to hear your excuses.' But with much more colorful language. Do you remember?"

He did. It was the night he ran away down the beach and ended up at Joshua's house. Colin felt sick to his stomach. He'd spent most of his life hating this man, or at least trying to. To find out now that Jasper was actually trying to somehow protect him . . . It was a hard pill to swallow.

"But what about the drinking? The women?" Colin asked, then regretted it. "I don't mean to upset you. Just forget the question. I shouldn't have asked you that."

"No," Ava said, "I'm not upset at all. I have longed for the day you would listen to me, ask questions, try to understand. There are many more things you need to know."

"Are you sure you're up to this?" he asked. "We don't have to talk about it anymore."

"I want to get it all out in the open," she said. "Your father never understood, even though

I have told him again and again that the truth would, indeed, set us free."

"Okay," Colin said. "But the second you feel sick or strange or anything else, you stop talking and I'll get a nurse or a doctor. Deal?"

Ava smiled. "Deal. You're a good son, Colin."

Colin shook his head. "No, I'm not."

"Yes you are," she said. "Now just listen. Your father did begin to drink when you were a very young boy. I found that odd since he was always so opposed to alcohol, didn't even like for me to have a glass of wine with a meal. I now know it's because his father and grandfather were raging alcoholics. Do you drink?"

"No," he said. "Not anymore. For the same reason."

"A good choice," Ava said. "Jasper's drinking stepped up when he went to work full-time for your grandfather. I tried to talk to him about it, of course, but he always said it was the stress from the job, from working for his father . . . any excuse he could come up with. What could I do except make his home life as pleasant as I possibly could? Even that didn't help too much. He constantly offered me a divorce, saying he understood if I wanted to take you and leave him, that he didn't expect me to stay under these circumstances. But the truth was, I loved your father. I always have. He is a good and decent man who got dealt a terrible hand. He didn't know how to love anybody because he never saw how it was done. And, by the way, he hasn't had a drop of alcohol in five years."

There was a piece of good news. "But the women," Colin said. "What about the women?"

"That . . ." Colin saw the hurt on her face, "That is something I cannot defend. But what I can tell you is that those days are over and have been over for a while. I have forgiven him. You need to do the same."

"But he hurt you, he disrespected you," Colin said. "How can I pretend that didn't happen?"

"It wasn't your pain. It was mine," Ava said. "I appreciate you trying to champion the cause, but it isn't your battle to fight. What happened was between two married people. Between your father and me. Not between your father, me, and you. I know you see me as the victim, but there are things that go on between married people that other people never see, not even the children. I will not defend his actions, but I will not say I was without blame."

"Mama," Colin said, "he cheated on you. How can you assume any responsibility for that? You *are* defending him, whether you realize it or not."

Ava stared at him for a moment before she answered. "Maybe I am defending him, and maybe it's because he wasn't the only person in this marriage who once made a bad decision.

I'm sure you understand that sentence and all that it means."

Colin stared at her blankly. He didn't comprehend the words at first. Then the full weight of her statement hit him. His mother had just confessed an infidelity of her own. He looked away from her quickly, shocked by this new knowledge.

"I know this is a lot to take in, son," Ava said. "But you needed to finally know the truth. Sometimes what you see or hear doesn't tell the whole story. We've all made mistakes . . . terrible, life-altering choices that have driven wedges between us. Your father and I mended our fences years ago. You and your father need to find a way to mend yours."

Colin couldn't answer her. There were too many emotions inside him, and he couldn't find his voice. He clenched his jaw and stared out the window into the darkness outside.

"I'm sorry if I disappointed you, Colin," Ava said, putting her hand on top of his. "No one wants to hear . . . intimate secrets from their mother. But you needed to know everything, and I simply could not allow you to continue to blame your father for all the ills of this marriage. My . . . indiscretion . . . occurred before his. I hurt him very badly, and frankly, I am surprised he stayed with me afterward."

Colin was terribly uncomfortable. Ava was right

when she said your mother's intimate secrets were difficult to hear. He could think of a dozen different places he'd rather be than sitting in this hospital hearing this confession tonight. Still, he was curious, no . . . he *needed* to know who this man was who made his proper and gentle mother stray from the confines of her marriage. Did he know the man? Did Jasper know the man?

"I know you must have questions," Ava said quietly. "I will do my best to answer them."

Colin looked at her for the first time since she shared her secret. Her face looked sheepish and guilty.

"I'm so sorry, son," she said. "I can't imagine what it must feel like to hear these things about your parents. I know you are mad and you have every right—"

Colin stopped her. "No," he said. "I'm not mad at you. Of course not. This happened between you and Dad. I can't judge you for your choices. I don't know what went on between you and Dad, or what made you . . . do what you did. I just . . . it's, well . . . hard for a son to see his mother as anything except . . . a mother."

"An astute observation," Ava said. "But I am also a woman who once felt very lonely and underappreciated . . ." Her voice trailed off for a moment. "I'm not trying to make excuses because there are none. I fell into an age-old trap

214

of presuming the grass was greener on the other side."

Colin felt an unexpected swell of compassion for his mother. She had screwed up. So had Jasper. So had *he*. In fact, the entire family could've rented a space on the psych ward of this very hospital and kept the doctors in business for years to come. It was a sobering thought to grasp just how dysfunctional your own family was. Even more sobering to know every single member of the family had contributed to the mix. No, it didn't magically fix the rift that had run so deep and long between Colin and his father, but for the first time in years, he didn't feel hopeless. Maybe there was some way to salvage this family. At least no one was keeping secrets anymore.

He bent over his mother and hugged her gently amid the IV and monitor cords. "I love you, Mama," he said. "Rest. Just rest now."

Chapter Nineteen

Jacey woke up early from a fitful sleep, if she could even call it sleep. Her first thought was about Colin and the terrible text message. *Sounded a little like a children's book,* she thought. *A very bad children's book.*

The same empty feeling she had in the pit of her stomach last night had returned with a vengeance as soon as she opened her eyes. She glanced over to see if Georgia was still asleep before slipping out of the French doors to the balcony. She sat on the chaise and leaned forward, looking down at the house where she'd seen Colin. Part of her wanted to see if he was there, part of her dreaded knowing, and all of her hated the way this entire thing made her feel. Such animosity for a woman she'd never even met and a raging desire to slap Colin's face or burst into tears at the thought of him were new and unwelcomed feelings. Maybe there was something to be said for living a vanilla life, after all. It had managed to keep these kinds of emotions off the table. She continued to stare at the beach house below. There was no sign of life on the deck or anywhere else. She turned back and looked at the Gulf.

Something must have made Colin change his

mind about her, and she'd lain awake most of the night trying to figure out what it could have been. She'd replayed every possible scenario over and over in her mind and come up with exactly nothing. It made no sense at all. Apparently he had just changed his mind. Was that routine amid the peaks and valleys of the world of romance? Was it normal for a man to *almost* tell you he was in love with you, then, "Oops, never mind"? And people said women were fickle. She realized she had very little experience with affairs of the heart, but even a girl without a lover's scar could tell this wasn't routine.

One thing was for sure: The euphoric feelings she'd had the past few days were gone, replaced by this awful, gnawing awareness that something wasn't right in the world. If this was what it was like to have a broken heart, then this would be her first and her last. No wonder Georgie was against dating again. Nobody wanted to feel like this. This heartache, coupled with the recent news of Lillian and Demarcus, had Jacey feeling down.

Jacey's friends were always amazed because she'd gone through high school and college unscathed by a bad breakup or unrequited love. The truth was, it surprised her too. She didn't think it was because she didn't want to fall in love. She just never met anybody who gave her the double whammy. She was either attracted to someone physically and not emotionally, or she was attracted to him emotionally but without a spark. Neither combination seemed to work. That wisdom was probably a bit beyond her years, but it had protected her when she watched her high school friends sob over breakups and check out of their lives for weeks, if not months, at a time. It was enough to make her wary of risking the same fate.

But when she saw Colin Jennings standing on the roof of a flooded house in tattered jeans and a white T-shirt, she was impressed. When she got to know him, the attraction, both physical and emotional, was so strong it frightened her. As she sat on the balcony trying to analyze herself, she thought it was probably why she had dated every man in the greater Baton Rouge area this past year. She'd been frantically searching for someone who made her feel the same way, but nobody had. Maybe nobody else ever would.

She forced herself to stop thinking about it. "No use in crying over spilled milk," her Granny always said. "Mop it up and move on." Now, if only she could put that plan into action.

Georgia slid the glass door open and joined her. "Good morning, my friend," she said, making a terribly loud moaning sound as she stretched and yawned.

"Why are you so chipper?" Jacey asked. "Didn't you get the memo? Your bestie has a broken heart."

"Oh, I remember," Georgia said. "But I'm not going to let it define her today. We're going to the pool in our cutest bikinis, and we're going to stretch out on our chairs and let people bring us things. All day."

"Can't I just sit here and nurse my wounds?" Jacey asked only half-jokingly.

"Do you want to end up the hot mess I was last year?" Georgia asked. "I didn't bathe for a week, remember? By the end of that week I smelled like vinegar, for some reason." Georgia shuddered at the memory. "There were food wrappers in my bed. I ate hummingbird cake and tuna sandwiches. I *hate* hummingbird cake. *And* tuna sandwiches. It took hours to get all the tangles out of my hair after I finally came out of my stupor. And the film on my teeth . . . It was like they were all wearing little sweaters. Do you really want to suffer the same fate?"

As sad as Jacey was, Georgia's words made her smile. "You really did smell bad," she said. "Maybe you're right. We should go out to the pool. Besides, I just shaved my legs. It would be a shame to waste it."

"There's the spirit," Georgia said. "Call room service and have them bring us bacon and eggs. I'll grab a quick shower."

"I think that is a superb idea," Jacey said, then went inside to order breakfast.

An hour and a half later they were lounging poolside.

"Just look at that blue sky," Georgia said. "What could possibly be wrong on a day like today?"

"Um, excuse me?" Jacey said. "Would you like me to give you a list?"

Georgia laughed. "Oops," she said. "I didn't mean to be insensitive."

Jacey smiled. "Yes, you did," she said. "But that's okay. I wouldn't have a clue how to act if you weren't saying something completely inappropriate."

"See?" Georgia said. "You understand me. Not everyone does."

"That's actually a little scary to think about," Jacey said.

Georgia laughed. "Oh, but you love me."

"I do. I don't know why, but I do."

"I still think we should go sniff around next door," Georgia said. "At least let me go. I can be subtle."

"Subtle? Like a bull in a china shop," Jacey said. "And no, absolutely not. Anyway, I thought we were moving on from that subject."

"So did I, but you keep checking your phone every thirty seconds," Georgia said. "I assume you are waiting for Colin to retract."

"I am not. I am checking to see if the sheriff has texted me or left a message."

"Okay, fine. I stand corrected," Georgia said. "Did you turn the ringer off? Is that why you need to actually look at the phone?"

Jacey made a face at her. "Shut up, Georgie."

"Fine, I'll just stay over here in my own little world and watch the seagulls while you reign as Queen of Denial. And I ain't talking 'bout a river in Spain."

"Egypt and other countries," Jacey said. "But nowhere near Spain."

"Whatever," Georgia said. "I'm a nurse, not a geographer. Is *geographer* a word?"

Jacey snickered. "Yes."

"I knew that."

"Right," Jacey said.

The easy and familiar comfort of banter with Georgia did seem to take the sting away from this morning. Jacey rested her head on the wicker lounge chair, and soon the warmth of the sun made her drowsy. That, and being tired from tossing and turning most of the night. Before long, she was sound asleep.

She dreamed of the boys, all four of them, and Lillian too. But it wasn't a scary dream or one that made her sad. Lillian was talking to her on the roof of the house, but they were surrounded by flowers and grass instead of water. It was a beautiful spring day, the sky a bright and dazzling blue, and there wasn't a cloud in sight. She and Lillian were both wearing sundresses and pretty hats, having sweet tea and cookies. The boys played baseball in the yard, squealing with laughter and youth. Lillian was telling her how much the boys loved Star Wars, how they loved to read and play sports, and she hoped Jacey would remember that. Jacey was writing it all down in a pink notebook.

"Wake up, Jacey, wake up."

The voice sounded so far away . . . She asked Lillian if she had heard it.

"Wake up! Your phone is ringing."

She opened her eyes and realized she was dreaming. Georgia was handing her the phone.

"Answer your phone," Georgia urged.

Fully awake now, Jacey swiped the phone and answered. "Hello?"

"Jacey?"

"Yes?"

"It's Roger Jefferson," he said. "How's it going today?"

"I'm fine," she said. "Do you have any news? I'm sorry . . . just anxious to see them."

"I do have news, and I'm glad you're anxious to hear it. Looks like you can visit tomorrow evening at the park down on Hiller Drive. Four o'clock," the sheriff said.

"Are you serious?" Jacey was so excited she was tapping her chest with her hand.

"I'm serious," he said. "It may have been

because I strongly suggested they let you visit." He laughed.

"Thank you, Sheriff," Jacey said. "Thank you so much. I don't know how I can ever repay you."

"No need for all that," the sheriff said. "You just follow your heart, you hear?"

"Yes, sir," Jacey said. "I sure will. Thank you again."

She hung up and turned to Georgia. "We can go to the park tomorrow at four to meet them."

Georgia smiled. "That is good news," she said. "See? The world is still okay, right?"

"It sure is," Jacey said, grinning broadly.

"How long can we visit? Did he say?" Georgia asked.

"No, and I didn't think to ask," Jacey said. "I guess until the foster parents get ready to leave. Surely it will be more than a few minutes."

"Should we take them something?" Georgia asked. "Toys or . . . ?"

"That's a great idea," Jacey said. "Let's go shopping!"

Georgia began gathering her things. "You know you don't have to tell me twice to go shopping."

Jacey suddenly remembered the dream she was having when the phone rang. She stopped packing her things and smiled at Georgia.

"Books," she said. "Let's be sure and bring them some books too."

Three hours later they were armed with books, puzzles, baseball gloves, Star Wars figurines, marbles, and a vast array of other things the clerk at the toy store said no boy should ever be without. Jacey had never felt such joy buying gifts.

"What was that?" Georgia said when they got to the car. "It normally takes you thirty minutes to pick out a T-shirt to buy, and even then you insist you've spent too much money on it. You blew through that store like a house on fire."

"That was maybe the most fun I've ever had," Jacey said breathlessly. "Do you think they will like it all? Are you sure I got enough? Do you think I got too much?"

Georgia raised an eyebrow as she continued trying to cram things into the trunk of her car. "It's a possibility," she said. "We should've rented a trailer."

Jacey laughed. "So I went a little overboard . . ."

"There," Georgia said as the last of it was finally loaded. She gave Jacey the sackful of books. "You're gonna have to hold these."

Jacey started scanning through them. "I hope all of these are age-appropriate."

"We were at a toy store, Jacey," Georgia said. "How bad could they be?"

"I guess you're right. Maybe I should skim over them tonight just the same."

"Already acting like somebody's mama," Georgia muttered. "Sucking all the fun out of things."

"What?" Jacey said.

"Oh, nothing," Georgia said. "I was just saying how exhausting it is shopping for kids. I'm thirsty. Let's get a smoothie or a shake or something."

"Yum," Jacey said. "Let's get a smoothie."

Jacey scanned her phone for a smoothie place, and they were already pretty close to one.

"Drive-through or inside?" Georgia asked.

"Inside," Jacey said. "I need to visit the little girls' room."

"Okay, I'll order," Georgia said. "You want the usual?"

"Yes, and add mango."

When she returned from the bathroom, Georgia was already waiting for her by the door.

"Take these," she said, handing her the smoothies. "I have to go too. The one on the left is yours."

Jacey leaned against the counter and watched a mother and her three kids wrestling at a table nearby. The smallest one, a girl, was crying. She apparently didn't want the green smoothie but the pink smoothie instead. Her big brother was sipping the pink smoothie and would stop every now and then to poke his tongue out at his sister, which only served to intensify the wailing. The oldest boy rolled his eyes and seemed embarrassed by the whole charade.

Jacey smiled but was cracking up on the inside. How perfect and natural and normal it was to see a mother and her children doing everyday things. She had never really paid attention to it before, but now it fascinated her. The mother was juggling food, drinks, a phone call, and kids without missing a beat. Jacey was witnessing the most noble of all the jobs on earth—being somebody's mama.

She took a sip of her smoothie and knew as soon as it hit her tongue that she'd made a terrible mistake. The fear and histamine hit simultaneously. She'd taken a drink out of the wrong cup. Jacey dropped the drinks in her hand and grabbed her throat. It was already happening. Her airway was closing. She was wheezing and could feel her tongue beginning to thicken. Her mind raced to recall that her EpiPen was all the way back at the hotel.

Georgia walked out of the bathroom, saw her, and quickly sprung into action.

"Where's the nearest hospital?" she shouted as people began to stare. "Where is it?"

Someone behind the counter said, "Two blocks

226

over," and pointed to the right. "Can we do something? Call an ambulance?"

"Does anyone have an EpiPen?" Georgia asked, putting Jacey's shoulder around her. "Hang on, hang on, girl. It's gonna be okay."

No one in the smoothie shop had an allergy pen, but they swarmed Jacey and Georgia to offer help. The boy behind the counter jumped over it and scooped Jacey up in his arms. "Where to?" he asked.

Georgia pointed at the Corvette. "Put her inside," she said. "What street do I use?"

"Go straight on this street. It's the fastest, but it's a one-way. The entrance to the ER is right there. Two blocks."

"Thank you," Georgia said, speeding off.

Jacey grabbed for Georgia's hand. She was scared to death but trying to remain calm. The wheezing had become even more intense, and she struggled for every breath.

"We're almost there," Georgia said. "So close, it'll be okay. Hang on. It's gonna be okay."

Jacey tried to concentrate on Georgia's words and not give in to fear. But it was getting more and more difficult to find air. The wheezing turned to grasping at nothing because there wasn't much getting through. She was barely aware of Georgia screaming at traffic and bobbing and weaving through the cars on the street. She heard horns and sirens in the background.

"Almost," Georgia said. "Hang on, almost . . ."

The last thing Jacey remembered was Georgia slamming the car into park and screaming, "Get a gurney and an epinephrine injection! She's in anaphylactic shock! Strawberries!"

Chapter Twenty

Jacey slowly opened her eyes and looked around, wondering where she was. Then she groaned. *Strawberries. Hospital.*

"Hello," Georgia said.

Jacey turned to her side to see Georgia sitting in a chair beside her bed.

"See this?" Georgia held up an injector pen. "This is called an EpiPen. People who are allergic to certain things find that having one on their person at *all* times is very useful. It also keeps the cops from chasing their best friend through the streets of Biloxi."

Jacey tried a half smile but felt like she'd been run over by a truck. "Sorry."

"I'm gonna let you slide this time since the officer was kind enough not to write me a ticket," Georgia said. "But if you hadn't been *almost dying in my car,* I would've surely gotten one." She paused. "Have you lost your mind? Why don't you keep the pen in your purse, Jacey? You could've died. You *almost* died. Do you understand that?"

"I'm so sorry," Jacey said sheepishly. "I just don't think about it. Honestly."

"As a nurse, I cannot stress to you enough the importance of having this with you 24/7,"

Georgia said. "And as your best friend, you scared to me death. It happened so fast I didn't know if we were going to make it to the hospital that was only two blocks away. If it had been any farther . . ."

"I know," Jacey said. "I promise, from now on, I will keep it with me. Always."

"Why did you drink out of my smoothie in the first place?" Georgia asked. "I told you which one was yours."

Jacey shook her head. "I don't know. I just wasn't paying attention. I was watching a mother and her children and . . . daydreaming, I guess."

"Don't do it again," Georgia said.

"I promise. And thank you so much. You saved my life."

Georgia waved her off. "Please," she said. "I got to drive really fast and was chased by the cops. Even if it was only for a block and a half. It you hadn't been beside me trying to die, it would've been fun."

Jacey laughed. "Seriously. Thank you. For everything you do."

Georgia shook her head. "Ditto."

"When can I get out of here?" Jacey asked.

"I'm working on that now," Georgia said. "In fact, let me go see what's going on."

Georgia went down the hall to the admitting area in the ER but failed to find anyone manning the desk. She'd managed to talk Jacey's doctor into releasing her because Georgia was an RN and assured him she could take care of her friend. She also had to promise him she'd fill the prescriptions he'd written for the auto-injectors before they left the hospital.

She walked a little farther down the corridor looking for any signs of life. When she rounded the corner she stopped short. Fifteen feet in front of her stood Colin Jennings and the woman from the beach, embracing in the corridor of the front lobby. She quickly ducked into the alcove by the bathroom door and hid.

"Thank you for coming, Julie," Colin said. "You've been there for me more times than I can count."

Julie. Georgia made a mental note of her name and strained to hear the rest of the conversation.

"I'm just glad you called," Julie said. "And I'm glad things turned out well."

"I love you," Colin said. "Be careful on your way home. I'll call you tonight."

"I love you too. I'll be expecting your call."

Georgia peeked around the corner to see if they were going to kiss, but all she saw was Colin reluctantly letting go of Julie's hand as she walked away. Georgia ducked back into the crevice, mad as a hornet and ready to sting. But she knew Jacey would kill her if she made a scene, so she backed up against the wall and watched the woman, Julie, walking down the hall. When she disappeared she heard the unmistakable sound of cowboy boots heading in the other direction. She peeked around again and saw Colin walking back toward the main area of the hospital.

"He's a snake . . ."

"Can I help you?" a male voice asked.

Georgia turned around to see a gentleman emerging from the men's bathroom. She was blocking his exit.

She flashed him a brilliant smile and pointed to the sign on the door. "This isn't the ladies room, is it?" She jogged down the hall back to the ER.

Georgia was as mad as she'd ever been in her life. Only a woman who had been cheated on could fully appreciate what she had just witnessed. She wanted to tear Colin limb from limb, then beat what was left of him with his torn-off limbs. He'd told that girl he loved her, when a few days ago he'd basically told Jacey the same thing. What a jerk. What a lying, cheating jerk.

She stopped suddenly when she got back to the ER waiting room. What was she going to tell Jacey? This would finish breaking her heart. Jacey didn't know it yet, but her heart was only a little cracked and scratched. It wouldn't be fully broken until she questioned every single thing she'd ever believed about men and relationships. Or when she wanted to sleep but was afraid she'd dream of him again if she did . . . Telling Jacey what she'd just seen would've been like serving her best friend some poison.

Why was Colin here anyway? Was he visiting the hospital in an official capacity—as a pastor? What a joke that was. If Colin Jennings was a preacher, then Georgia was a ballerina. All 145 pounds of her. But he had thanked that woman for coming, so maybe someone in his family was here. She turned around and jogged back toward the hospital entrance, hoping to check with the front desk and see if she could get any answers. If it was one of those pink ladies, she'd have trouble getting any information, but she was sure she could manipulate a candy striper.

Ah . . . a candy striper.

"Hi," Georgia said. "I'm trying to see if they admitted a patient here. Last name Jennings."

The girl scanned the computer. "Hmm," she mused, all cheerful and happy. "I only see an Ava Jennings. Is that her?"

"It sure is." Georgia smiled. "Can you tell me why she's here?"

The candy striper looked around. "I'm not supposed to."

Georgia winked. "Oh, I know," she said. "And you're doing a great job." Georgia whipped her nursing ID out of her purse and flashed it quickly. Too quickly for the girl to see the Baton Rouge General tag. "I'm actually an ER nurse. I was just checking to see how she was doing." Georgia turned slowly, hoping the girl would take the bait. She did.

"Wait," Candy Striper said. "She had bypass surgery this morning. Poor thing. She's only fifty-seven years old, currently in the ICU. Shall I call for you?"

"No, I'll check on her. But thanks so much," Georgia said. "Have a great day."

So this must be Colin's mother, Georgia decided. That's why Colin came to Mississippi in such a hurry. And that Julie girl must've come to sit with Colin during the surgery. So she'd been in his life awhile . . . probably the girlfriend before he met Jacey last year. Then why did he go looking for Jacey? Maybe they had broken up but recently reconciled. Or maybe Colin was a player. Who knew? There were too many questions for her to decipher, but she still thought it best not to tell Jacey any of it just yet. She would mentally file her facts and suspicions, saving them for the day Jacey needed to know the truth about this guy. That day would come eventually.

Georgia walked down the corridor until she reached the ER again, and this time she found somebody to talk to. After being assured Jacey would be released in a couple of hours, she went back into the room where Jacey was watching TV.

"Where have you been?" Jacey asked.

Georgia fiddled with the contents of her purse to avoid eye contact. "Oh, you know, she said. "Just trying to find somebody around here who could give us the green light. Tell us when we could blow this joint."

"Well?" Jacey asked.

"Well, what?"

"Can we leave?" Jacey asked.

"Oh," Georgia said. "Yes, well, not yet. In a couple of hours. What are you watching?" She turned her attention to the television.

"The news," Jacey said. "It's the only channel I can get. I have to wonder why they would put a news channel in an emergency room. I mean, people come here when they're having heart attacks. The news is bound to make it worse. Nobody wants to see all this. I knew there was a reason I didn't watch the news. Just listen to some of this." She turned the up volume.

"No, thanks," Georgia said. "I get all the news I want in the ER. You know I don't watch that mess."

"I'm going to the bathroom," Jacey said. "They must've given me a ton of fluids. She just pulled the IV out a few minutes ago."

"That's what happens when you don't keep your EpiPen with you," Georgia said. "You remember that."

Jacey stuck out her tongue at Georgia. "Where's the potty?" she asked.

"Right outside the door to your left," Georgia said.

A moment after Jacey turned the corner, a picture of a lovely woman with short, stylish gray hair and a warm smile came across the TV screen. The cheerful blonde reporter on the local news channel said, "There are reports that Ava Jennings, a local philanthropist and chairperson of two Biloxi charities and board member of several more, has been hospitalized today to undergo open-heart surgery. Mrs. Jennings is the wife of Jasper Jennings, the CEO of Jennings Construction. We at WBYR wish her a speedy recovery and a heartfelt thank-you for all she has done for this station and this city."

Georgia dove across the bed to the remote and turned the TV off. *This woman must be a huge deal around here.* And Jennings Construction? Even she had seen their trucks going up and down the highways and Interstate 10. No wonder Colin had no trouble funding his life and his little building projects. This was why he hadn't answered her when she'd grilled him. He didn't have to work because the money was already in the bank. Georgia was both irritated and intrigued. She would Google their names later tonight at the hotel to see what else she could find out about Colin and his family.

"Why are you in my bed?" Jacey asked when she came back in.

"This nursing stuff is exhausting," Georgia said. "You sit in the chair awhile and let me recover from the stress of this morning."

Jacey laid back in the recliner. "You know," she said, "I've been thinking about Colin today."

Georgia's eyebrow shot up. "You have my attention," she said.

"I know you said to leave it alone and put it out of my mind and all that stuff," Jacey said. "And I am trying to—I promise I am. But I can't help but think he is just like me. He probably just got scared. You know what I mean? Maybe it got really . . . real. It made me run away too. Maybe he just needs some time to think."

"No," Georgia said. "He's nothing like you. He didn't need time to think."

"How do you know?" Jacey asked. "Maybe I should just call him and tell him it's okay if—"

"Do not call that son of a—" Georgia cut herself off. "Don't call him, Jacey. It's not cool to call a guy after he has told you he needs a break or used some other lame excuse. Leave it alone."

Jacey was a little surprised at Georgia's zeal. She was really mad at Colin. "You really wanna punch him, don't you?" Jacey said.

"You have no idea," Georgia answered.

Jacey shrugged. "I'll give it a little more time."

"Yes," Georgia agreed. "Let's give it a little more time."

Jacey looked at Georgia and could tell she was really seething. Jacey had known her long enough to see that. She chalked it up to loyalty and the "cheating fiasco of 2014," as Georgia dubbed it. She didn't press the issue because Georgia could still be sensitive about it now and then.

"So . . . I'm starving to death," Jacey said. "What do you want to eat?"

"Anything but strawberries," Georgia said.

Chapter Twenty-One

Colin paced back and forth in front of the window in the ICU waiting area, his head jerking up every time the door opened. They were waiting for the okay to visit his mother, but it seemed to be taking an outrageous amount of time. Patience had never been his strong suit, and today he was in short supply. He glanced at his father.

Jasper was sitting in a chair in the corner, his hands folded in his lap. He'd stayed very quiet for most of the day. Colin wondered whether he should approach him or not, try to start a conversation. But every time he thought he could, he changed his mind. Ava had told Colin enough for him to know he'd been wrong in many ways about his dad, but reaching out seemed too raw, too unfamiliar to him. Maybe he should wait on Jasper to make the first move. Or maybe his mom would tell his father that she and Colin had talked about the truth. Surely that would propel Jasper into a conversation with him.

But what if his mom didn't make it? No, he couldn't think that way. Of course she was going to make it. The surgery had gone well and she was "resting comfortably" in recovery— whatever that meant. When the surgeon had come out to tell them the surgery was successful, the relief had almost buckled his knees. Colin had been sure they were going to lose her . . . maybe because of his guilt, remorse, regret, or something. He'd been in these situations before, praying with frightened parents, children, aunts, and uncles as they waited for news about their loved ones. And he'd tried to pray all morning when she was in surgery, but his prayers seemed dull and without direction. It left him restless and agitated.

Thank God Julie had been there during the surgery, or else he'd have gone stir-crazy. She came in like a chatty ray of sunshine and talked nonstop. It wasn't the first time she had helped save him.

"These things are routine now," Julie had said, referring to open-heart surgery. "It's like having your wisdom teeth pulled these days."

"You ever had your wisdom teeth pulled?" Colin asked.

"Well, now that you mention it, no." Julie laughed.

"I have," Colin said. "Not pleasant."

Jasper chuckled, a sound that surprised Colin. He hadn't even realized Jasper was listening to their conversation.

"I remember that," Jasper said. "You must've been about eighteen. Right before you left for college. You caused quite a ruckus the night after. Standing up in the bed, then trying to jump off the balcony. The pain pills didn't agree with you at all. After they finally knocked you out, I sat in a chair in your room all night and watched you sleep."

"I don't remember," Colin said.

Jasper smiled. "I knew you didn't."

Colin smiled back at his father. "Thank you."

"You're my son," he said, picking up a magazine.

Julie smiled. Colin saw her face and wondered if she'd noticed the gentle moment that had just passed between him and his father. After the doctor came to tell them Ava's surgery had been a complete success, Julie picked up her things to leave. Colin walked her out.

"Thank you for coming," he said.

"Where's your girl?" Julie asked.

"What?"

"If you love her, Colin, you need to invite her into this."

"She's had enough to deal with," he said. "She doesn't need more."

"Do you love her?" Julie asked.

"I don't know," he said. "Maybe. I'm not sure."

"I see. Our circumstances cloud our true feelings sometimes."

He thought about her words as he walked her to the first floor. He said good-bye, wondering all the time if Julie was right about Jacey. Should he invite her into all this confusion? He honestly didn't know. He missed her and wished she were here to share some of the burden . . . but Jacey was still fragile. She needed time to process the last year. Throwing more fuel onto an already burning fire seemed selfish. He'd made the right decision. Maybe. He began pacing again.

Finally the door opened, and a sweet little old lady in a pink outfit said, "Jennings family?"

Colin sprang to her side, Jasper close on his heels.

"You can see your mother now," she said.

Colin and Jasper followed her to the doors of the ICU.

"She's awake and off the ventilator already," the Pink Lady said. "That's very good news. She'll be a little groggy, but everything is fine."

They stepped into Ava's room, and Jasper walked to the bedside. He picked up her hand and kissed it.

Colin stopped in his tracks. His presence made him feel intrusive. *This should be a private moment between the two of them,* he thought to himself. He turned to step outside, but his father stopped him.

"Colin," he said, reaching for him. "Come over here so she can see you."

Colin went to his mother's side.

"My handsome men," she whispered.

Colin felt his eyes fill with tears. "I bet you

wouldn't say that if you had your glasses on," he joked. "Neither one of us looks too good."

Ava smiled. "Go home," she whispered. "Rest."

"Not a chance," Colin said.

"Me either," Jasper told her.

Ava closed her eyes. "Stubborn. Just alike."

Colin and Jasper looked at each other, then back at Ava.

"Okay, you two," a voice behind them interrupted. "That's enough. We need to let her rest. You can visit again in three hours."

"We've only been here for two minutes," Colin said.

"And that's only because I am Nurse Nice-to-You," she said. "I can turn into Nurse Run-for-Cover very quickly. Now, shoo. Get out."

Jasper bent to kiss his wife and Colin squeezed her hand.

"We'll be right outside, Mama," he said.

She shook her head. "I'll be right here," she said weakly, her voice barely above a whisper.

They slipped out the ICU door and back to the waiting room. Jasper went back to his chair in the corner, and Colin followed after him.

They sat in an uncomfortable silence. There was so much to say to each other, but neither knew where to start.

Jasper finally picked up a discarded newspaper and began to read.

Colin took his phone out of his pocket and

began to scroll. He thought about Jacey and the hasty message he sent to her. He pulled it up, read it again, and regret punched him in the gut. Why had he said something he did not mean? Then, to add insult to injury, he'd said it through a text message. What kind of coward does that?

He excused himself and stepped outside the waiting room to call Jacey. He needed to explain himself to her as soon as possible. When he dialed her number it went straight to voicemail, but he decided not to leave a message. What would he say: "This is Colin, and I'm an idiot"? He waited a few minutes and called again with the same result. She may well have been screening his calls now.

"If I were her, I wouldn't answer the phone either," he muttered.

He leaned back against the wall. Maybe it really was for the best. There were other things to focus on right now. He needed to stay in Biloxi for a while, at least until Ava felt better. He didn't want a houseful of staff to take care of his mother, because that job belonged to Jasper and to him. They would make sure she had everything she could possibly want or need to get her back on her feet.

There was also Jennings Construction to think about. Jasper would need help, for a while anyway. Colin wanted to lend his father a hand. He knew it would go a long way toward mending their relationship. They both needed this time together.

But he did need to tell Jacey what was going on and why he'd said what he said. The last thing on earth he wanted to do was to hurt her. He loved her—of that he was very sure. And he needed to tell her so. He called again, but this time he left a message.

"Jacey, I am sorry for that text message. Please forgive me for sending it. So many things have happened in the last few days. Please call me. I do . . . love you. Call me."

He put his phone back in his pocket. Surely she'd answer him, if only out of curiosity. He wouldn't reach out again until she did.

Chapter Twenty-Two

Jacey felt like she was waiting for her favorite celebrity to arrive. She smoothed her T-shirt over her body and flipped her hair with her hands. She fidgeted and fiddled with the bags of toys beside the park bench.

"You need to calm down," Georgia said. "You're gonna wear holes in those bags."

"What's taking so long? We've been here for an hour."

"An hour and ten minutes, to be exact," Georgia said. "Because you made us leave so early. It's still twenty till. They aren't late. We were way, way, way early."

"I wanted to make sure we got here on time."

"Nailed it. It must be ninety-eight degrees out here." Georgia wiped her face. "I looked adorable when we left, but now I'm wilted."

"The boys won't care," Jacey said. "How do I look?"

"The boys won't care," Georgia mocked.

"I wish Colin . . . ," Jacey began. "Never mind."

Georgia didn't say anything. She was still infuriated with Colin, and even more so now. Jacey had been in the shower last night when her phone rang. When Georgia picked the phone up to see if it was the sheriff, she saw that it was

Colin. Georgia let it ring until he hung up, and when he called back she considered answering it and telling him exactly what she thought about him. The third time she stared at the phone until it stopped ringing—hoping he got the picture. But then she heard the voice message buzz.

She looked at Jacey's phone for a long time trying to decide what to do. She picked it up, then put it back down. She couldn't listen to Jacey's phone messages. Doing so would be a colossal invasion of privacy, and Jacey was a grown woman. It wasn't Georgia's place to run interference for her. She could make up her own mind about Colin. But what if he was trying to smooth it all over now, after what she'd heard him tell that Julie girl? *I love you.*

When she finally gave in and listened to the message, Georgia was outraged. What a snake. She was right that he was a liar and a cheater. Georgia didn't know what kind of scheme he was trying to run on Jacey, but if he cheated once, he'd cheat again. She contemplated for a few minutes, then deleted the voice message and call record. She threw the phone back on the bed and stared at it, wondering if she'd done the right thing. Of course she had, she told herself. She wasn't going to let him toy with Jacey's emotions. Especially not now. Jacey was inexperienced in the fine art of "players," but Georgia had enough game for all of them. She'd protect her friend even if she didn't realize she needed protecting. One day Jacey would thank her for it.

"Did you hear me?" Jacey asked, poking Georgia's arm. "No smart remark? I said his name."

Georgia shrugged. "A moment of weakness," she said. "It'll pass. I wish this sun would pass behind a cloud."

Georgia tried to change the subject. The more she thought about it, the more guilt she felt for erasing the phone calls and voicemail. She knew how Jacey felt about the man, but in the end, she hoped her actions were for the greater good. She thought about her own misery last year and was convinced she was doing Jacey a favor. At least, that's how she justified it. He didn't deserve Jacey's affection, and she sure didn't deserve his brand of "love."

"It is hot," Jacey agreed. "It's the price we pay for living in the South. God's country."

"God's furnace," Georgia said.

Jacey grabbed Georgia's arm. "Georgie," she said. "Look! It's them!"

Jacey stood up when she saw the boys walking across the park with a woman and an older boy.

The boys saw her too. And they started to run toward her.

Jacey headed toward them. When they met, she knelt down and wrapped them all in her arms. All four of them began talking and crying at the same time, while the outsiders could only look on. Even Georgia was touched by the scene.

Jacey wiped at her tears. "Let me look at you all," she said. "You've grown so much. All of you. You look so big!"

"You look just the same, only not dirty," Derek said.

Jacey laughed. "That's about the best compliment I have ever gotten," she said, grabbing him again.

"They talk about you quite a bit," the woman said. "Seems like you made an impression."

Jacey stood up. "I'm so sorry," she said. "I'm Jacey Lang. And this is my best friend, Georgia. It's so nice to meet you. Thank you for bringing the boys to see me."

"My name is Penny Evans," the woman said, "and this is my son Michael."

"Hi, Michael," Jacey said.

"I can't stay long," said Penny, a tiny woman with a pinched mouth and no-nonsense clothes. "You'll have about an hour to visit."

Jacey thanked her but didn't have a good feeling about her at all. Maybe Penny just didn't meet people well. She would try to give her the benefit of the doubt.

Jacey looked at the boys, all smiling up at her. "I would've gotten here sooner if I could've, guys."

"Michael, and what's your name? Georgia?

Why don't we give Jacey and the boys some time alone?" Penny asked. "Let's go sit at the picnic table under the shade."

"That's a great idea," Georgia said, but she raised a brow when she looked at Jacey. She turned back to the boy. "How old are you, Michael?"

"I'm twelve," he said.

They walked away chatting while the boys and Jacey sat on the ground.

"I can't believe you're here," Dewayne said. "We asked everybody to find you."

"Mrs. Ernestine told me," Jacey said. "She misses you all very much."

"Can you take us to see her?" Dewayne asked.

"Maybe one day soon I can," Jacey said.

"Is that how you found us?" Dewayne asked.

"Well, it's a long story, and one day I'll tell you all about it. But I sure am glad I'm here. Are you boys doing okay?"

They all nodded their heads. "I can tie my shoes," Devin said.

"I can hit the ball over the fence," Derek offered.

"We are doing okay," Dewayne said. "But not great."

Jacey was struck by the maturity Dewayne displayed. He couldn't be any older than ten, but he acted like a small adult—thoughtful and serious. It was easy to see how protective he was over his younger brothers, simply from his body language. Like a miniature father. He'd seen too much in his young life.

"I'm so sorry about your mother and Demarcus," Jacey said.

The two smaller boys didn't really respond to that, but Jacey could tell it affected Dewayne. "I miss her," he said finally. "She thought you were the best."

"I thought she was too," Jacey told him. "She loved you all very, very much. She told me that over and over. I know she would be so proud of all of you."

"You should see how far Derek can hit a baseball, Jacey," Dewayne said quickly.

Jacey made a mental note not to mention Lillian again unless he did. The loss was obviously still too raw for Dewayne.

"And Devin can do a lot more than tie his shoes. He can brush his own teeth and get dressed by himself too," Dewayne continued. "Come here, Devin."

Devin walked over to his brother, and Dewayne wiped a little cookie crumb from his face.

"That's better," Dewayne said. He kissed his brother's cheek.

Jacey wanted to cry again. Dewayne had taken the place of both his father and his mother for the two smaller boys. He was their cheerleader and caretaker, and if Jacey had to guess, their only source of affection. It was too much for a small boy to be responsible for. He needed to be a kid himself.

"What about you, Dewayne?" Jacey asked. "What do you like to do?"

Dewayne shrugged. "I read a lot," he said. "I'm going to be a doctor when I grow up, so I have to do really good in school now. I'll need some scholarships and a job as soon as I'm old enough to work so I can save up some money."

Jacey smiled. All noble aspirations. But what about ball games and bicycles and frogs and spiders? He didn't deserve any of this. It broke her heart to hear him talk this way. He was a child, and he deserved a childhood.

She and Dewayne took the little boys to the swings and slides across the park and played for the hour. She finally convinced Dewayne to have a good time and not worry about pushing his brothers on the swings. He let his guard down for a little while and seemed to enjoy himself playing tag and sliding from the "super duper big slide," as Devin called it. Devin wouldn't have any part of it—said it was too high for him—but he loved watching his brothers shoot out of the tunnel at the end of the slide.

When Michael came to tell them it was time to go, the two little boys began to cry. Dewayne became very quiet.

Jacey walked with them and held their hands.

"It's okay," she said, though she felt like crying too. "I'll be back. I promise."

"Sometimes people don't come back," Derek wailed.

Like cutting my heart out, Jacey thought. "I promise. I will come back as soon as I can."

"Don't promise if you can't," Dewayne said. "Just tell us."

Jacey put her arm around him. "I am telling you right now: I am coming back. I don't break my promises."

Jacey walked to where Penny and Georgia sat, the little ones still clinging to her and a resigned Dewayne holding his head down. It would take years of unbroken promises to make Dewayne a believer again.

"Thank you for bringing them, Penny," Jacey said. "I can't begin to tell you how much I appreciate it. I would love to see them again as soon as possible."

"Well, we'll see," Penny said, looking at the boys and back at Jacey. "It disrupts my schedule."

Jacey didn't particularly like her tone, but she couldn't afford to make the woman mad by asking what that meant. "Well, I am so grateful to you," she said, knowing she'd have to go into beholden mode if she wanted to see the children again. "This is a very nice thing you are doing for them. And for all the others you foster."

Penny nearly smiled. "Well, we'll be seeing you."

"Oh, wait!" Jacey said. "I nearly forgot. We brought them some things."

"Jacey, no," Georgia said quietly.

Jacey looked blankly at her friend. "What do you—"

"Just leave it alone," Georgia said.

"Tell Jacey good-bye," Penny said, taking the little boys by the hand.

"Bye," they said in unison, still sniffling from their tears.

Jacey and Georgia watched them walk to their car, the boys looking back every few steps. Jacey waved every time. When they got out of earshot, Georgia whispered, "She is a nutcase."

"What do you mean?" Jacey whispered back, still smiling and waving.

"Let them leave first," Georgia said. They watched Penny strap them into their car seats and drive away.

"Sit down," Georgia said. Jacey sat down at the picnic table and waited for Georgia to speak.

"I'm just gonna throw some quotes out there for you," Georgia said. "First one: 'Oh, we don't let the boys play with commercial toys. They are satisfied with homemade glue and old newspaper.'"

"What?" Jacey asked. "They can't play with regular toys? How do you even make glue?"

"Oh, wait, I'm not finished yet," Georgia continued. "Next one: 'We don't encourage friendships outside the home, nor do we allow our children to play sports, as they're a waste of time.' I nearly busted my gut at that point."

"I can't believe you didn't," Jacey said. "I wouldn't have blamed you."

"And my personal favorite," Georgia said, "'Our children aren't allowed to eat anything after they leave the table. I feed them three meals a day, no snacks. If they don't like their food, they can go to bed hungry.'"

Georgia stopped and looked at Jacey, waiting for her response. She got one immediately.

Jacey grabbed her phone and dialed Sheriff Jefferson. When he answered, she said, "Sheriff, it's Jacey Lang. What do I have to do to begin the adoption process?"

Chapter Twenty-Three

One week after her surgery, Ava Jennings was recovering well enough to go home. Colin had been staying at the house since the day after her surgery and was busy getting everything ready for her return. He and their maid, Evie, stocked the refrigerator with healthy foods, had gone to the farmer's market for fruits and vegetables, and made sure her favorite flavored waters were in the house.

Evie had been with Colin's family since he was a baby. In fact, Evie was just about the only person Colin had been afraid of when he was growing up. Something about the way she could look at him and say, "Boy!" still put the fear of God in him. She called him out whenever he needed it, and she'd do it in front of anybody. Colin respected her and loved her.

Evie brought Colin to the master bedroom to collect the things his mother would need downstairs. Ava said she wanted to be downstairs in the den while she recovered, not tucked away in her bedroom, so Evie was spitting out orders for things they would need to build her a "nest."

"You don't put no other slippers 'cept them beside that sofa," Evie said. "She don't like but that one pair."

"How can she tell? They're exactly the same," Colin said as he sorted through the slippers. "Just different colors."

"I think so too," Evie confessed, laughing. "But these pink ones are her favorite, so take them. And take this bed jacket right here, and the afghan off the hope chest."

Colin gathered everything she pointed toward.

"We need her hand lotion from the bathroom, her hairbrush, and her Bible from the bedside table," Evie said.

Her Bible. *She has probably spent hours and hours praying for me,* Colin thought. "Is that it?" he asked.

"I'll tell you when that's it," Evie said, surveying the room.

"You're getting mighty bossy in your old age," Colin said.

"Old age? I can still peel a peach tree limb and make you a believer."

Colin laughed. "You probably could. And I could probably have you arrested for child abuse for making such threats at me."

"You call the 911, little boy," Evie said. "You gonna need them when I get through with you. If you ask me, you didn't get near enough switchings when you were little."

Colin smiled. "I have to agree with that assessment."

"Now, get that hand mirror on the bathroom

counter, and don't come back telling me you can't find it."

Evie finally decided they had all they needed from upstairs, so they started down to the den. "Is there a wheelbarrow in the house?" Colin asked. "I think I need some help."

"Hush, boy," Evie said. "You all right. Now make it look nice downstairs. I got to go tend to the soup."

Evie disappeared into the kitchen, and Colin began making his mother a "nest."

Jasper had called earlier saying they would be home within the hour, and Colin was beyond ready for his mother to return. Having her back in the house would be an affirmation that maybe things were beginning to work out. There were so many things to talk about . . . things he should've been saying all along had his anger and pride not prevented them. Never again would he let that happen. Every time he thought about not being aware of his mother's illness, he wanted to punch a hole in the wall.

While Ava was in surgery, Colin asked his father to explain just how sick his mother had been.

"There were days she couldn't even make it up the stairs," Jasper told him. "So we slept in the study." He said that whenever Ava tried to walk down to the beach, she'd stop to rest at intervals and sometimes had to call him to come help her back. If only Colin had known . . . he would have been here with her. He would've picked her up and carried her to the shore of the Gulf. But he was busy being noble and self-righteous—running away from problems he should've faced. From now on, Ava Jennings would only need to pick up the phone if she needed him.

Colin wasn't sure how to make a nest for his mother, but he gave it a shot. He pulled the heavy oak coffee table closer to the leather sofa and placed all her things from the bedroom within an easy grasp. He placed the remote controls for the air-conditioning, TV, and lights on the end table beside her. He ran upstairs and got more pillows in case she wanted to elevate her feet, then filled up a water carafe and put it next to the remotes.

He sat on the sofa to wait and took his phone out of his pocket for the tenth time today. He checked the ringer again. Maybe Jacey just hadn't had time to answer. Or she was trying to decide what to say. Maybe she thought he was crazy. Who was he kidding? Maybe she just didn't want to answer. He couldn't blame her if she never wanted to talk to him again.

He needed the opinion of a male counterpart. He had already asked Julie what she thought about the text he sent Jacey, and she made her opinion perfectly clear. She called him an idiot and the most insensitive man she'd ever known.

Surely Joshua would understand where he was coming from, so Colin dialed his friend and waited.

"How's your mom, man?" Joshua said.

"On her way home," Colin told him.

"That's good news. I'll come see her in the next few days."

"She'd love to see you," Colin said. "But first, let me get your take on something."

"Go ahead," Joshua said.

"Say I told a girl I was falling in love with her," Colin said. "And then I sent a text message a couple of days later saying that maybe I should back off from the relationship because I needed some time to think." Colin paused. "You still with me?"

"Still here," Joshua said.

"Then say I left a voicemail a few days later, telling her that I love her and asking her to call me."

"I'm assuming this is you sending a message to Jacey, the elusive love of your life?" Joshua asked.

"It is."

"So you want me to tell you why she hasn't called?"

"How did you know she hasn't called?" Colin asked.

"If you were her, would you call you back?" Joshua asked.

Colin thought about it. "I was in a bad situation," he said finally.

"And then you put her in one."

"Thanks for nothing, man," Colin said.

That wasn't exactly what Colin wanted to hear, but he knew Joshua would tell him the truth. Julie hadn't just been speaking from a female point of view. She was right. He was an insensitive idiot, and he had two votes to prove it. This was about to become an epidemic in his life. He had walked around for years thinking he had all the answers, only to find out in the last two days he didn't even understand the questions.

Now . . . what could he do about Jacey? He would charge up to her front door on a fiery steed if he had to. Whatever it took to make her listen. He wasn't going to lose her a second time.

Colin heard the front door open. "We're home!" Jasper called.

When Colin got to the foyer, Ava was walking slowly with a pillow held tightly against her chest. "That pillow has become your security blanket," Colin said, reaching gently for her elbow. Together, Colin and his father walked her toward the den.

"This pillow is my new best friend," Ava said. "Don't you dare let it get more than a foot away from me."

"We've got you all set up in the den," Colin told her. "Evie had me bring everything but the bed down from your room. She's in the kitchen making homemade chicken soup and fresh lemonade. And if I'm not mistaken, there's a berry cobbler."

"All of my favorites. Bless her sweet heart," Ava said. "I wish I could say that sounds good, but nothing does."

"Your appetite will come back," Jasper told her. "The doctor said it's normal not to want very much at first."

Ava shuffled into the den and sat down slowly on the sofa. Jasper covered her legs with the afghan, and Colin adjusted the pillows behind her neck. Then they both stood beside the sofa and stared at her.

"What are you doing?" she asked.

Jasper and Colin looked at each other, then back at Ava.

"Go away," she said. "Shoo! People have hovered over me for an entire week. Enough. Go."

Jasper and Colin reluctantly walked toward the kitchen together.

When they got to the archway leading to the kitchen, Jasper turned back to her. "Do you need—"

"No, I do not need," Ava interrupted. "Go away."

"I put some magazines on the—"

"Thank you very much, son," Ava said. "That

was really sweet of you. Now go away and take your father with you."

"It is good to see y'all, Mr. Jasper," Evie said when they walked into the kitchen. "How's our girl?"

"She is feeling pretty good and glad to be in her own house," Jasper said.

Colin sat down at the marble island and grabbed an apple. "Mom can be very forceful when she wants to be," he said. "I don't think I've ever seen her like this."

Jasper smiled and shook his head. "You don't know the half of it," he said. "Your mother once talked a police officer out of giving her a speeding ticket, and before he left, he apologized for stopping her in the first place."

"My mother?" Colin asked. He couldn't see the proper lady Ava Jennings shaming a cop into an apology.

"Yes, your mother," Jasper said. "She is quite a woman."

"Yes, she is," Colin agreed.

"Evie, I don't know if Ava is going to eat, but that soup smells delicious," Jasper said. "How much longer?"

"You stop that, Mr. Jasper," Evie said. "You stay outta this soup. I'm 'bout to go visit with Ms. Ava for a minute and then come back in here so she can get some rest. I counted every noodle in that pot, so you best stay away from it."

Jasper laughed.

Colin was surprised at the sound of Jasper laughing. He couldn't remember the last time he'd heard that sound. He looked at the crow's feet around Jasper's eyes. His father had weathered so many storms, fought battles Colin knew nothing about, carried scars deep within himself without asking for mercy or offering excuses. He was his own man: He couldn't be bought and he couldn't be broken. Colin felt a sense of pride creeping into the space where his anger had lived all those years. Maybe there was a chance they could salvage their relationship after all.

Chapter Twenty-Four

Exactly one week after visiting the boys at the park, Jacey was back in Shreveport. Project Triple Boy was about to become reality, and she needed to tell her parents all about it. Needless to say, they were quite surprised—but after the initial shock wore off, her dad was on board right away.

"We've been over and over it, and I am not questioning your judgment," Chris Lang said. "I just want you to make sure, once and for all, this is absolutely what you want. It won't be like a plant or a fish. These are children. You can't forget to feed them or water them."

Jacey laughed at her dad's analogy. "I am sure it's what I want, Daddy. You are going to love them. Both of you are."

Though her father had been supportive, her mother, Lisa, was still trying to wrap her head around it.

"Of course we will love them," Lisa said. "They are children. But, Jacey, sweetheart, this is a huge responsibility. You don't know anything about raising children. Who's going to help you with them? And three of them? You've always been responsible and trustworthy, but you're so young. I just think you've bitten off more than you can chew."

"They aren't babies, Mama," Jacey said. "I don't need anyone to help me with them. It isn't like I'll have infant triplets and nighttime feedings and diapers to change. They are little people. I'm not even sure they will allow me to adopt them yet, but I have to try."

"I am just so worried you will find it much more difficult than you expect," Lisa said. "And you want to buy a house too? You aren't married. You aren't even in a relationship. Maybe you should wait until—"

"I can't wait," Jacey interrupted. "The boys certainly can't wait, and I don't need a man to help. I know I can raise these children and love them and provide for them. I am not trying to be disrespectful, but I didn't come up here to ask for permission. I came to ask for your blessing, but I am doing this with or without it."

Lisa sighed and pursed her lips.

Jacey almost laughed looking at her. When her mother's lips pursed, everyone in the house knew she was irritated. Those lips had made Jacey and her brother turn around on a dime and spin out of a room.

But Jacey knew her mother was just afraid she was making a rash decision. Lisa was a worrier, and this past year had tested her limits. Lisa had stayed at the condo for two weeks after Jacey was discharged from the hospital and would've stayed longer if Jacey hadn't finally made her leave. Jacey had found much comfort in her mother's presence, but she needed to recover on her own. Georgia wouldn't allow her to bathe in self-pity, whereas Lisa had almost encouraged it. It had caused a bit of tension between her mother and her best friend. In the end, Jacey knew she had to "suck it up," as Georgia was so fond of saying. She sent Lisa back to Shreveport . . . and those lips had never been tighter than they were the day she left.

"Mama," Jacey said, "I know you are worried that this is just some crazy idea. It isn't like me to do something without thinking about it and planning it for a year. I've never done anything like this before. But I've changed since the accident, and I hope I've changed for the better. I don't want to watch my life just pass me by anymore. I want to write about people who do worthwhile things, but I also want to *do* some of them myself. These boys . . . They are special. They are bright and friendly and hopeful, even though they haven't had much to hope for. Their mother was the only stable thing in their lives, and now she's been taken from them." She took Lisa's hands in hers and leaned closer to her. "I have a real chance to make a difference in their lives, and they will make a difference in mine. How can that be wrong?"

Lisa didn't answer right away, but Jacey saw her face soften. "How can we help?"

Jacey jumped from the chair, ran around the table, and crushed her mother in a hug. "Thank you, Mama," she said. "You are going to love your grandsons!"

Lisa looked at her husband. "Grandsons?" she asked. "Do you think anybody is running a special on Botox?"

Chris and Jacey laughed.

"You're gonna be the hottest grandmaw on the block," Chris said.

"Oh, I don't think I'll be 'Grandmaw,'" Lisa said. "Maybe Nonnie, or Nanna, or Nonna, even. Let's see. I have a book somewhere around here about what Southern children call their grandparents . . ." Her voice trailed off as she walked into the living room.

Chris looked at Jacey and smiled. "That didn't take long," he said.

"Do you think she's really okay with this?" Jacey asked him.

"Honey, by this time tomorrow those boys will have new wardrobes and a swing set in our backyard, and everybody in this subdivision will know she's going to be a grandmother."

Jacey hugged her father. "Thank you, Daddy. For everything."

Jacey and her parents spent the rest of the evening online looking for houses near Baton

Rouge. She wanted to buy a place with a couple of acres of land, someplace where the boys would have room to grow and play and call their own. Her parents offered to help with the financing, but Jacey turned them down. She had always been frugal, and sharing a place with Willow and Georgia had allowed her to save a lot of money. She wanted to do it on her own.

They came up with three properties for Jacey to look at when she got back to Baton Rouge. Two of them were okay, but the third one was absolutely perfect. The log house had four bedrooms and two baths on three acres of land just outside Baton Rouge in Prairieville. There was even a small barn and a garden out back. Jacey couldn't wait to see it in person.

The next morning she left for Baton Rouge—leaving her proud father and teary-eyed mother behind.

"We are so proud of you," her father said. "Those boys don't know it, but they are the luckiest little fellas in the world."

"Thank you, Daddy," Jacey said.

"I've decided on Nonna," Lisa said, dabbing her eyes. "It sounds elegant."

Jacey laughed and hugged her mother. "Of course it does."

The four-hour drive from Shreveport to Baton Rouge left her plenty of time to think. She had so much to do. She had spoken with the Realtor in the morning and was able to coax her into showing Jacey the log house late in the evening. She didn't even want to look at the other two. She hoped the house was what it appeared to be online. It was within her budget, convenient to the city, yet private. It was close to some good schools and a nice park. She really wanted this house.

Tomorrow she would have to go back to Biloxi to attend her first class to become certified to adopt. These classes were over the course of a few weeks, and she could easily make the two-hour trip to Biloxi to attend. She called Penny after she got her class schedule and arranged park dates with the boys for those days. Penny, while not exactly thrilled, finally agreed. "It might be nice to get them out from under my feet for a while," was the actual phrase she used. Her tone infuriated Jacey. She couldn't believe she would have to wait at least six months before she could take the boys away from this woman. There was no telling how much damage that woman could do to them in six months. She didn't think they were being physically abused, but emotional abuse was just as bad. Especially since they had gone through so much already.

Penny refused to let them talk to her on the phone, but she said Jacey could write them letters. Jacey asked if she could e-mail them, but Penny gave an emphatic no. She said they did not believe in technology, and the boys would be better off for it in the long run. So Jacey wrote letters to each of them, being very careful of her words, assuming Penny was going to read them first and only hoping the boys would get to read them at all.

She turned on the radio and flipped it to her favorite station. Of course, a sad love song floated through the airwaves.

"Colin," she whispered.

Even his name hurt her. So much had happened in the past few days—she hadn't allowed herself any time to think about it. But driving down this stretch of road, Adele's voice serenading her, she couldn't shove the thoughts away anymore. She loved him—she was sure of it. She wanted to call him and demand he tell her what had happened. That was a fair question, wasn't it? Didn't he owe her that much? It was Colin who had pursued her—not the other way around. Why had he even bothered? She was doing fine before he showed up. Sort of. Maybe. Not really.

Okay, he had helped her. She had to admit it. Even if he didn't realize it, he had helped her regain her memory of the accident, and for that she would be forever grateful. But seeing him again had jolted things inside of her she'd never had to deal with before. Her memory was the least of it. Just being in the same room with him made her feel different somehow. And waking up beside him . . . It was hard to imagine a better place than being in his arms. It would be hard to let that go. But she had no choice. She had reached out to him, and he had rejected her. She could not and would not pursue it anymore. Neither her pride nor her aching heart would allow it.

She sighed deeply and switched the radio channel to a comedy station. No more Adele for her today unless Adele wanted to pay for the therapy she'd surely need after one more sad song. Before long, she found herself laughing at a radio comic who had plenty of jokes about his children.

Jacey got into Baton Rouge during high traffic time and drove straight to her bank. She had a meeting with a mortgage broker before the appointment with the Realtor. Thankfully, that process went smoothly, and she made it to Prairieville just as her Realtor drove up. Jacey had called Georgia to meet them there, and she pulled up behind them. Before Jacey could even turn off the ignition, she knew this was the place she wanted.

"It's beautiful," Jacey said as she stepped out of the car. "And perfect."

"Hush," Georgia whispered. "You don't want to act too excited. She'll up the price five thousand dollars."

"I love it!" Jacey exclaimed even louder.

Georgia rolled her eyes. "She's just being silly,"

she said to the Realtor. "She says this about every house we've seen. This one is like . . . I don't know . . . the fifth one today. Right, Jacey?"

Jacey ignored her and hurried to the front door. "I knew this was going to be the place," she said. "I could just tell from the pictures."

"I give up," Georgia muttered.

Jacey ran through the house like a kid at Christmas. The kitchen was lovely—a mixture of exposed logs with a modern backsplash, a huge island with bar stools, and French doors that opened to an outdoor kitchen and a large fenced-in backyard. The den was spacious with hardwood floors and beautiful built-ins. She could already see the boys wrestling on the floor and watching cartoons. She hurried down the hall to the bedrooms and peaked inside each one. This was the house, and she didn't even want to look at another one.

Jacey came back to the kitchen where Georgia stood with her hands on her hips beside the Realtor.

"I'll take it," Jacey said, smiling broadly.

"I'm stunned," Georgia said dryly.

After discussing the fine points of the purchase, the Realtor locked up the house and left Jacey and Georgia standing in the driveway.

"Is there a phrase stronger than 'eager beaver'?" Georgia asked.

Jacey laughed. She didn't care what Georgia

or the Realtor thought about her enthusiasm. This house was exactly what she wanted, and she couldn't wait for the paperwork to go through so she could get started inside.

"Wow," Georgia said. She leaned against her car. "I started looking for a new condo this morning. This is really happening."

Jacey shook her head. "It really is."

"No more roomies," Georgia said.

"I can't believe we've known each other seven years," Jacey said. "We were such little snot-nosed brats back then."

"And my hair . . . ," Georgia said. "What was I thinking? No wonder he was fooling around."

Jacey laughed. "It wasn't that bad, and it surely wasn't the reason he fooled around."

"You're right. It was probably this twenty extra pounds," Georgia said.

"Stop it," Jacey said. "He was a bad apple. That's all. Looks like both of us picked one."

Georgia didn't respond. Should she tell her about Colin's phone calls? She asked herself that question at least ten times a day. She was carrying around a tremendous amount of guilt for erasing Colin's message but was equally convinced it was the right thing to do. Most of the time, anyway. She couldn't tell Jacey now, amid her buying a house and going to adoption classes and adjusting to her new life. It was best that she keep it to herself. At least for now.

"There's all kinds of time for men," Georgia said. "Right now we need to focus on making the inside of this house exactly what you want it to be. Do you have any idea what kinds of things the boys like? I mean, movies or characters or things like that?"

"All of them love Star Wars," Jacey said. "Lillian had taken them to see it right before the flood. They talked about it nonstop on the roof."

"Shall we buy Star Wars–themed bedspreads and curtains, or do you have something else in mind?" Georgia asked.

"You know, I think that would be awesome," Jacey said.

"Then let's go shopping," Georgia said. "The bedroom stuff is on Aunt Georgie."

"Aw, Georgie, you don't have to do that."

"I do, actually," Georgia told her. "I intend to practice on your kids before I get my own. Someday. Maybe. Anyway, I'm going to see if I can buy their love."

Jacey laughed. "Deal. Do you want to buy my love? Because I've had my eye on a new Coach purse."

"You're on your own," Georgia said. "Now let's go spend some of my hard-earned emergency room money."

The next few weeks were consumed by moving into her new house and preparing for the adoption. Jacey had been through three home inspections by the State of Mississippi and was returning to Biloxi once a week to go to the classes. She actually enjoyed the classes even though they were heartbreaking on many occasions. There were so many children in the United States waiting for adoption, especially older children. Most people wanted infants. Older kids practically had zero chance of being adopted . . . or what Jacey deemed "being rescued."

Penny continued to frustrate and annoy her. The boys were less and less their cheerful selves every time she got to see them. She had been careful not to mention the adoption in front of them, because she didn't want them to suffer yet another disappointment if something were to fall through. On this day, however, she changed her mind.

"Dewayne, what's the matter, honey?" Jacey asked as they watched Devin and Derek play on the swings in the park. "Is school going okay?"

"Yes, I like being at school," he said.

"Is something else wrong?" she prodded gently.

Dewayne didn't respond.

"Something at Penny's house?"

"Nothing," he said, looking at Penny as she sat at the picnic table under the trees.

Jacey looked over at her too. "She can't hear us," she said. "You can tell me. I promise."

"She said you don't really care about us,"

Dewayne blurted out. "She said she heard you were going to try to adopt us, but you probably changed your mind by now. She said you thought you were better than she was, all pretty and neat. Or something like that. And you didn't want a bunch of kids to mess up your life. She said you were just being nice when you came to see us."

If someone had poured a bucket of tar over her head she couldn't have been angrier. "She said what?" Jacey asked through clenched teeth.

"Please don't tell her I told you, Jacey," Dewayne said, his eyes round with fear.

Jacey calmed down when she realized how scared he was. "It's okay, buddy," she said. "I'm not going to say anything. I promise. I just don't understand why she would've said something like that when none of it is true."

Dewayne shrugged. "She said she was the only white woman who would put up with black kids because God doesn't like black kids to live with white people. She said nobody wanted black kids, and you would take us back in two days if you ever adopted us. Or maybe you'd just split us up and keep the little ones."

Jacey put her hand up. "Stop, Dewayne," she said.

He put his head down. "I'm sorry."

"No, that's not what I meant," Jacey told him. "Look at me."

Dewayne lifted his head.

"It *is* true that I'm trying to adopt you," Jacey said. "But I'm trying to adopt *all* of you. I didn't say anything because I didn't want you to be disappointed if the judge were to say no for some reason. But I would never, ever separate you from your brothers. Do you hear me? I want all three of you, and I am working as hard and fast as I know how to make that happen."

Dewayne began to smile. "You promise?" he asked. "You *promise?*"

"I do promise," Jacey reassured him. "And just so you know, Penny is wrong. God doesn't see color. Only people do, and only ugly people at that. God only sees our hearts. So don't worry about what Penny says. I just need you to hang on and help your little brothers to hang on, okay? Be nice to Penny. Don't upset her, do what she says. Okay? I'll try harder to make this happen faster. I promise."

Dewayne threw his arms around her, and Jacey squeezed her eyes hard to stop the tears.

"It's going to be fine, baby, just hold on. Keep your brothers close."

"I will," he said.

As soon as the boys left with Penny, Jacey called Roger Jefferson.

"Sheriff?" Jacey said. "It's Jacey Lang. I know you may not be able to help me, but is there any way you know of to speed up this adoption process?"

Chapter Twenty-Five

Colin stood on the shore with his mother and watched the Gulf waters gently caress the shore.

"This view never gets old, does it?" she asked.

"It doesn't," he agreed. "I'm just glad you are able to enjoy it again."

"Me too," Ava said. "Where did your father go?"

Colin pointed up the beach. "Where do you think?"

Ava shook her head. "Can you believe how he acts with that dog?"

Colin laughed. "I can't believe he lets him in the house. Yesterday he was in his lap asleep in his recliner."

"I saw that too," Ava said. "The man has reinvented himself over the past few months. In fact, I think we all have."

Colin couldn't argue. The house on the bluff above them contained more laughter, more joy, and more hope in the past few months than it had in the last thirty years. Getting to know his father was a gift he'd never expected and one that couldn't be equaled. Jasper was still reserved, but Colin thought some of that was just his personality. He was nowhere near the closed and aloof man Colin had known his entire life. In fact, Colin found him to be quite funny at times, especially when he teased Ava. It was obvious Jasper adored her.

"Dad?" Colin called. "We're going up. You coming?"

Jasper waved and jogged their way, his rescue mutt from the pound close on his heels.

"Shall I carry you up?" Colin asked as they began to climb the wooden stairs to the yard.

"Not today." Ava smiled. "I think I can make it all the way."

"Don't push it," Colin warned. "I'm right behind you."

"I promise I'll tell you if I need help," Ava said. "I do not want another stay in Biloxi General. I don't care for the room service."

"I wasn't crazy about it either," Colin said.

He watched his mother carefully ascend and marveled at the progress she had made. A month ago she couldn't climb the first ten steps without help. Yesterday she had made it almost to the top before asking for help.

"How are you doing, Ava?" Jasper asked behind them as the dog raced past them all.

"Good," she said. "Almost there."

"Don't push it," Jasper warned.

"You two are the same exact person sometimes," Ava said. Within a few minutes, Ava made it all the way to the yard without stopping. She was clearly elated.

"The first time in years," she said. "I didn't think I would ever do it again." She did a little dance move Colin had never seen before.

"Did you just . . . *dance?*" Colin asked.

"She used to be a fabulous dancer," Jasper said, grabbing her hand. He began spinning her around in the yard while the dog danced and yapped around them.

"Who are you people?" Colin asked.

"The hippie parents no one ever told you about," Ava said as Jasper kissed her neck and made her giggle.

"I've seen enough. Y'all should get a room." Colin walked to the house with their laughter trailing behind him.

Colin went to his bedroom and checked his e-mail. He'd gotten much more proficient at computers over the past couple of months. Working in an office would do that for you. He sometimes still had a hard time believing he was behind a desk at Jennings Construction, but someone had to step up—and Jasper was consumed with Ava's recovery. That left Colin at the helm. Of course, he had an exceptional board of directors whom he trusted and relied on to guide him as he learned the ropes.

If someone had told him a few months earlier he would've been living back at his parents' house and working for his father, he would've told them they were crazy. For years he couldn't even imagine being in the same room with his father, much less living underneath his roof again. But circumstances sometimes had a way of figuring things out for a man when he was too mule-headed to figure them out himself. This had certainly been one of those times.

Colin and Jasper were still working on their relationship, but it was a thousand times better than it had ever been. Ava said part of their problem had come from being too much alike. Both of them stubborn and hard-headed, unwilling to bend—and in some ways, still insecure little boys. It wasn't exactly a flattering picture, but Colin reluctantly agreed with her. One morning, a few days after Ava came home from the hospital, Jasper had walked out onto the patio and approached Colin with a cup of coffee in his hand. "Do you have a minute?" Jasper asked.

"Sure," Colin said.

Jasper slid a wrought iron patio chair from the table and joined Colin. "I need to talk to you, son," he said. "I need to apologize."

Colin paused a moment, then took a sip of his coffee. "You don't have to say anything . . . we have both—"

"Yes, I do," Jasper said. "I haven't been the father I should've been to you. I was gone too much, I wasn't around when you needed me . . .

and I wasn't around when your mother needed me either. I have suffered the consequences for those failures."

Colin knew he was speaking about Ava's affair, and he could see the shadow of hurt on his father's face.

"I'm sorry, Dad," Colin said. "I know it must've—"

But Jasper cut him off again. "No, don't be sorry for me. I got what I deserved. You can't walk around thinking you're untouchable, but that's exactly what I did. I gave nothing to Ava . . . All I did was take. And I expected her to accept that. I gave nothing to you but insisted you respect me. It doesn't work like that. I was wrong, son, and I'm sorry."

Colin had longed to hear these words from his father for years. In his imagination, this moment would resemble a scene from a movie where the music swells and the hero rides away. Instead, what he felt was a deep sense of regret over things he'd done himself . . . Years of shoving both his parents away from him and refusing to listen to anything they had to say . . . Regret for calling himself a minister and proclaiming the courage of forgiveness, all while declining to entertain the thought . . . He was a fraud, at best.

"I'm sorry, too, Dad," Colin said.

Jasper stood up and opened his arms, and

Colin walked into them. Tears were shed that morning, without promises, without declarations of change, but with much silent hope for the future.

Colin closed the laptop, lay down on his bed, and closed his eyes. And just like every time he closed his eyes, her face appeared. *Jacey.* What had he done? It was the same question he asked himself every night. He gave back the one thing that had kept him sane the last year. Jacey was sweet and kind and generous and loving. And the worst part? She had trusted him. He had taken that trust and thrown in back in her face. Would she ever be able to understand that he had done it for her? Would he ever get the opportunity to explain?

He was still surprised Jacey had never returned his call or answered his message. She wasn't the type of girl to accept things at face value. Of course, her silence could be an easy way of letting him down. There was always the possibility that Jacey did not feel the same way he did. Maybe he had misread all the signals. He was a little rusty in the romance department, so it wouldn't be hard to mistake the way she looked at him . . . especially the way she'd looked at him in his trailer that morning. No, he was sure of it. That was more than desire. He could tell the difference.

The overthinking had come full circle again tonight. He had to stop dancing with this same devil. He was constantly aware of her absence, so he either had to let her go or show up in Baton Rouge and demand an answer. But just like he always did, he talked himself out of that too. The ball was in her court. He'd already made the gesture.

He got up and went downstairs in search of something else to occupy his mind. He found his father in his study painting fishing baits—a hobby he had once loved and recently began to practice again.

"Can I help?" Colin asked.

"Of course," Jasper said. "Pull up a chair."

Colin picked up a dry bait and started to polish it. "These are really good, Dad."

"Thank you, son," Jasper said. "I had forgotten how much I enjoy this."

"I need to find a hobby," Colin said.

"That should be an easy fix. What do you like to do?"

Colin shrugged. "I like to build houses. Pretty large hobby, huh?"

"So build houses," Jasper said.

"I'm working for you right now," Colin said. "There'll be time for that. Later."

Jasper didn't respond.

They sat in silence and painted, each of them preoccupied with his own thoughts.

• • •

During supper that night, Colin got ambushed. *Ambushed* was the term he'd used in the past when Jasper began grilling him out of nowhere about anything from his grades to his girlfriends. Only tonight, it was friendly fire.

"Son," Jasper said, "your mother and I would like to talk to you."

The words still had enough power to make him immediately uncomfortable.

"What's wrong?" Colin asked.

"Nothing is wrong," Jasper said. "We want to know how long you intend to stay here."

"Are you kicking me out?" Colin asked, only half-joking.

"Not so much kicking you out as kicking your—"

"Jasper!" Ava said. "Don't say that. You can stay here indefinitely, Colin. You know that. But your father and I are—"

"Worried about you," Jasper finished.

"Why?" Colin asked.

"Because you are miserable," Ava said.

"I'm not miserable," Colin said. "I love being here. This is my home, and you need me here."

"We appreciate everything you have done for your mother and me," Jasper said. "We couldn't have gotten along without you these past three months. But your work here is done."

"I can look for an apartment," Colin said. "Or

move in with Joshua until I can find one."

"This isn't about moving out of the house," Jasper said. "This is your home. It will always be your home."

"Then what is it about?"

"Son, is there a woman in Louisiana you need to see?" his father asked.

Colin stared at his father, then looked at his mother. "How did you know about that?"

"Joshua visited today while you were at the office," Ava said. "He might have mentioned something."

Colin shook his head. "I'm gonna kill him," he said.

Jasper leaned back in his chair. "Son, let me tell you how you lose a woman you love. You ignore her. You make her feel like she doesn't matter. You put everything else before her. You make her unimportant."

Colin put his head back and sighed. He didn't really want to get into this with his parents. Who talked about their love life with their mom and dad? Then again, at this point, what could it hurt?

"I told her I loved her," he said. "I told her, and she didn't respond. What more can I do? I *told* her."

"It isn't what you say, Colin," Jasper told him. "It's what you do."

"That's just it. I don't know what to do,"

Colin said. "If she wanted to see me, she'd call, wouldn't she?"

"I wouldn't," his mother said.

Colin looked at her. The female mind was a mystery to him. "Why not?"

"Because I'd wait for you to convince me I wasn't wasting my time," Ava said.

"Don't let another minute go by," Jasper said. "Trust me. You never want to grieve a person who is still alive."

Colin weighed those words and wondered how hard they had been for a man like his father to say. Maybe they were right. Maybe that's what he needed to do: go to Jacey and bare his soul. Lay it all on the table. It had been months. He needed to see her, hold her, tell her. He needed to convince her.

He stood up. "I think I'll . . . Are you all right? You feel good?" he asked his mother.

"I'm fine," Ava said. "I feel better than I have in years."

"Dad?" Colin said. "The company?"

"Will still be here when you take care of your other business," Jasper said. "Go."

"Are you sure?" Colin asked. "Because I can—"

"Get out of my house, Colin," Jasper said.

Colin smiled. "Yes, sir."

Colin took the stairs two at a time and packed a duffel bag. He was headed to Baton Rouge.

Chapter Twenty-Six

Colin arrived in Baton Rouge shortly after nine p.m. He drove straight to Jacey's condo but discovered no one was there. Neither Jacey's nor Georgia's vehicle was home. He pulled up in the driveway and turned off the ignition. He'd wait.

Thirty minutes later a car pulled up beside him, but it didn't belong to either of the women. A man and woman got out.

"Can I help you?" the man asked.

"I'm looking for the girl who lives here," Colin said, a little puzzled.

The man and woman exchanged a glance.

"I'm the girl who lives here," she said.

"I'm sorry," Colin said. "You live in this condo?"

"Yes," she said. "Is something wrong?"

"What happened to the other girls?"

"I'm not sure. I never met them."

"Look," the man said. "She just bought this place a week ago. Is there anything else you need?"

"No," Colin said. "Sorry I bothered you. My mistake."

He got inside his truck and backed out of the drive. She had sold the condo. Where had she gone? And where could he start looking? Where was she? *This is just like last year,* he thought. He'd let it happen again.

Then an idea struck him. Georgia probably wouldn't answer his call, so he'd go to the hospital where she worked and ask her in person where Jacey was. He made a U-turn in the street and headed to Baton Rouge General.

Colin pulled into the ER parking lot and went inside. "Can you tell me if Georgia Bankston is working tonight?" he asked the woman manning the desk.

"Georgia doesn't work here anymore," she said cheerily.

"What? Where did she go? To which hospital?"

"I'm not sure," cheery girl answered.

"Is there someone around here who would know?" he asked.

"Actually, all of the old staff left at the same time," she offered. "Something about pay raises and hours. I don't know. I think they were trying to make a statement, but the joke's on them. They just hired a whole new staff. Including me."

"I see," Colin said.

"Anything else I can help you with?" she asked.

But he was already halfway out the door.

Not this again. Colin felt a sinking in the pit of his stomach. She couldn't just be gone. He got in his truck and headed east. There was another hospital on Bluebonnet Avenue, so he would try there next. He would try them all until he found Georgia. She would have answers.

Two hours later Colin sat on his bed in his hotel room and fell backward against the pillows. He'd struck out. He went to every hospital in Baton Rouge and asked for Georgia Bankston, and everyone told him the same thing. There was no Georgia Bankston in their ER. Maybe it was policy and they couldn't tell him. He understood that. But there had to be some way to locate at least one of the women. He'd start over again tomorrow and again the next day and the next if need be. But he wasn't leaving Baton Rouge without seeing Jacey.

Chapter Twenty-Seven

Jacey tucked the boys in their sleeping bags on the floor of the den and lay down on the sofa. Sometimes she still had to pinch herself to make sure she wasn't dreaming. The adoption wasn't final yet, but they were here with her and would be all hers in a few months.

Things began to happen very fast after Jacey called the sheriff last month. Turned out, there were already complaints lodged against Penny and her husband. Everything from withholding food and basic needs to hitting some of her foster children to "emotional trauma," as the paper read. Jacey's caseworker was able to convince a judge it would be more harmful to put the boys in another foster home when there was someone waiting to adopt them. Jacey had already completed the necessary classes, had passed three home inspections with flying colors, and was just waiting to bring them to their new home. In the end, the judge agreed. The day she picked them up at the group home was the happiest day of her life.

"Hi, guys!" Jacey said in the visiting room of the children's home.

They were a little withdrawn from being yet again displaced, but they were happy to see her.

They hugged her with their normal enthusiasm, and Devin climbed in her lap.

"Hi, Jacey," Dewayne said. "Do you have to leave soon or can you stay with us awhile?"

"Well," Jacey said, "that's what I've come to tell you. We talked to a very nice judge who thinks it would be best for all of you . . . and for me, too . . . if you came to live with me."

The boys didn't react at all. They just looked at her.

"Did you hear what I said, fellas?" Jacey asked. "You're coming home with me, to your new house."

Dewayne burst into tears, and his little brothers followed suit. The little ones probably had no idea why they were crying, but they fed off of their big brother. Jacey cried with them, then laughed and cried some more.

"Well? What are we waiting for? Let's go get your stuff," Jacey said.

They raced down the hall and packed their things, which took only minutes. They didn't have much—basically the clothes on their backs and a few more items. It broke Jacey's heart to see their meager belongings, but they were going home to three closets full of clothes and shoes and dressers full of socks and underwear. Their Nonna had made sure her "three little soldiers," as she dubbed them, were already taken care of.

Jacey laid her head on the sofa pillow and

looked down at them sleeping soundly in their sleeping bags. They had been here for two weeks now and were adjusting very well. They loved their rooms with the Star Wars theme and played exceptionally well together. But come nighttime, the little ones ditched their beds and slept with Dewayne. She asked her caseworker if that was something she should worry about, but she assured her they were fine. Except when it stormed. Thunder scared Devin so much he wet the bed a couple of nights after they had arrived at their new house. Dewayne came into her room in the middle of the night to tell her.

"Jacey," he whispered, shaking her gently. "Wake up."

Jacey popped straight up in the bed. Since getting the boys, she'd learned the meaning of sleeping with one eye open.

"What's wrong?" she asked.

"You promise not to be mad?" Dewayne asked.

"I'm not going to be mad," she assured him. "What's the matter?"

"It's raining and thundering," Dewayne said. "It scares them. I don't like it much either. But Devin wet the bed. Penny used to make him sleep in his wet pajamas. He's crying and afraid to tell you."

Jacey jumped out of bed, visions of Penny running through her mind. Sometimes she wanted to choke the woman. She ran into Dewayne's room and scooped Devin up. "It's okay, baby," she said. "We'll fix it."

She ran a bath and quickly bathed him, then got him a new set of pajamas.

"I'm sorry, Mommy," Devin said.

Jacey stopped. He had called her *Mommy*. She bit her lip—so hard she thought it would bleed—trying to keep the tears from her eyes. Mommy *may be the sweetest word in the English language,* she thought to herself.

"What are you sorry for?" she asked. "You didn't do anything wrong. You had an accident. Remember yesterday when I spilled the pitcher of Kool-Aid on the floor? Same thing. You just spilled some tee-tee."

That made him giggle.

"Guess what, boys?" Jacey said. "I think we'll have a slumber party tonight."

"What's that?" Derek asked.

"It's where you sleep on the floor, right, Jacey?" Dewayne asked.

"Right," she said. "Grab your pillows. I'll grab the sleeping bags and I'll meet you in the den."

Since that night, if it rained, the boys asked if they could have a slumber party. Tonight was their third one in two weeks.

Jacey picked up her phone and checked the time. It was two a.m. She would've worried they would be too sleepy to go to school when they got up in the morning, but she knew better. All three of them loved school, and Jacey was surprised at how well they did in all their subjects. Her caseworker told her foster children sometimes had a difficult time in school, but not these boys. They were very smart and eager to learn.

Another surprise? How quickly her maternal instincts kicked in. She fought the urge to drive by the school ten times a day to see if she could spot them on the playground and make sure they were okay. They begged to ride the bus, but she took them every morning and picked them up every afternoon. She promised them she'd let them ride the bus after the first of the year, but she already didn't like the idea.

She checked the weather on her phone. The storm would pass in an hour or so, and she hoped the boys would sleep through it. Devin seemed to be the only one who was really affected. The caseworker thought since he was so young, in time the memory of the flood and being on the roof during the driving rain and lightning and thunder would fade. Jacey hoped she was right, but when it stormed, she still thought of those days and nights. And of Colin. Always Colin.

She had decided she was going to call Colin and tell him about the adoption the day after she got them home. No matter how he did or didn't feel about her, she knew he'd want to know about them. He was the first person who had been completely supportive of her looking for the boys. He deserved to know she had them. She had picked up the phone to call him while the boys played outside when Georgia told her something that devastated her . . . something Jacey wished she'd have heard about months earlier.

"Jacey, don't," Georgia said. "Just don't."

"I only want to tell him about the boys," Jacey said. "I'm not calling to pledge my undying love to him."

"But you are," Georgia said. "You may not realize it, but that's exactly why you're calling him."

Georgia had seen right through her, so Jacey didn't deny it. "So what if I am?" It had been months since she had spoken to him. She was tired of pretending she didn't care, pretending she didn't miss him.

Georgia walked to the French doors and watched the boys playing. She bit her lip and turned around. "Jacey, I have to tell you something," she said. "And the only way to do it is to blurt it out."

"What is it?" Jacey asked, a little frightened at the tone in Georgia's voice.

"The day you drank my smoothie and we went to the ER," Georgia began, "I saw Colin in the hall at the hospital."

"What?" Jacey asked. "Did you talk to him? Why was he there? Do you know?"

"No," Georgia said. "Of course I didn't talk to

him. And he didn't see me. I did some snooping around and found out his mother was there. She had heart surgery. But Colin was with that woman. That same woman from the beach that night. I saw him hug her. And I heard him tell her he loved her before she left. She said it too. I'm so sorry. I should've told you, but I didn't want to hurt you."

Jacey handled the information like a champ in front of Georgia. She even thanked her for finally telling her, even though she chastised her for waiting. But later Jacey did cry. That night after Georgia had gone home and the boys were asleep, she lay in her bed and cried for the man she loved and the relationship that never was. She cried because she knew she would never feel the same way about another man. She cried most of the night, but the next morning she woke up with resolve. She didn't need Colin or any other man because there were already three of them living in her house. Those were her men now, and she'd spend the rest of her life making sure they grew up to be honest, hardworking, and faithful. She was raising future husbands and fathers, and she was determined to raise them well.

Chapter Twenty-Eight

Colin called Julie the next morning. Since Julie was a paralegal, she would certainly have some tricks up her sleeve for locating Jacey.

"How do I find somebody in Baton Rouge?" he asked.

"Have you lost her again, Colin? This is getting ridiculous."

"Look, she moved from her condo, she and her friend. They sold it," Colin said. "Her friend is a nurse, so I went to every hospital in Baton Rouge looking for her last night, and they all said she didn't work there."

"They can't give out employee information to you, Colin," Julie said. "It's against the law. You know how many crazies there are running around?"

"What do I do?" he asked. "I'm out of ideas."

Julie sighed. "You say they sold a condo?"

"Yes," Colin said. "A couple of weeks ago."

"Go to the courthouse and tell them you want conveyance records for her and her friend. Vendee, not vendor. If they bought another place, it'll be recorded in the county courthouse. Or parish, I guess in Louisiana. There will be an address on the deed. If it isn't, then go to the assessor's office and get it."

"Don't I need some kind of credentials for that?" he asked.

"It's all public record," Julie said. "Anybody can look it up."

"Okay," he said. "Thanks, Julie. Love you."

"Love you too," she said. "I don't know why, but I do."

Colin chuckled and ended the call. Off to the parish courthouse.

Thirty minutes after he arrived, he had all the information he needed. He was very surprised to learn Jacey had bought a house right outside Baton Rouge in a town called Prairieville. It was actually a house and a few acres of land. Had she and Georgia bought it together? Why else would she need such a big place unless they were both living there? But that seemed unlikely to him. He had heard both of them talking about buying their own separate places after their friend got married. They thought it was time to get out on their own. But Jacey had gone in a surprising direction when she bought this house.

Colin put the address in his GPS and began driving toward Prairieville. He decided not to call her and tell her he was coming. Maybe catching her off guard was the best way to handle this. If he called her, she'd have too much time to prepare for him. He would be able to tell by the look on her face if coming to see her was a mistake or not.

He was nervous. He had to admit it. One way or the other, he was driving into his future. The rest of his life would depend on what she said to him today . . . but he had to find out, he had to know. He wanted her. Only her. That was the only sure thing.

He knew the first order of business was to apologize for his erratic behavior. Surely she would forgive him after he told her the whole story, which was what he should've done in the first place. Jacey was compassionate, so she would understand. And deep in his soul, he knew she loved him. He'd always known it, even though he'd let the doubt creep into his mind time and time again. That's all it was: doubt. The closer he got to her house, the more his confidence grew.

He pulled into the driveway and killed the engine. This house was even bigger than he imagined. Her car was parked in the garage. He took a deep breath and got out. Then he walked up to the front door and knocked. In a few seconds, the door opened.

Jacey couldn't believe her eyes. "Colin," she said, just above a whisper. "What are you doing here?"

"I came to see you," he said, smiling. "You were hard to find."

"I just bought this place." She stood in the doorway, her heart pounding, frantically trying to mask her emotions.

"Can I come in?" he asked.

She looked behind her at the toys strewn on the floor and the boys' laundry waiting to be folded. She didn't want him to see any of it. Not because the house wasn't spotless, but because it was none of his business.

"I'll come out," she said and shut the door behind her.

"Oh, okay," he said.

"Let's sit on the porch," she offered.

They sat down in the rockers, each waiting for the other to speak first. "How have you been?" he finally asked.

"Fine," she said, "I'm fine. How are you?"

"Good," he said.

Jacey couldn't hold his gaze for too long, so she looked away. She wanted to throw herself into his arms and tell him that she loved him, even though she knew he loved someone else. Her feelings seemed so desperate and pathetic.

"Jacey, I need to apologize to you," he said.

She stiffened in the chair. "No, you don't."

"I do," he insisted. "I need to tell you everything. If you would've just returned my call. I wanted to . . ."

Suddenly she was furious. *He* needed. *He* wanted. What about what *she* needed and wanted? She wasn't going to give him the satisfaction of cleansing his guilt. What did he want from her?

Was he going to tell her how sorry he was for loving another woman, even though he'd *told* her he was falling for her? Then what? Was she supposed to demand some sort of consequence so he could serve his time and feel better about himself?

No. Not just no, but no way. She couldn't listen to it and didn't want him to barge in. Not into her lovely new home, where there were only happy memories to be made. She didn't want the shadow of this . . . toxic thing to be a part of the legacy of this house. Maybe it was childish, or maybe it was the most mature thing she'd done in her life. Whichever it was, she didn't care. But he had to go. Now.

"You need to leave, Colin," Jacey said quietly but firmly.

"But, Jacey, I came to tell you—"

"I don't care why," she interrupted. "Don't you get that? It's done. It's over. It doesn't matter anymore."

"It wasn't just because of the flood, Jacey." Colin attempted to explain even though she didn't want to hear it. "It was more than that, we shared—"

"Nothing!" Jacey almost shouted. "We shared nothing. It was a freak flood, and we just happened to be two of the people affected by it. We weren't the only ones it touched, Colin. We knew each other for a brief period of time on a shoddy roof over a muddy sea. That's it. Let's not make it more than it was."

"I'm sorry you feel that way, but I'd still like to explain," he said. "Why won't you just let me tell you?"

"Because none of it matters," she said. "It's done. I'm okay. In fact, I'm more than okay. I'm seeing somebody, and it's getting kind of serious." Why she said it, she didn't know. Maybe to save face, maybe to buffer the rejection she still felt, maybe to hurt him if she still had the power to. For whatever reason, she said it.

Colin looked surprised. "I didn't know," he said.

"Well, now you do," Jacey said. "And actually, I'm expecting him anytime now, so I'm glad you came by. I appreciate the sentiment, but really, we don't have to do this."

He stood up slowly. "It was good to see you, Jacey," he said. "And congratulations. I hope it works out."

"It will," she said. "And good luck to you." *Please get out of here,* she thought. *Please, before I lose it, just get out of here.*

He began walking toward his truck but turned back to her.

"I'm sorry if I hurt you. It wasn't intentional. That's what I came here to say. That and—"

She put up her hand to stop him. "Water under the bridge," she said. "No apology necessary."

He stood there another second without speaking, then asked, "Did you find the boys?"

Dear Lord, how many times was she going to lie today? "No, I was never able to. I had to give up. I'm sure they are doing okay."

"I really wish you would've returned that call." He opened his truck door just as it began to rain. "Good-bye, Jacey."

She watched him back out of the driveway and whispered, "Good-bye, Colin."

She went back into the house, locked the door, and sobbed.

Chapter Twenty-Nine

There was a reason they called it heartache. He could've sworn there was a knife sticking six inches into his chest. It was actual, literal pain.

So she was seeing someone else. The thought of her with another man was infuriating. His jaw clenched. He rolled the window down and briefly stuck his head out into the rain. He didn't know why . . . maybe trying to wash his sins away. The sin of omission, his Catholic friends called it. He was too late. He'd lost her because he wouldn't open his mouth, and there was no one to blame but himself. For the first time in years, he was sorry he had quit drinking.

He called Joshua's cell to tell him he was going to stay at his house. He knew Joshua was at a coaching conference this week, so he left a voice message. "I need to crash at your house for a day or two. Thanks, buddy." He needed to be by himself for a few nights.

He steered the truck toward I-10 and punched it. Back to Biloxi.

Jacey cried until there was nothing left to cry, mad at herself the entire time. Her heart was betraying her head. Ever since Georgia told her about the scene in the hospital, Jacey had assured herself she didn't need Colin, didn't want him. And most of the time she believed it. But today, when she found him standing at her door . . .

Why had he come here? Why hadn't he just left it alone? She was getting better every day . . . until he showed up. And why did he have to look so good? He was thinner and looked a little tired, but he was still as attractive as he'd ever been, maybe even more so now. Was it because she loved him? Still? It wouldn't have mattered if he'd only had three teeth and no hair. She loved him, and that made all the difference in the world.

Why couldn't she just stop loving him? She vaguely remembered asking Georgia that very question about Buck on one of Georgia's particularly bad nights. "Why can't you just stop loving him?" She now understood just how ridiculous that question was.

She dialed Georgia.

"Hello?"

"Did I wake you up?" Jacey sniffled.

"Yes, but what's wrong?" Georgia asked.

"Colin was here," Jacey said. "He just left."

"I'll be there in ten minutes."

What did he feel like he needed to explain? He kept asking her to let him explain. Why would she want to listen to him talk about another woman? And what would he say anyway? *You see, Jacey, there's this other woman, and I know*

I told you I was falling for you, but I was actually in love with her. So anyway, I came to explain it all to you so we could still be friends and maybe we could paint rainbows later and watch the unicorn races. Or maybe we'll go digging for a pot of gold and build a big ole house and we'll all live in it together . . . Exactly what part of that needed an explanation? He had chosen someone else. Did he really need to drive to Louisiana after four months to tell her that? The time span and his deafening silence had spoken volumes. No further clarification needed.

She went to the porch to wait for Georgia and watch the rain. Maybe if she stood in it, it would wash away the pain. She stepped into the yard. *Nope. No dice.* Why did every terrible day in her life have to be accompanied by rain? She used to love rain. Now it just reminded her of pain and sorrow and struggle. Maybe they could all move to the desert where it never rained.

Georgia drove up and jumped out of her car.

"What are you doing?" she asked. "Get out of the rain. Are you crazy?" Georgia grabbed her arm and dragged her back into the house.

"Maybe," Jacey said. "Maybe I am crazy. Or just pathetic because I still want a man who no longer wants me."

"Jacey . . . It's okay. You're going to be okay. Let me go get you a towel."

"He said he wanted to explain it all to me," said

308

Jacey loudly so that Georgia could hear her from the linen closet. "I don't know what he wanted to explain or even how you are supposed to explain something like that. And he kept asking me why I didn't return his call."

Georgia slowly walked back into the den. "He said what?"

"He asked me why I didn't return his call," Jacey repeated. "Um, maybe because he never called? Could that be it?"

Georgia handed her the towel and sat down on the sofa.

"Anyway, why couldn't he have texted me the explanation?" Jacey rubbed the towel over he hair. "He felt quite comfortable rejecting me in a text message, so telling me about lover-girl could've been done with similar ease."

Georgia was silent. And guilty.

"I was getting so much better, Georgie," Jacey said. "I was beginning to accept that it wasn't meant to be. I mean, I have the boys. I have this new house. We're doing great, you know? Then he had to show up. Here. I didn't even think to ask him how he found me. Wait . . . you didn't . . ."

Georgia put up her hand. "Not me. I haven't seen him or talked to him. I promise. I've been at my new place for two weeks, you know that. I have no idea how he found you."

"Thank you," Jacey said. "If you had told

him how to find me, that would've been a total betrayal."

Georgia felt sick to her stomach. She had to tell her about the phone call. She had to.

"You know what really bothers me most of all?" Jacey asked. "I think he thought I was going to fall into his arms and forgive him for everything and ride off into the sunset. I think I really shocked him."

"I need to tell you—" Georgia began.

"But I got him, and I got him *good*."

"Why?" Georgia asked. "What did you say?"

"I'm not entirely sure where this came from," Jacey said, "but I told him I was seeing someone else and that it was serious."

"You did what? Why would you do that?"

"Frankly, Georgie, I'm surprised you aren't roaring with laughter. It sounds exactly like something you would say."

"You never lie to anybody," Georgia said.

"Whose side are you on?" Jacey asked. "Because it feels a little bit like you are taking up for him. And I'm not sure I like it."

"Of course I'm not taking up for him," Georgia said. "It's just . . . it's just that maybe you should have let him talk."

Jacey put her hands on her hips, then threw them in the air. She began pacing angrily around the kitchen. "Why would I have let him talk? To hear him lie to me again? Or tell me all about

310

his girlfriend? She may be his wife now, for all I know. Maybe he came to tell me they got married, or maybe they're having a baby, or maybe he thought I should—"

"Stop," Georgia said. "Stop it and listen to me. He *did* call you."

Jacey stopped in her tracks. "What?"

"He called you the night before we went to visit the boys at the park," Georgia said. "You were in the shower at the hotel. He called you three times."

"Why didn't you tell me?" Jacey demanded.

"That's not all," Georgia said. "He left . . . a voicemail. And I listened to it. Jacey, I'm so sorry. I was trying to protect you . . ."

"What did he say?" Jacey asked quietly.

"I swear I was only trying to—"

"What did he say?"

"He said he loved you, he was sure of it, and he apologized for the text message he'd sent." Georgia's eyes filled with tears. "He asked you to call him back. I'm so sorry . . . I thought I was helping. I'm—"

"No," Jacey said, tears springing to her eyes. "You don't get to be sorry. You don't get to apologize. Why would you keep that from me? It was calculating and just . . . wrong. I'm not a child, Georgie. I am a grown woman."

"You don't know what it's like to hurt so much you want to—"

Jacey cut her off again. "I don't know what it's like to hurt? Are you kidding me? I was in a constant state of turmoil for a year. My whole life was pain, physical and mental. I had *crippling* panic attacks, and you thought I couldn't handle emotional trauma? This is my *life!*"

"I'm so sorry. I was trying—"

"Trying to help, I know," Jacey said. "You're always just trying to *help*. Do me a favor and stop helping me, Georgia."

"I didn't want him to use you," Georgia said, the tears falling down her cheeks. "You don't know how it feels to be betrayed by someone who is supposed to love you."

"I think I just found out," Jacey shouted back at her.

Georgia began to cry in earnest.

Jacey knew she had just delivered a terrible blow. "I'm so mad at you. So mad. Please just leave me alone. Just stay in here and leave me alone for a few minutes."

Jacey went back to the front porch and slammed the door behind her. She was furious with Georgia. Absolutely furious. Even in her anger she knew Georgia was only trying to protect her, but it was still deceptive and manipulative. She never would have done anything like that to Georgia. She always told her when Buck called or left messages or sent flowers. Even when she knew Georgia would throw the vase out the back door. Georgia should've told her . . . She should have gotten her out of the shower and told her he called.

Jacey knew her friend was still smarting from a breakup that had happened nearly two years ago, but now it was spilling over onto everyone else. It was as though Georgia were still stuck right in the middle of it. Her intentions had been good, but her methods were maddening.

Jacey sat down in the rocker. Had Colin's voice message really said he loved her and that he was sure of it? He'd said today that he could explain . . . But she had been terribly mean to him and then lied to him. She was ashamed of herself for that, and that she'd done it for no other reason except to hurt him the only way she knew how. She'd lied about having a boyfriend and lied about the boys. So who was manipulative and deceiving now? It was all a matter of perspective, and hers was nothing to brag about right now.

Jacey went back inside and saw Georgia standing at the kitchen window. She turned around when the door opened.

"Jacey . . ."

"Stop," Jacey told her. "I'm still mad at you . . . but I know why you did it. I know it came from a place inside you that loves me and doesn't want to see me hurt. You have loved me and cared for me as much as any blood member of my family would. So I apologize to you for what I said about betraying me. That was wrong and hateful and I'm sorry. Okay?"

Georgia nodded her head.

"But I want you to find some way to let go of what happened between you and Buck," Jacey said. "The way you cling to the pain and misery like a shield from the rest of the world isn't healthy. You should be better by now, but you aren't. If you need to go to therapy, I'll go with you. I'll take you. I'll hold your hand. But you have to find a way to fix it."

Georgia began to cry again. "I loved him so much," she said. "I loved him for nearly my whole life. Since I was twelve years old."

Jacey went to her and put her arms around her. "I know," she said, smoothing the back of Georgia's hair. "You got a raw deal, honey, and you didn't deserve it. But you have to let go. You just have to."

Georgia pushed away from her. "I would never, never hurt you on purpose," she said. "I promise you I thought I was doing the right thing."

Jacey shook her head. "I know you did," she said. "And I really do appreciate that, more than you know."

"I was so mad at him, Jacey. I wanted to punch him in the face and knock his two front teeth out."

"That sounds like the Georgie I know." Jacey

chuckled. "But guess what we're gonna do instead?"

Georgia wiped her face with the towel around Jacey's shoulders. "What?"

"Well, I may be absolutely nuts," Jacey said, "but we are gonna pick up the boys from school and head to Biloxi. The man I love needs to explain himself, and no matter what—if he loves me, doesn't love me—I still have the best friend in the world and three unbelievable kids. Whatever happens, I'm gonna be all right."

Chapter Thirty

"Are you sure you don't want me to stay here with the boys while you go to Biloxi?" Georgia asked. The carpool line at the boys' school seemed to stretch on for miles. "Doesn't that make more sense? You can be alone with Colin and hear him out."

"No," Jacey said. "I don't want to leave them here while I'm there. It's important they feel safe and secure, especially right now. I don't want them to think I just up and decided to go somewhere else. People leave them all the time. Not always by choice, but still."

Georgia shook her head. "I get it," she said. "But don't they have school tomorrow? Is it okay to take them out? Do you have to report that?"

"The teachers have an in-service tomorrow, so there is no school. And I can take them by child services tomorrow for their visit while we're in Mississippi."

"Then this works out great," Georgia said. "Hey, do the kids have any pictures of their mother and brother? I thought about that this morning while I was in the shower for some reason."

"I called the paper in Biloxi and was able to buy a copy they had," Jacey said. "I had copies made and framed three of them. I put one in each of the boys' rooms. Dewayne is the only one who talks about her very much. I saw him sitting on his bed staring at the picture a few days ago."

"Jacey, what you have done for those boys . . . It's probably the most noble thing I have ever witnessed. I'm so proud of you. And I'm so sorry for what I did."

Jacey shook her head and smiled. "Stop, it's done, over," she said. "Now, don't get me wrong. I am still mad at you. But sometimes I think about the nights right after the accident, when I was still in the ICU . . . and how every now and then I would wake up. Sometimes I saw Mama in the room, and sometimes Daddy . . . but I *always* saw you. You don't throw away that kind of friendship because of a well-intentioned mistake."

Georgia smiled. "I couldn't leave you with nurses I didn't know," she said. "And, Jacey, I have worried myself to death over that phone call for months. I've lost sleep over it. I've come so close to telling you so many times."

"Well, we're going to find out today what he has to say," Jacey said. "And then, whatever happens, we're gonna work on you. Starting with a date."

"A date?" Georgia asked. "I don't want to go on a date."

"It's time," Jacey said. "You're moving on,

whether you want to or not. Even if I have to drag you to a restaurant or a movie to meet a guy and physically put you in the chair. Now, do you want to find a date for yourself, or do you want me to find one for you?"

Georgia pondered that for a moment. "You know, Colin told me months ago he wanted me to meet someone, a football coach. You think that offer still stands?"

"I think there's only one way to find out," Jacey said. "If I like what Colin has to say, we'll inquire about this mystery man. And if I don't, well . . . I guess after you call the coroner to pick up the body, we'll try to find him anyway."

Georgia laughed. "I'm glad you are keeping a sense of humor about this."

Jacey sighed. "The truth is I am scared to death. I don't know what I'm about to find out. He's already told another woman he loved her . . . so I'm not sure what I'm expecting. But hearing him out seems like the right thing to do."

"I think it's a great decision," Georgia said. "Just one thing: Where is he?"

Jacey looked a little surprised. "Okay, until you said that, it never occurred to me where to look. Do we just drive into Biloxi, stop at a 7–Eleven, and say, 'Do you happen to know Colin Jennings and where I might locate him?'"

"Let's just start at the last place we saw him," Georgia said. "The house on the beach."

. . .

Colin threw his bag on the bed in Joshua's guest room and fell beside it. He couldn't stop thinking about what Jacey had said to him. He couldn't stop thinking about how pretty she looked or how good she smelled. He couldn't stop thinking at all.

Why hadn't he gone to her earlier? Would he never learn? He was still treating people like they were disposable. Just as he had done with his parents. Just as he did with everybody. It was the worst kind of self-indulgence, like pressing the hold button on somebody else's life until he felt like answering the call.

Today he understood just how much he'd hurt Jacey. He'd seen it on her face as soon as she opened the door. Part of it was surprise, but most of it was pain. She looked wounded, although she tried to hide it. He'd have to live with the knowledge that he had done that to her. He'd hurt her, and that hurt had turned to anger. She had been ready to throw him off her property and was mad enough to physically attempt it. He was responsible for the look on her face and the venom in her voice.

He walked onto the deck and watched the Gulf roll and spin and spill its waves against the shore. He suspected if someone cut him open and looked at his heart, it would look just like the waters swirling in front of him. He bypassed the gate and jumped over the deck railing, onto the path that led to the beach, and began to run. Nothing could soothe the soul like running in sand.

He glanced up the beach to the house on the bluff. He wondered what Ava and Jasper were doing this evening and felt a tug of homesickness. That almost made him laugh. The only bright spot in this whole mess was knowing he could jog all the way there, run up the steps, and be invited into a loving home. There he would find parents who would listen if he wanted to talk, a nurturing mother because he finally allowed her to be, and a sage father whose advice was now welcomed and not ridiculed. He turned up the speed. He couldn't get there quick enough.

"What time is it?" Jacey asked.

"Six thirty," Georgia said. "We should be there soon."

"We'd already be there if you hadn't packed everything in your house," Jacey said. "There's a good possibility we'll only spend one night. Let's face it: How long does it take a man to make a Dear Jane speech?"

"You have gotten so pessimistic in the last couple of hours," Georgia said. "And you know I always overpack."

"Where are we gonna stay, Jacey?" Dewayne asked.

"We are staying at a hotel on the beach, fellas. Won't that be fun? You can play in the sand tomorrow and build sand castles, and maybe we'll find a pizza place to go to."

"Yay!" came the collective cheer from the backseat.

"Tonight Aunt Georgie is going to stay with you awhile," Jacey said. "Is that okay? I'll be right next to the hotel, but I have to go visit a . . . friend."

Dewayne looked at his little brothers. "That's okay," he said. "Can we order room service, Aunt Georgie?"

"How did you know about room service?" Georgia laughed.

"Mama took us to Gulf Port once and we stayed in a hotel," Dewayne said. "She called it a vacation, but I think she was just hiding from my daddy. Anyway, she let us call and order room service."

Sweet boy is missing his mama, Jacey thought. "I bet that was fun."

"Of course you can order room service," Georgia said. "And after supper, you can order ice cream and pie and cake and candy."

"Georgie!" Jacey scolded as another collective "Yay!" rose up.

"Hey, what are aunts for?" Georgia asked.

An hour later the boys were watching cartoons and occasionally jumping on the bed. "Boys, I told you to stop that," Jacey said. "One of you is going to fall and get hurt."

"What is it about parenthood that automatically turns you into a joy sucker?" Georgia asked.

Jacey rolled her eyes. "Why do aunts believe that cake and an IV of soda can be supper?"

"We ordered burgers too," Georgia said. "Now go put this on and see how you look."

"Where did you get this?" Jacey asked as she looked at the flowing strapless dress. The fabric was beautiful and light, the colors muted and subtle. Not the usual kind of thing Georgia wore.

"I got it a few weeks ago at Ted & Daisy's. The day I decided I was going to lose twenty pounds," she said. "It's my inspiration outfit. You may as well wear it until I can. And it's perfect to wear on the beach . . . the wind gently blowing through your hair, the dress flowing behind you in the breeze. It's very Lifetime Movie Channel, don't you think?"

Jacey raised a brow. "Who are you?"

"Just go put it on," Georgia said. "Stop spoiling this for me. I'm trying to make amends."

"Stop it!" Jacey called from the bathroom "I don't need you to make amends."

"I wish you would've let me get a room with a balcony," Georgia said. "We can't even see the house from in here."

"I have three kids now, Georgie," Jacey said. "I

can't have a balcony on my room. What if they get too curious and lean too far over the edge?"

"Like I said, joy suckers," Georgia muttered under her breath.

"Look, Aunt Georgie," Derek said. He turned a flip in the air over the bed.

Georgia sucked in her breath. Okay, that one scared her. "Noooooo," she whispered. "Don't do that."

Jacey came out of the bathroom and twirled. "Okay, how do I look?"

Georgia clapped her hands. "It's perfect," she said, and it really was. The dress hugged Jacey's slim body in all the right places, then gracefully billowed around her legs. "It'll kill him. What's the plan?"

"What do you mean?" Jacey asked.

"I mean, what's the plan? What are you going to say? Do?"

Jacey drew a blank. "I have no idea," she said. "I haven't thought about it."

"Are you kidding me?"

"I guess . . . I'm just gonna go over there and knock on the door and hope for the best," Jacey said.

"Well, there you have it, ladies and gentlemen. The plan of the century." Georgia shook her head in disgust.

"It's okay," Jacey said. "Really, it is. I have zero expectations about this. I am here to hear the man out. I owe him that much. That flood will always bind us together, and I shouldn't have reacted the way I did today. He deserves better than what I gave him."

Georgia shook her head. "I'm proud of you, Jacey."

Jacey smiled at her, then stood in front of the full-length mirror to assess the outfit. "You sure I look okay? This isn't too much?"

"You look amazing," Georgia said. "And besides, you said yourself there is a possibility of getting seriously shot down. You may as well look good on the ground."

"That actually wasn't helpful, but okay," Jacey said. "I have my phone and I'll keep you updated. Boys, come give me a good night kiss. You'll be asleep when I get back."

"Wanna bet?" Georgia cracked.

Jacey shot her a look that Georgia had dubbed "the mama glare." She knelt down to hug the boys. They leapt from the bed to shower her with kisses.

"You promise you're coming back?" Devin asked.

Jacey hugged him tightly against her. "I promise," she said. "Now hop back on the bed. Your supper will be here any minute."

"Good luck or break a leg or jingle bells or whatever it is you say to somebody in this position," Georgia said.

Jacey held out her fist and Georgia bumped it. "Here goes nothing."

She took the elevator to the ground floor and walked out the back to the pool area. It was too cool to swim, but there were a lot of people on the decks and at the bar. She walked through the gate and onto the beach, and as soon as she turned toward the house, she saw it. Colin's truck was parked behind the house.

She stopped in her tracks. Maybe she hadn't really expected to find him, and now that he was nearby, this whole idea seemed crazy. Did she really want to go through with this? Risk having her heart ripped out again just to hear what he had to say? What possible excuse could he have for saying "I love you" to two women at once? Nothing could justify something like that. She began to lose her nerve. *Maybe I shouldn't do this . . .*

She turned to go back to the hotel, but stopped again when she thought about the voicemail Georgia had erased. Had Jacey been a part of some competition she knew nothing about? If so, that might be the biggest insult of all.

"Stop it," she said out loud. "Stop trying to make it make sense, because it doesn't. Nothing about this has ever made sense. Just go hear what the man has to say."

She marched over to the house, up the steps

to the deck, and was surprised to find she could see inside the place. The back of the house was covered in huge floor-to-ceiling windows. She walked up to the door and knocked, her heart pounding as she waited for an answer. But there was no movement inside. She knocked again with the same result.

She sat down in one of the chairs on the deck. She texted Georgia to give her the news, then made herself comfortable. He had to show up sometime, and she wasn't moving from her spot until he did.

Colin left his mom and dad feeling much better than when he arrived. He told the whole story, starting with the flood and ending with this morning's showdown.

"Perhaps she needs some time," Ava said. "Women are a mystery, Colin. Even to me."

"She's had months," Colin said. "I think I just messed up. That's all. I don't think I can do anything about it."

"I think you did too," Jasper said.

"Jasper!" Ava said.

"We're telling the truth around here now, aren't we? You made a mistake, son. If she won't listen to you when you try to tell her, write her a letter. Women aren't going to throw a letter away without reading it. They are the nosiest people on the planet."

Ava stared at him. "Remember the cookies you asked me to bake? No."

"Now, Ava, I wasn't talking about you," he said.

Colin laughed. "You may be onto something, Dad."

"With all this technology, letter writing is a lost art," Jasper said. "Write your girl a letter. If she doesn't answer, then you've done all you can do."

"Thanks for lending an ear," Colin said. "I'm gonna head on back to Josh's."

"You want your father to drive you?" Ava said. "Maybe *you* can make him some cookies."

Colin laughed. "Thanks, but I think I'll run back," he said. "And don't make him do time for that, Mom. You know he's crazy about you."

Ava smiled. "Well, we'll see."

Colin made his way down the wooden steps to the beach and began running back to Joshua's house. He thought Jasper's idea was spot-on. He could write Jacey a letter and explain everything that had happened. A giant redwood may have to give its life for the paper he'd need to complete it, but he was going to write it just the same. If she didn't reply, he would learn to live with the loss. But at least he would know he'd done everything he could.

He made it back to the house in about ten minutes. He was surprised he could still run the entire way. It had been so long since he'd tried. But he needed to shave some time off that. He really needed to get back to the gym and start—

"Hello, Colin."

His head jerked up to see Jacey standing on the deck of Joshua's house. And he'd never seen a more beautiful sight.

Chapter Thirty-One

At first he thought his mind was playing tricks on him, conjuring up some lovely mirage because he wanted to see her so badly. But here she was. Standing on Joshua's deck wearing a beautiful dress that moved gently around her legs with the autumn breeze. The moonlight cast a soft glow over her face and tinted her hair a shimmery golden brown. Maybe she really was a mirage. No one could look this . . . perfect.

"Jacey?" he said. "What are you doing here? How did . . ."

She walked slowly across the deck and opened the gate by the steps. "You said you needed to tell me something," she said. "So . . . tell me."

Colin ran his hand through his hair and stepped onto the deck.

"I can't believe you're here," he said. "I thought, after today, well . . . I didn't expect to see you again. Can I get you anything? Water, a drink, anything?"

"You can tell me why I'm here, Colin. That's all I want."

Colin gestured to the French doors. "Let's go inside," he said. He opened the door and motioned her inside, then followed close behind her.

"Sit down," he said. "You sure you don't want anything? I've been running, so I need some water, but I can fix you anything . . ."

"Talk to me," Jacey said, taking a seat on the sofa. "Please."

Colin grabbed a bottle of water from the refrigerator and sat in front of her on the ottoman.

"I can't tell you this story without starting at the beginning," Colin said, "so you may be here awhile."

"Okay," Jacey said. "But first . . . I want to apologize for today. You caught me off guard, and I really didn't mean to come off the way I did. I know I sounded just awful, and I really am sorry."

Colin took her hands into his. "No, Jacey," he said. "You don't have anything to apologize for. It's on me. All of it is on me."

The touch of his hands on hers made her want to cry. His hands were strong, but gentle. They had shoved her into a boat, sheltered her in a storm, held her when she cried, and caressed her face. But she pulled hers away, reluctantly. She couldn't think straight when he was touching her.

Colin leaned away from her and began to speak. He started by telling her about his childhood, about his relationship with his parents—or, in his father's case, the lack thereof. He didn't try to whitewash anything . . . told her every bit of the good, the bad, and the ugly. He spoke of his unchecked anger and his lack of respect for his parents. He told her about Jasper's constant absence and his mother's apathy toward it. The only thing he left out was the truth of his parents' affairs, believing there was no point in sharing secrets that didn't belong to him. And he was honest with her about his college years . . . all the women, the drinking, the poor lifestyle choices he'd made.

Jacey was a little surprised to hear most of the things he said because the Colin she knew was so far removed from the one he was describing. But she kept her questions and comments to herself for the time being. She let him talk because she knew he needed to.

Colin described meeting Julie, and how their friendship turned him around. "I was so lost," he said. "I didn't care about anything except the next thing that would make me feel better—be it a woman, a bottle of Scotch, or a fast vehicle. I was searching that night for something . . . redemption, I guess. Julie probably saved my life, though she would say it was all part of a divine plan. I was in a downward spiral, destination Rock Bottom, with no way or intention of stopping myself. Julie stood up to me, called my bluff, and put me in my place. That was a first for me."

Colin clearly loved his friend, and Jacey was

thankful Julie had come into his life when she did.

"When I left Baton Rouge, the day after you spent the night at my trailer," Colin continued, "it was my intention to go home and have it out with my father once and for all. I just couldn't take it anymore. I had found you again, and that was enough for me. But then my mother got sick. Well . . . she got sicker, and I thought it was my fault. I said some things to her that day I never should've said and . . . well . . . to cut to the chase, she ended up in the emergency room and had heart surgery the next day."

This was the day Georgia had seen him with the other woman. Should she interrupt him here and ask the question? She decided against it. There would be time to ask him later, and maybe he'd tell her without any prompting.

"I was in bad shape, Jacey," he said. "I still couldn't stand to be in the same room with my father. I started to question my commitment to the ministry, and I knew I was really none of the things I presented myself to be. And I couldn't drag you down with me. I needed to get my head together, but my mother was about to have her chest cut open. I wanted to call you. I wanted to ask you to be with me, but I just couldn't. I knew you didn't need any more chaos in your life . . . It sounds childish when I say it out loud, but I made a rash judgment call when I sent that text. But I thought I was doing you a favor."

Jacey really wished people would stop doing her favors. "You broke my heart," she said quietly.

Colin felt like a traitor. "I know I did," he said. "And I am so sorry. If you will let me, I will spend the rest of my life making it up to you."

Jacey looked at him without answering, still more than a little confused. She was beginning to understand why he'd sent the first text message. The stress of his circumstances was enough to jolt anybody into another plane, and the strain from the tug-of-war with his father was equally frustrating, she was sure. But there was another problem far more prolific.

"What about the girl?" Jacey asked.

"What girl?" Colin said.

"You know what girl," Jacey said. She appreciated his explanation, but the important question lingered. "Please don't bare your soul to me and then lie about the woman. It defeats the purpose."

"Jacey, I have no idea what you're talking about," he said. "There is no girl."

"Colin, please, don't lie to me," Jacey said. "Especially not now. I was in that same hospital the day your mother had surgery. Georgie and I were in Biloxi looking for the boys. We stopped at a smoothie shop and, long story short, I landed in the ER."

"You were here?" he asked.

She waved him off. "I was still in the ER when Georgie saw you down the hall," Jacey said. "She saw you with a girl. The same girl we saw at this very house from our hotel balcony right over there." She pointed to the hotel. "Georgie heard you tell her you loved her. *That* girl."

Colin finally understood. "That wasn't a girl," he said. "That was Julie."

"Who is Julie?" Jacey asked.

"Julie is my friend, my dear friend," he said. "Julie with the Bible from the bar."

"Julie was the bar Bible girl?"

"Yes," Colin said. "I do love her, and I always tell her so. But there's never been anything like *that* between us."

"So the girl you were hugging on that deck"—she pointed outside—"and the girl you were talking to in the hospital was . . . your friend. And that's all?"

Colin nodded his head. "Yes," he said. "And I do love Julie, but I am *in* love with you. Only you, Jacey."

Jacey sprang from her seat on the sofa and flung herself into his arms. "I'm in love with you too," she said.

Colin held her, the relief flooding through him. He felt the way he did the day he saw the boat coming around the bend to save her. They were going to make it. He pulled her away from him and kissed her, thoroughly and completely.

And when he was done, he kissed her again.

"Well, that was worth the wait," she said, her voice shaky and her knees weak. She was glad she was sitting and not standing.

He pushed her back gently. "But, wait. What about the other guy? You told me you were seeing somebody and . . ." Colin paused, assessing Jacey's face. "You lied to me, didn't you?"

Jacey grinned sheepishly. "I did," she confessed, "but it's your fault."

"Okay, I'll accept that," he said, pulling her back to his lips. "I can't tell you how much I have thought about this," he said, his mouth against hers.

"Me too," she said, straining her body against his, every part of her alive and aware.

"We'd better stop now. I don't want the first time to be like this. In somebody else's house, on an ottoman."

Jacey laughed. "That's very gentlemanly of you."

Colin kissed her lightly on the lips. "I aim to please," he said.

"How did you find me?" she asked. "How did you even know where to look?"

Before he could answer, they were interrupted by the sound of wailing. It sounded like World War Three had broken out on the beach. Jacey knew in an instant what it was.

Colin jumped up to open the gate. "I'm so sorry," Georgia said, rushing past Colin to get to Jacey. She held Devin, inconsolable in her arms, and a sobbing Derek by the hand. Dewayne stood behind her, dry-eyed but bewildered.

"Devin woke up crying, then Derek started in," she said in a frantic tone. "Dewayne tried to help, but they only wanted you." She looked behind her. "Hi, Colin."

"Hi," Colin said, visibly confused.

Devin whipped around in Georgia's arms and spotted Colin for the first time. Then Dewayne noticed him, and Derek too.

"Colin?" Dewayne said. Colin knelt down on one knee and opened his arms, and Dewayne ran toward him. Derek jumped on Colin's back, and even Devin wriggled out of Georgia's arms and joined the party. Colin looked up at Jacey, the questions clearly written on his face.

"I forgot to tell you," she said, smiling. "I adopted them. In eight more months, they will be all mine."

Colin fell backward on the floor and allowed himself to be consumed by the adoration of three giggling, spirited, and energetic little boys.

There were still questions to be answered and curiosity to be satisfied . . . but tonight, Colin and Jacey knew all they really needed to know.

Chapter Thirty-Two

"Your home is beautiful, Ava," Lisa Lang said. "I can't tell you how much we appreciate the invitation to join you for Christmas."

"And I can't tell you how much we love your daughter and the children," Ava said. "They have transformed our lives in a matter of months."

"Speaking of, what is the shrieking coming from the other room?" Lisa asked.

"I imagine that would be Colin teaching the boys how to slide down the bannister, although I am afraid to look," Ava said.

"I don't think I will either," Lisa said.

"Colin!" Jacey's voice echoed from the foyer. "Have you lost your mind? Boys, get down from there! Every one of you is going to break your neck. Colin, don't you dare let them get up on that bannister again, do you hear me?"

Ava and Lisa listened and smiled.

Jacey came into the kitchen where the women were still chuckling. "Do you know what Colin was letting the boys do?" she asked.

They shook their heads.

"They were sliding down the bannister," she said. "They could've killed themselves. It's like watching four kids instead of three when they're together. And I don't know who the worst influence is—Colin on the kids or the other way around."

She walked out of the kitchen, and Ava and Lisa laughed out loud.

"Young mothers," Lisa said.

"She'll relax," Ava said. "Give her some time. When Colin was a baby, his bed collapsed with him in it. When I uncovered him, he was smiling. But I almost called an ambulance."

"When Jacey was a baby, she slid out of my lap and onto the floor while I was giving her Tylenol. I almost called the National Guard."

In the foyer, Jacey continued to scold Colin—but he could only grin at her motherly tone. "I'm sorry, Jacey, but that's like a rite of passage. Every kid needs to slide down a bannister."

"Not with a marble floor beneath them," Jacey said.

"Did you want me to put some mattresses down?" he asked. "I will."

"I want them to *not* slide down the bannister," she said.

He kissed her quickly. "Okay, I promise, no more bannisters."

"Thank you," she said, pulling him back to her lips. "That one was too fast."

"Ewwww!" The joint disgust echoed behind them as the boys witnessed their affection. Jacey pulled away from Colin and laughed.

"Come on, guys," Colin said. "I want to show

338

you how to get down the bluff without using the steps."

Jacey shook her head. "Are you kidding me?" she muttered as they all dashed outside.

Her cell phone jingled and she fished it out of her pocket. It was Georgia.

"Hello, my friend. What are you doing?" she said.

"I'm waiting for Joshua to come back to the car," she said. "We stopped at the store to get a bottle of wine to take to Mom's house."

"Oh, so you two decided to spend Christmas together," Jacey said. "I approve."

"Jacey . . . he's wonderful," Georgia gushed, "and I mean *wonderful*. He's thoughtful and generous and asks for my opinion about things. He's . . . perfect. So now I'm just waiting for him to mess up."

"No." Jacey laughed. "You can't think like that."

"It's hard not to."

"Listen, Colin says he's a real stand-up guy. He's no cheater. Now, don't do anything crazy to run him off."

"Like what?" Georgia asked.

"Like be yourself." Jacey laughed.

"Ha-ha, you're so funny," Georgia said. "Oops, here he comes. Oh my, he looks like a Greek god. I have to go, bye."

Jacey was still smiling after they disconnected.

Georgia was going to make it. She and Joshua had been dating for a couple of months, and she'd never seen Georgia this happy and relaxed. Joshua was good to her and for her. The fact that he was a football coach was just lagniappe. Georgia loved football and had already attended a couple of his games. Joshua had told Colin he knew Georgia was a keeper when she told him at halftime that his defense should blitz the rest of the game if they wanted to win. The strategy worked.

Later that night the Jenningses and the Langs gathered in the den to open presents. Jacey sat with a beautifully wrapped package in her lap, looked around the room, and counted her blessings. Her father and Jasper were working on Devin's new motorized jeep in one corner. Colin and the two smaller boys were playing with their new puppy, the golden retriever Jasper had given them. They had argued for thirty minutes about what they were going to name her, but finally decided on Princess Leia as a salute to the Star Wars character. Leia was currently licking Derek's ear, and he was in the throes of a giggle fest. Ava and Lisa were sharing cookie recipes and comparing cooking notes. Jacey wondered if there was another time in her life she'd been this happy, but she couldn't remember one.

"Okay, ladies and gentlemen, if I could have

your attention, please," Colin said. "Boys, are you ready?"

The boys ran to his side, and they all walked to Jacey and stood in front of her.

Jacey smiled. "What's this?" she asked.

"One, two, three," Colin said, and they all bent down on one knee in front of her.

"Ready?" he asked.

They began singing "My Girl" to her in perfect pitch and tone. Jacey was completely enchanted, as was the rest of the audience. When the song was over, Colin turned to Dewayne. "You still got it?" he asked.

Dewayne smiled, took a small box out of his pocket, and gave it to Colin.

Still on one bended knee, Colin opened the box. It held a beautiful antique diamond ring.

Jacey's hand flew over her mouth. They hadn't even talked about this.

"Jacey," Colin said, "I love you and I love these boys. It would be my honor to be your husband and their daddy. Will you marry me?"

"Please?" Devin added, which cracked up the room.

Jacey opened her arms and invited all of them in. "Yes, yes, yes, and yes." She laughed and cried. "I will marry you."

Epilogue

June sixth was cooler than normal in Mississippi. The temperature was holding steady in the lower to mid-eighties. It was the perfect temperature for an outside evening wedding looking over the Gulf.

Jacey had peeked out the window earlier and saw several people she recognized walking to the large white tent, including Mrs. Ernestine Harrison. She was dressed to the nines and being escorted by none other than Sheriff Roger Jefferson. The boys were going to be so excited to see her. Jacey had taken them to visit not too long ago, and they had loved it.

Ava and Lisa—the wedding planners, as they liked to call themselves—had done a beautiful job getting ready for today. There must have been a million white lights in the trees on the lawn that would come on when twilight fell. Vintage and rustic features adorned every table and chair. The guests would feast on the bounty from the Gulf with all the trimmings. And magnolias were everywhere.

One day months earlier, Jacey was sitting at the table with Ava and Lisa talking about the wedding flowers when Colin walked in and listened to their conversation.

"Lisa and I think roses would be best," Ava said. "Pink-and-white tea roses. They will be beautiful."

Jacey didn't really have a preference, and she trusted the opinion of both her mother and soon-to-be mother-in-law. "That's fine with me," she said.

"How about magnolias?" Colin said. "I don't know much about flowers, but magnolias are nice."

"Why on earth would you want magnolias, son?" Ava asked.

He bent down by Jacey's chair and kissed her cheek. "Because she rode into my life on a magnolia limb full of flowers. That limb stayed on the roof with us for days, and I can still smell them. Can we have magnolias?"

Jacey smiled. "We sure can," she said.

"This isn't just an ugly dress, Jacey," Willow said. "It's almost criminal."

Jacey stared at herself in the mirror of Ava's bedroom. In a few minutes, she would walk down the stairs on her father's arm and marry the man of her dreams. She was too happy to care what Willow thought of her matron of honor dress.

"Hey," Georgia said. "You knew this was coming, Willow. You knew this was coming and you should've waited longer to get pregnant. You didn't plan well."

"I didn't know I was going to have to wear hot-pink spandex," Willow said. "Or I would have."

"It isn't spandex," Jacey said. "It's *supposed* to fit that way."

"Um, I don't think so," Willow said. "It's like I have two butts. One in the back and one in the front."

Georgia laughed out loud. "It sure does!" she said.

"Just because you've lost twenty pounds and are trying to look like a Victoria's Secret model now doesn't mean you can laugh at the pregnant chick," Willow said.

"I look so good in this dress I can't believe it," Georgia said. "Here, take a picture so I can text it to Joshua."

"He'll see you in ten minutes," Willow said. "You're so full of yourself."

"It's because I'm so hot," she said.

"Will both of you just stop and look at me, please?" Jacey asked. "All I want you to be is jealous. Just jealous."

Willow and Georgia stood on either side of her.

"You look unbelievable," Willow said.

"You do," Georgia agreed.

There was a knock on the door, and Willow went to see who it was. She came back and handed Jacey a box with a bow on top.

"What's this?" she asked.

"I don't know," Willow said. "Your future father-in-law said it was a gift from your future husband and you may want to wear it for the ceremony."

Jacey opened the box and found a note. She flipped the paper over and read it out loud. "Remember the locket Lillian wore? It's only fitting that their other mother has one too."

Jacey pushed the tissue away to reveal a beautiful gold locket. She opened it to find a tiny picture of the boys. She put her hand over her heart and felt tears beginning to sting her eyes.

"No, no, no," Georgia said, running to fetch a hankie. "No crying. You'll mess your up makeup, and it's perfect. Do not cry."

"Help me put it on." Jacey asked her.

The locket looked beautiful with her strapless gown. She traced her fingers over it. "I promise you, Lillian, I will never let them forget you," she whispered.

Julie stuck her head in the door and smiled. "Are you ready? It's about that time."

Jacey picked up her bouquet of beautiful white magnolias and smiled at her new friend. "I am," she said.

They walked out into the hallway, and Jacey took her father's arm. She thought back over the past couple of years as they made their way down the aisle to Colin. He was so handsome and such a good man. Their boys were standing beside him, waiting. Life was so precious and so uncertain. She'd spent twenty-five years afraid of love and afraid of taking a chance, but a flood opened her heart and filled it with more love than she'd ever known.

Author's Note

After the completion of this novel, two things happened that were both tragic and coincidental.

First, a friend of mine lost her husband in an incident similar to the one that is described in the pages of this book. I was afraid this book would somehow cause her and her family more heartache, but was assured by her it would not. So I want to say thank you to Suzanne. My prayers are still with you all.

Second, the flood of 2016 devastated parts of my beloved Louisiana. It started raining one day . . . and it just would not stop. Neither my family nor I were directly affected by this unprecedented disaster, but we knew many who were. Hundreds of the flood victims are still struggling to recover. A portion of the proceeds of this book will be donated to this cause.

Below you will find the addresses for organizations that continue to assist in that recovery. Please consider lending a hand. And thank you, from the resilient, proud, and undivided State of Louisiana.

Judson Baptist Church
32470 Walker Road North
Walker, La. 70785
RE: Flood Relief

Christ Community Church
PO Box 1113
Denham Springs, La.
70727

Discussion Questions

1. Both Jacey and Georgia help the other see things in their lives that they can't figure out or admit on their own. Who in your life fills that role? Can you think of any significant steps in your life that you wouldn't have taken without that friend's encouragement?

2. Jacey is concerned that the expectations and pressure of being a preacher's wife would be too much for her. Have there been any times in your life when you feared the expectations of a position or relationship? Were your fears worse than the reality?

3. Have you ever been affected by a natural disaster like a flood? How did you—or your community—respond?

4. Have you or anyone close to you suffered from PTSD? What advice or encouragement would you give to someone who was experiencing it?

5. Jacey ultimately adopts the boys to ensure that they are loved and cared for. Do you know anyone who has adopted a child? Was it a situation of a family specifically looking for a child to love, or more similar to Jacey's, where they saw a need and realized they could fill it?

6. Do you think the red tape that surrounds adoption is too much, too little, or right on target?
7. Do you think Georgia should have deleted the messages on Jacey's phone? If you were Jacey, could you have forgiven her for it?
8. Jacey has terrible allergies but doesn't take the seemingly logical step of keeping an EpiPen with her. Why do you think that is? What things are difficult for you to remember to do even though you know you should?
9. Envision Jacey and Colin's family three years from now. What do you think it will look like? Where do you think they'll be?

Acknowledgments

Once again I find it hard to accept all the accolades that come with having a book published without sharing them with my family. They are my backbone, my cheerleaders, my support system, my reality checkers, and they can put me back in my place just that fast. I adore every last one of them, even if we do move around like a weird human covey of quail . . .

Emily Davidson, if you look up the phrase *best friend* in the dictionary, there's a picture of you beside it. I love you, my BFF.

JW, you thermostat-touching, muddy-boot-wearing, candy-smacking, dirty-truck-driving, last-Coke-drinking, slow-walking, slow-talking, slow-moving cowboy . . . Thank you for being the chill to my hustle. It balances beautifully in the end.

Brady and Camille, you two are the great loves of my life. This world has become magical since you arrived.

Georgia Boswell, you inspire me, you amaze me, and you make me smile. Strong women are my heroes, and you're at the top of that list. I "heard" your voice every time Georgia spoke in the pages of this book.

And Jacey Dunbar . . . Your beautiful face just would *not* get out of my head. She is you.

And thank you, Courtnie Clark Graves for all your help. You sure got the best prize. Give our future all-American a kiss.

About the Author

Celeste Fletcher McHale lives on her family farm in Central Louisiana, where she enjoys raising a variety of animals. Her hobbies include writing, football, baseball, and spending much time with her grandchildren.

Center Point Large Print
600 Brooks Road / PO Box 1
Thorndike, ME 04986-0001 USA

(207) 568-3717

US & Canada:
1 800 929-9108
www.centerpointlargeprint.com